MW01126804

More

Than You

Know

Written by E.M. Jost

This is a work of fiction. Names, characters, businesses, places, events, locales, and incidents are either the products of the author's imagination or used in a fictitious manner. Any resemblance to actual persons, living or dead, or actual events is purely coincidental.

© 2020 Elizabeth Jost

For all the women who have fought through the storm and have come out stronger on the other side.

Love isn't perfect. It isn't a fairy tale or a storybook, and it doesn't always come easy. Love is overcoming obstacles, facing challenges, fighting to be together, holding on and never letting go. Love is work, but most of all, love is realizing that ever hour, every minute, every second of it is worth it because you did it ... TOGETHER. -Unknown

Forward

Many subjects in this book are heavy and difficult to speak of or read. None of them should be taken lightly. The pain of heartbreak and infidelity, anxiety and depression and suicide is a real thing that far too many people face. The guilt and trauma that results is a vise, holding onto you for a long time. The first step to move past the pain is admitting that it is OK to not be OK. Trauma and heartbreak happen too frequently. This pain can lead you to believe that nothing will ever be the same or get better. Accepting help from those around you, whether friend, family member or a professional is the first step to recovery. To understand that infidelity is not OK and that it's not a part of every relationship is a difficult step. To build trust takes years after your trust has broken. But understand that your broken trust should remain with the person who broke it and not the person trying to help you heal. Anxiety and depression are real things and very common. It's OK to talk about them and it's OK to get help, whether through therapy or medication. Do what helps you and don't worry about what others think. They are not the ones who are hurting. And please reach out to someone, anyone, if your thoughts stray to the idea that the world would be better without you or if you think that death is the only way to stop your pain. Know that there is someone out there to help you. Love is tricky and often a painful experience. Not everyone gets their happy endings. Books, movies and TV shows are supposed to show you the unrealistic side of things because that's what they are for. Entertainment. Not reality. Enjoy them, but do not expect the outcome. Remember that at the end of the day, you are stronger than you think and that you are doing your very best. Thank you for reading my book.

Present

Chapter 1

The soft morning sun came slipping through the blinds, causing Jenn to blink slowly awake. She let her eyes adjust and stared up at the unfamiliar ceiling fan circling above her. She blinked, trying to remember what had happened the night before. She glanced around the room, trying to find something that was familiar. She slowly rolled over to face the man from last night, struggling to remember his name. Was it Jim, Mike, or Jeff? She knew that it was something generic like that.

"Ugh, I have to stop getting into these situations," she whispered to herself.

Luckily, he was still asleep and snoring softly. Jenn rolled in the other direction and slowly slid from the bed. Her clothes were lying on the floor in a path from the door to the bed.

Picking up the clothes and making her way to the bedroom door, Jenn snuck out into the dark hallway. Judging by the sunlight coming through the windows it was still early. She peeked into another bedroom before she found the bathroom. Pulling the door shut quietly, she began to dress and then splashed cold water over her face. The eye makeup she had perfected last night was smeared, making her look like a raccoon. She sighed as she tried to wipe away the black smudge but only made it worse. She pulled out her phone and turned it on. The battery charge was almost down to zero, so she had to figure out her escape path quickly. Unfortunately, she had no idea where she was so calling a cab was out of the question.

Trying to stay as quiet as possible, she opened the bathroom door and went to look for her shoes. Stepping out of the bathroom, she nearly collided with the man from the night before.

"Oh, sorry, didn't see you there," she mumbled, feeling slightly embarrassed by getting caught sneaking out.

"Yeah, I noticed you were out of bed and came to check on you. Are you OK?" he asked. She smiled. He was just as good looking in the morning as he was last night.

"Oh, totally fine. Just trying to find my things." She began to pick at her fingernails, a bad habit she had when she was nervous.

"You were trying to sneak out without me knowing, weren't you, Jenn?" he asked with a sly smile. She looked up at him and her cheeks flushed. He reached out and took her hand, gently pulling her towards the kitchen. "At least let me make you breakfast before you go."

Jenn sighed, allowing him to guide her. "OK, if you insist."

She followed him and began scanning the countertop

for a piece of mail or something personal since she still could not remember his name. Thankfully, there was a letter on the kitchen table where she took a seat. His name was Mike. Jenn pouted to herself, wishing that his name was less common. She watched him as he fixed breakfast, letting her guard down slightly. Finally, a man that knew how to treat a woman right.

"So, Mike, that was fun last night, right?" she asked with an almost instant regret. She cringed and hoped that she didn't sound like someone digging for a compliment.

Mike turned around with a smile. "I did have fun. You are an entertaining woman for sure."

He turned his back and returned to the stove. She rested her head in her hands and stared, letting her thoughts get the better of her. She shook her head to snap herself out of her daydream. She assumed that he probably did this with all the women he took home from the bars.

He went about the breakfast preparations in silence and Jenn pulled her phone back out. She had a missed call and a text from her best friend, Riley.

The text sounded both angry and amused: *Hope you had fun. Call me in the morning, so I know you are alive.*

She felt like the worst friend ever, but Riley had told her to go for it. It worked in their friendship, since Riley was more down-to-earth and levelheaded than Jenn. Riley had been in a relationship since college and only came out with Jenn to make sure she was safe. Nothing really stopped Jenn from doing stupid things, but at least she didn't end up on the side of the road somewhere. Even though they were opposites, they had been friends since junior high.

"Must be a good text," Mike said as he walked towards the table carrying two plates of food. He set one down in front of her and she thanked him. She picked up her fork and took a bite, smiling and repressing the need to let out a groan of delight. He was an excellent cook. Jenn could tell he was staring at her, so she looked up from the plate. He was busy watching her with a crooked smile.

"Delicious, thank you so much," she managed to say while taking a few more bites.

"You're welcome, you earned it." She looked up at him again, feeling embarrassed and vulnerable.

They continued their breakfast in near silence, the awkwardness of the situation washing over her. She finished the food and set her silverware on the plate.

"Well, Mike, thank you for a fun evening and for a nice breakfast. You have my number if you ever want to hang out again." She stood up and turned to grab her purse from the counter.

Mike stood and walked over with outstretched arms. She awkwardly slid her arms around his shoulder and gave him a quick kiss on the lips. Gently, she pushed away from him and turned towards the door. Without looking back, she opened the front door and stepped out into the bright morning sun. Rummaging through her purse, she found her sunglasses and hastily put them on.

It took her a moment to adjust to the brightness and figure out where she was. Across the street was one of her favorite coffee shops which she frequented on workdays. Looking down the street she realized that she was a few blocks from her work. She slipped her jacket over her shoulder and began walking in the cool autumn morning. A few cars drove past as she pulled her phone to call for a ride. The phone was dead. She continued to walk until she reached the front doors where she worked.

She sighed and shook her head, feeling embarrassed to show herself to her coworkers in this state. She pushed the front doors open to a small reception area.

A blonde woman looked up from her computer and smiled. "That's a good look for you."

"Good morning, Caroline, my cell went dead. Can I just borrow the phone for a moment?" Jenn asked.

"Of course, Jenn." Caroline handed the phone to her across the desk with a judgmental smirk. Jenn rolled her eyes and quickly dialed Riley's phone number.

She answered after a couple of rings. "Hey Jenn,

where are you? I was getting worried."

"Oh, you know, hanging out at work in my very best walk-of-shame outfit." Jenn smiled to herself. She could just imagine Riley's expression of exacerbation and amusement. Luckily for Jenn, Riley never judged.

"Can't wait to hear this story," she said, "I'll be there in 15." Jenn thanked her and hung up the phone. She turned back to the desk and a staring Caroline. She wasn't even trying to hide the smirk anymore.

A short brunette woman walked around the corner into the reception area. Jenn sighed, silently wishing she could disappear into the wall.

"Morning, Betty." It was the most fake cheerful tone she had.

"Oh, morning Jenn. Didn't realize you were working today?" Betty replied, looking Jenn over from head to toe.

Jenn inhaled, "Nope, cellphone died. Just calling for a ride." Betty and Caroline exchanged glances.

Betty turned back to Jenn, "Another one, Jenn?" She smiled, and Caroline giggled.

"Oh, to be young and single," Caroline quipped. Jenn looked away and out the front window. Caroline was only one year older than she was. She looked back towards Caroline and noticed she was resting her chin purposely on her left hand so that Jenn could clearly see the huge diamond ring glistening from THAT finger.

"What can I say?" she muttered and turned back to the door. Betty patted her shoulder and walked back around the corner and out of sight.

Jenn wasn't ashamed of her private life, but it was tiring trying to defend herself, so she just stopped commenting. Caroline clicked her tongue and went back to her computer. Jenn sat down in the waiting area and picked up a magazine and started flipping pages. She began to feel the annoyance bubble in her chest, and she turned the magazine page a bit too hard causing it to rip. She closed her eyes and took a deep breath.

Jenn wished that people would stop paying so much attention to her private life. Opening her eyes, she stared at the magazine page without really reading it.

The soft clicking of the computer keyboard continued behind her, punctuated only by an occasional sigh from Caroline. The phone rang, and Caroline answered with one of those annoying fake customer service voices, "Thank you for calling DRC, this is Caroline, how may I direct your call?" It made Jenn smiled.

A familiar blue car pulled up outside and Jenn set down her magazine. Without looking back, she gave Caroline a wave and headed out the door. She quietly opened the car door and slid into the passenger seat, trying not to wake the baby or the toddler in the backseat.

Riley glanced her way with a smile, "Morning, sweetheart."

"Hey," was all Jenn could say. Riley pulled out and drove off in silence. Jenn leaned her head against the window and watched the buildings fly by.

"You need me to stop and get some breakfast for you?" Riley asked with her motherly tone.

"Um, no thanks. Mike made me some." Jenn responded. She felt the weight of Riley's stare. Riley let out a small giggle. Jenn felt suddenly embarrassed.

"Oh my god, you said a name and had breakfast? Who is this guy?" Riley was ecstatic.

"No one, no one. Just a guy. I don't really remember much about him. He was dressed nice," Jenn stuttered. "Stop looking at me like that."

Riley smiled and turned her focus back onto the road. "I'm just saying, I thought you usually left before breakfast and forgot names just as fast." She pulled up outside of Jenn's apartment building. Putting the car in park, she turned toward her friend. "Could this be a first? Like, a second date thing?"

Jenn sighed. "Ri, you know that I don't do second dates." She picked up her purse and opened the car door.

"Jenn, come on. It's been long enough. You have to try again." Riley said as she put her hand on Jenn's. Jenn loved Riley, but she did not understand her point of view. Riley got her happy ending. She married her college sweetheart and had two children in quick succession. She did not understand what Jenn had been through.

"Thanks for the ride, Riley. I'll call you later," she said as she closed the car door.

"Jenn…" Riley started to say but the slam of the door cut her off. Jenn walked towards the apartment door without looking back and heard Riley's car pull away as she dug into her purse, searching for her keys. Jenn took a deep breath and opened the door. She hated getting upset at Riley. Riley was the only one who knew the whole story and had stuck by Jenn's side, good or bad. She made a mental note to send her a text later, apologizing.

Making her way to the kitchen, she tossed her purse on the counter and plugged her phone into its charger. She leaned against the counter, resting her head in her hands. She secretly agreed with Riley, but she would never openly admit to it. It had been five years since Jenn's was had been turned upside down.

She glanced down at her phone and saw a text alert. Her stomach flipped a little and she let her guard down, hoping that Mike was checking in on her. Pushing the text icon on her phone screen, she smiled fleetingly, then frowned. The text was from her friend, Jake, asking if she wanted to grab coffee after work in the morning. She was slightly annoyed that she let herself get her hopes up. She quickly texted back a yes and set her phone down.

Glancing at the clock on the wall, Jenn realized she needed to get a shower and rest before work later that night. She was lucky to have strange hours. It made her social life a little easier. She stood in front of the mirror, staring at herself for a few moments. It wasn't that she didn't enjoy herself and it wasn't as if she didn't want what Riley had.

More than anything, she wanted a relationship. More than anything, she wanted a family of her own. The problem was that she had had it, or almost had it and it had blown up in her face. She hated thinking about it because it made her both very mad and very sad. It had taken a long time for Jenn to resurface after her ex tore her heart to shreds.

She took a deep breath and shook her head to refocus. Turning her back on her reflection, she climbed into the shower. The warm water washed over her, and she suddenly realized how tired she was. She quickly washed up and turned the water off. Wrapping herself in a large towel she made her way into the bedroom. Without pulling the blankets back, Jenn flopped onto the bed and closed her eyes. Her head still spinning from the thoughts coursing through her brain, she drifted off to sleep.

10 years ago

Chapter 2

Jenn and Riley had been dreaming about going to college together since they became best friends in junior high. They started a list of colleges that had everything they both wanted and that were just far enough away from home to make them feel independent.

With a stroke of luck, they found a small college near St. Louis that had the athletic and educational programs they both wanted. They were accepted without issue and were promised spots on the volleyball team. As the summer ended after senior year, they packed up Riley's car and headed off to their first year of college.

The excitement was almost too much. The girls talked and giggled for the entire two-hour journey to Eastern College. It was mid-day when they pulled into the busy parking lot outside of the dorms. People were bustling around, emptying their cars and making their way towards the buildings. Jenn stood next to the car and smiled while Riley pulled bags out of the trunk.

"Don't worry Jenn, I got this," she muttered as she pulled a particularly big bag out. Jenn smirked

and walked over to help. They gathered their bags and headed in the general direction of the dorms.

Following the crowd, they found the check in area and got the keys to their dorm and a packet of information. Juggling her bags and keys, Jenn dropped her packet, the paperwork spilling across the sidewalk

"Here, let me get that," a voice called from behind her. A tall, dark-haired guy rushed past her and began picking up the scattered papers. He stood up and turned towards Jenn with a smile. "There you go." He continued to smile at her as she took the papers. "I'm Kevin and this is my roommate, Curt," he said while motioning towards a blonde guy standing behind Jenn and Riley.

"Thank you, I'm Jenn and this is my roommate, Riley." Jenn set down her bag and extended a hand to Kevin.

"Oh, how formal," he smirked. "Well, I suppose we'll see you at orientation." He winked at Jenn and then motioned to Curt to follow him. Jenn stared at his back as he walked away.

"Jenn, close your mouth! That's just embarrassing," Riley said as she bumped into Jenn's shoulder, waking her from her daydream. Jenn shook her head as she picked up her bags and followed Riley into the dorm.

The rest of the afternoon was spent unpacking and organizing the dorm room. Jenn couldn't help but wonder where Kevin was living on campus. After rearranging things a few times, the girls stood back and sighed with relief.

"Well, I'm starving," Jenn said as she grabbed her purse off the bed. "Let's go eat." After locking the door, they made their way across campus toward the dining hall.

About halfway across the quad, Jenn heard someone call her name. "Hey Jenn! Come over here!" She turned to see who was talking and saw Kevin sitting with a group of guys. She glanced at Riley and shrugged before walking toward the group. "Hi again," he said with a smirk and patted the ground near him. Jenn sat down, and Riley followed suit. Kevin introduced them to the group, Jenn nodding to each. She didn't have a great memory for names, but she recognized Curt from earlier that day. "So, where are you girls from?" Kevin asked.

"Small town in central Illinois," Jenn answered.

"What brings you to Missouri?" Kevin asked.

Jenn went into her story without divulging too much information. "Riley and I have been planning this since junior high. We made a list of all colleges that had the necessary components. Athletics, academics, size. This one covered it all." She smiled at Riley and squeezed her hand.

"Oh, so you're an athlete?" Kevin asked as he looked around at his friends. "What we have here is a good portion of the baseball team."

Jenn glanced at Riley and then back at Kevin. "We play volleyball." They stared at each other for a moment, in silence. "Well, we were just heading in to grab something to eat," Jenn said while pushing off the ground. "Maybe we'll see you around campus." She pulled Riley up and began to turn away.

"You can count on that," Kevin called after her as she walked away. Riley giggled, and Jenn elbowed her in the ribs.

"Oh boy, you are in trouble," Riley said as she gave a wry smile. Jenn shook her head. Riley and Jenn had promised to focus on school and volleyball once they made it to college. They were both unattached when they left high school, and both planned on staying that way for the foreseeable future. What Jenn did not see coming was meeting a cute guy her first day and really wanting to get to know more about him.

"No, no. No trouble. Just another boy. And you know that athletes are players. I mean, look at him." They both turned back to the group that was sitting in the center of the quad. Jenn looked a little longer than she should have and caught Kevin's eye. "Damn it!" she whispered and grabbed Riley's arm. They picked up their pace as they headed to the dining hall.

Chapter 3

Jenn stayed true to her promise. She and Riley went to class and to volleyball practice. They focused on studying and playing. However, Kevin did not back down. He seemed to always be there. He managed to sit with Jenn at meals, he bumped into her frequently on campus and he was at every one of her volleyball games. Although she saw him talking to different girls around campus, he seemed to pay the most attention to her.

She was cleaning up after a Friday night game when Riley came up behind her and made her jump. "I'll give it to him, he is persistent," Riley said. Jenn looked up from her bag and saw Kevin waiting next to the stands. Against her better judgment, she smiled.

"He's just supporting the team. He understands what it's like to be a college athlete," Jenn replied, feeling warmth in her cheeks.

"Sure, OK," Riley muttered as she helped Jenn pick up some equipment. They walked to the equipment closet in silence. She locked the door and turned around. She and Riley almost ran straight into Kevin, causing Jenn to gasp and step back.

"Sorry, didn't mean to sneak up on you. Curt and I were going to grab some pizza and wondered if you two would like to join us?" Jenn glanced sideways at Riley, who smiled and nodded.

Jenn sighed and looked back at Kevin. "Sure, give us 15 minutes to change, please." Kevin gave a thumbs up and turned back towards the door where Curt was waiting.

Riley grabbed her arm, "Oh, come on, it's just pizza. Look at them. I mean, wow," she said breathlessly. Jenn rolled her eyes and adjusted the bag on her shoulder. They walked together towards the locker room. After changing they headed to the front of the gym, where Kevin and Curt were waiting. Together they walked a few blocks to a local pizza parlor.

Jenn wasn't quite ready to let her guard down, but Riley was excited enough for them both. She and Curt talked for what seemed like hours, discussing their pasts and what they wanted to do in the future. Jenn watched them with a smile on her face. It was nice to see people click like that. She and Kevin talked on and off about all sorts of things, but it was awkward. It wasn't that she wasn't interested in him, she just didn't want to start anything right now. In the back of her mind, she always saw male athletes as womanizers. And she wanted to focus on school and on volleyball. She had to for the sake of her scholarship. Curt and Riley left the restaurant holding hands, walking in front of Jenn and Kevin.

"So, I think we've lost our roommates," Kevin said,

letting out a small laugh.

"Yeah, they get along well, don't they?" Jenn smiled at Kevin and quickly looked back at the ground.

"What about you?" he asked as he stopped.

Jenn slowly turned to face him. "Look Kevin, I don't know what you are expecting. I'm trying to focus on school and adjusting here. I don't know how a guy would fit into that." She glanced down at her feet and noticed that he had taken a step closer to her.

"I'm not asking for you to give up studying or playing. I understand, I am on scholarship too. But Jenn, clearly there is an attraction between us. You can't deny that." He took another step toward her. She felt her stomach tighten, shyness taking over the moment. Her mind was racing a million miles per hour, something it tended to do when she was nervous. She finally looked up at him and he was standing dangerously close to her.

"I'm not denying, just questioning what that means," she said softly. He smiled his crooked smile and placed his hand under her chin, so she couldn't look down again.

"Maybe we should stop thinking for a moment." He leaned down and softly kissed her lips. She closed her eyes as her stomach fluttered like a hundred butterflies. She let her shoulders relax and raised her arms, looping them behind his neck. Jenn didn't know how long they stood there before she heard someone clear their throat. She opened her eyes and pulled away from Kevin. Riley and Curt were standing a few feet away.

"We thought we lost you two. Turned around and you were gone," Riley said with the biggest smile. Jenn brushed her hair back with her hands and began to slowly walk back towards campus. Curt and Kevin exchanged nods and Riley hooked her arm with Jenn's and leaned into her. She whispered "Wow!" in Jenn's ear and squeezed her arm. Kevin and Curt walked together and began talking about their weekend plans while the girls walked in silence. Jenn's mind was still racing, and she didn't really know what to say.

Once they made it back to campus, they exchanged good nights and walked toward their dorms. As soon as the door closed to their room, Riley exploded. "Oh my god, girl. That looked like a scene from of one of those Hallmark movies you love." Jenn fell back onto her bed and stared at the ceiling.

"Riley, it felt like it, too. The world stopped. Like, literally stopped around us." Jenn burst into a fit of laughter as Riley sat on the bed next to her.

"I told you that you were in trouble," she said as she lay down next to Jenn on the bed. They stared at the ceiling in silence.

"I didn't even check on you. So, you and Curt?" Jenn said, turning her head towards Riley. Riley had a huge smile on her face and began talking about Curt. Jenn smiled and nodded, only half listening. Her mind kept wandering back to the kiss. She had kissed boys before, but nothing ever felt like that. She didn't know what to think about it, but she knew that it was the start of something big.

Later that night while she was studying, a message popped up on her computer.

Well, that was fun. Hope to do it again soon.

Jenn sat and thought about it. She wanted to experience everything that she could at college. That's what you were supposed to do. Was dating not part of those experiences?

She typed back after a few minutes, *Maybe we should.* She leaned back in her chair, waiting for a response.

The chime sounded for a new message and she peered at the screen. *I look forward to it.*

She smiled and rubbed her eyes. It was late, and she could hear Riley snoring behind her. She turned off the computer and climbed into bed, even though she knew that sleep would not come easily. After tossing and turning for an hour, her mind slowed down enough to let her drift off to sleep.

Present

Chapter 4

The alarm sounded on her phone and Jenn slowly blinked awake. She felt like she hadn't slept at all. She picked up her phone and checked the time, 7 p.m. Sometimes she regretted working third shift. She rolled out of bed and made her way to the bathroom, running her hands through her hair as she walked. It was matted on one side and she struggled to pull her fingers through. She splashed some water on her face and brushed her hair. She got dressed for work and headed to the kitchen to make something to eat.

After she ate, she poured herself a cup of coffee and sat at the kitchen table to read the newspaper. Her phone chimed for a new message and Jenn picked it up. She assumed it was someone from work or Riley, but she was pleasantly surprised to see a message from Mike.

Just checking in to make sure you made it home safe. Didn't want to write earlier, I assumed you were sleeping. Thanks for a great night and I hope to see you again.

Jenn sighed. She wished that Mike would just be like all the other guys and never call again. He got what he wanted, and so did she. What more could there be here? A small knot formed in her chest. She didn't like this feeling of nerves and uncertainty. She didn't allow herself to feel that. She started to reply and stopped herself. Setting down her phone she hit her speed dial and speaker button.

Riley answered after a few rings. "Hey, what's up? I just got the kids in bed."

Jenn sighed again, "Mike texted. He was checking in to make sure I made it home safe."

Riley was silent for a moment. "Is that a bad thing?" she asked.

"Ugh, Ri, you know I don't like this." Jenn put her head in her hands.

"What? Don't like that a nice guy was checking in on you? A guy that you obviously had a good time with. You gave him your real number, that's a first." Jenn sat up quickly. Riley was right, Jenn never gave her real number.

"Crap, you're right. I didn't realize I did. I must have given it to him last night when I was drunk. Crap."

She could hear Riley laughing. "Or, you could have done it on purpose?" Jenn stared at the wall.

Had she done it on purpose? "No, no way. No. Definitely drunk Jenn wasn't thinking clearly."

Riley paused for a moment, "Jenn, I'm going to say it again even though you hate hearing it. It's not a bad thing. It is a good thing. It's time. Five years, Jenn, five years. You deserve to try again. You deserve to be happy." Jenn hated when Riley did this, which was quite often. She sat in silence for a few moments.

"Ok, I hear you. But what makes you think this guy is any different from…him…?" Jenn could not bring herself to say his name.

Riley sighed loudly. "How do you know that he is not, if you don't even give him a chance?" Jenn hated when Riley was right, even though throughout their friendship she was right most of the time.

"Damn it. I will kill you when this backfires. I love you, but I will kill you," Jenn relented.

Riley clapped her hands and let out a yelp.

"Riley, relax. You'll wake up your kids," Jenn said with a chuckle.

Riley shushed herself and giggled. "Write him back, just see. I'll be here for you through it. I always am." Jenn smiled to herself. It was true. Riley stuck by her side through everything. She was one of the only reasons Jenn was still here.

"Ok, here goes nothing. I have to get ready for work, but I will call you tomorrow," Jenn said. They exchanged goodbyes and hung up. Jenn took a deep breath and picked her phone up. She pulled up the message from Mike and sat staring at the screen. She didn't know what to say. Keeping it simple, she typed

It was fun, thanks. Give me a call tomorrow evening and maybe we can meet up again.

She paused for a moment before hitting send. Once she hit send, she knew she couldn't take it back. Her finger hovered over the button. She closed her eyes and pushed send, her heart beating a little faster than usual. She set the phone down and cleaned up her dishes. Her phone chimed, and Jenn's heart skipped. She walked back to the table and picked it up.

Looking forward to it.

Jenn couldn't help but grin. She was going to give this a fair chance, at least.

She finished her coffee and placed the empty cup in the sink. Gathering her work things, Jenn grabbed her purse and headed out the door. She worked at a small rehab center downtown as a nurse, covering the 9 p.m.-9 a.m. shift. She also hated driving, so she took the bus, which meant leaving the house almost an hour before the shift started to make sure she got there on time. She liked the extra time, though, and the quiet of the bus late at night. It gave her time to think and to listen to music.

She turned on her Spotify and put on headphones. Leaning her head against the cool bus window, she watched the lights go by and reflected on the choice she just made. It would be her first real date in five years. The thought made her chest tighten. She hated that her mind always went to the negative outcomes, but that was merely based on all her experiences. The bus came to a stop on the corner near her work and she thanked the bus driver as she exited. She slipped the headphones and phone back into her purse as she walked towards the front door.

Scanning her badge at the front door, she sighed as she walked in. The nice thing about night shift was that she didn't have to deal with the judgmental Caroline. She walked past the front desk and down to the break room.

Tossing her bag into a locker, she jumped as someone tapped her on the shoulder.

"I hear you had to do the walk of shame to work this morning." She turned to face her coworker, Nicole. She was one of the only coworkers who knew all about Jenn's past. The rest were just kept up to date on Jenn's surface issues.

"Yeah, and I see Caroline still can't keep her mouth shut." Jenn smiled and closed her locker. Another thing that Jenn liked about third shift was that there was less staff there. Even though she went out frequently, Jenn was not a huge people person. She loved being a nurse and caring for people, but spending a large amount of time with a lot of people was exhausting. Jenn and Nicole clocked in and headed out to the nurses' station. They got the report from the previous shift and walked together on their first rounds, checking in on each patient.

They went about their nightly routine, chatting about recent events and plans for the weekend. "So, I met a guy and his name is Mike. He's calling me later and we're going to go on a date." Jenn told Nicole during their last rounds of the night. Nicole stopped in her tracks with her mouth open. Jenn rolled her eyes and let out a small laugh.

Nicole shook her head, "Whoa, whoa, whoa. We have a name and a second date? Do I need to do a neuro check on you?" Jenn shoved her arm and kept walking. Nicole took a few fast steps to catch up. They walked in silence for a bit, checking in each room.

"I think it's time." Jenn stopped outside the last room and stared at the ground. "I'm so sick of not feeling anymore. It's not who I am. I'm sick of letting him ruin everything." She sniffed and looked up at Nicole. She hated that she cried when she was angry. Jenn cried a lot, but the fact that she couldn't even get angry properly really made her mad.

Nicole put a hand on her shoulder. "It's about damn time," she said and pulled Jenn into a quick hug. Jenn wasn't really a touchy-feely person, but she accepted the embrace. They finished walking to the desk and sat down to finish charting.

The sun shining through the windows as they

finished their night. The next shift arrived soon after and the girls reported off to them. Nicole had finished her report first and she waited for Jenn so they could clock out together.

"So, are you going to head home and get some sleep before the big night?" Nicole asked as they walked outside.

"I promised Jake I'd meet him for coffee first," Jenn said as she slipped her sunglasses on. They shared a quick hug and said goodbye, turning and walking in opposite directions. The coffee shop was a few blocks from her work and close enough to Jake's job that they often met in the morning. Jake was a physician's assistant at a local hospital, and he worked third shift as well. Their morning coffee time was another one of Jenn's routines.

She and Jake had also been friends since high school. They dated briefly during their junior year but decided that they were better off as friends. He was her best guy friend and they stayed in touch throughout the years. They went off to different colleges but made sure to visit each other as much as possible and spent time together during breaks. It was a stroke of luck that they ended up living in the same city after graduation and happened to work in similar fields.

She walked in and saw him waiting at a small table in the corner of the coffee shop. He stood as she approached and gave her a quick hug. He was already had his coffee, so she headed up to the counter to order. "Did you want anything to eat?" she called over her shoulder.

"Sure, get me whatever you're getting." Jenn ordered a coffee and two scones and walked back to the table. Jake thanked her as she sat down. She sipped her coffee and took a bite of the scone as they sat in silence for a moment.

"So, anything exciting happen at the hospital tonight?" she asked, finally breaking the silence.

"Oh, same stuff as usual. I did figure out one mystery, so I'll count that as a win." Jake sipped his coffee and smiled. "How about you?"

"Oh, nothing out of the ordinary," Jenn replied. She slowly sipped her coffee and smirked. "I did have to do the walk of shame into work this morning to borrow the phone."

Jake looked at her with a quick look of shock before letting out a nervous laugh. Jen noticed a flash of something in his eyes but couldn't figure out what it was. "Really? I bet Caroline had a field day with that."

Jenn looked at him for a moment before shrugging. They talked for a little while before Jenn began to yawn. Jake picked up Jenn's empty cup and plate, placing them in the dirty dish bin. They walked together to the bus stop, something Jake always did even though he had to walk the other direction back to the hospital. They stood together until the bus got there. "Any plans tonight?" Jake asked.

Jenn blushed, "Yeah, I have a date," she replied without looking at him. It was silent for a moment before she heard him let out a small laugh.

"I'm sorry, did I hear the word date come out of your mouth?" Jenn looked at him and noticed that same flash in his eyes. She leaned her head into his shoulder and let out a sigh.

"I know, hell has frozen over for sure." He wrapped his arm around her shoulder and pulled her closer momentarily.

"About damn time" was all he said. She looked up at him and smiled.

"You're the second person to say that today." The bus drove toward them and stopped. Jenn pulled him into another hug and then stepped back, looking at him. His smile seemed strained. She squeezed his hand and they exchanged goodbyes.

"Good luck!" Jake called after her as she stepped onto the bus. She sat down and waved from her seat, giving him a thumbs up as the bus drove away.

Jenn pulled out her phone and turned her music back on. She closed her eyes briefly and just listened. At that moment, she was an odd mixture of nerves and calmness. Jake had that effect on her. She was genuinely happy that he had stayed in her life, unlike most of the other people she knew in high school. Not only was he smart, he was a genuinely nice person and was always there for Jenn when she needed him. She kept her circle of friends small and she liked it that way.

The bus pulled up to the corner outside of her apartment. She gathered her bag, thanked the bus driver and stepped off the bus. She stopped inside the lobby to grab her mail before heading upstairs to her apartment. She tossed her work bag into her front closet and headed into the kitchen for another cup of coffee. Jenn's vice that came with working third shift was drinking entirely too much caffeine. She flipped through her mail and opened a rectangular envelope. Two photos fell from the card inside and Jenn smiled at the two small boys smiling back.

She opened the letter and read; *your nephews wanted you to put these on your fridge.*

She picked up the photos and walked over to the refrigerator immediately. The front was mostly empty aside from a few small school photos of her nieces and nephews, a medium-sized family photo from Riley and several pictures of her and Jake. She stood back and crossed her arms, looking from photo to photo with a huge smile on her face. At that moment, Jenn felt happier than she had in a long time. It wasn't that she was always sad, but she constantly had a sadness pulling at her. She had been in a dark place for so long that it was hard work pulling herself back into the light.

She glanced down at her watch and realized she needed to shower and sleep before Mike called that evening. She made sure to plug her phone in so that she would be ready for his call and she jumped in the shower. She let the warm water run over her as her exhaustion finally hit. She brushed her teeth and climbed into bed. She drifted off as her mind slowed down, thinking of what was to come and fighting off thinking about the past.

7 years ago

Chapter 5

Kevin did not want to commit to being Jenn's boyfriend at first. They went on dates and spent a lot of time together, but he made excuses whenever she brought up the term boyfriend. After several months of dating casually, he agreed to be exclusive.

He was Jenn's first real boyfriend. He was her first for a lot of things. The first time meeting a boy's family and spending the holidays with them. Her first experience with most things physical. He was her first real love. The only time they spent apart were weekend nights when there were parties, since Jenn didn't drink that often.

By senior year they were living together with Riley and Curt off campus in a small apartment. They were a great support system for each other, whether it was with sports or academics.

It was Jenn's dream come true. Her best friend was dating her boyfriend's best friend. She hoped that they would all get married and end up living next door to each other in the suburbs, raising their kids to be best friends as well.

Riley and Curt talked about marriage and kids all the time, but Kevin never fully joined the conversation. He said that he wasn't sure about the future, that he preferred to live in the present.   Jenn accepted this because she was so happy with everything happening in her life, even though there was always a nagging in the back of her mind.

She was doing well in school and was one semester away from finishing the nursing program. She had made the all-conference team in volleyball and received an honorable mention as an All-American. Riley had made second team all-conference and the team had made it to the first round of the national tournament before losing. Her senior year was shaping up just the way she had always imagined.

****

Jenn and Kevin planned to stay with his family for a week over Christmas break and then travel for a week to Jenn's home. Riley was doing the same with Curt so that they would end break in their hometown, to celebrate together. Riley and Jenn hugged goodbye and headed off to their boyfriend's cars. Jenn climbed into Kevin's car and leaned over for a quick kiss before he started the ignition. Kevin took her hand as they pulled out of the apartment parking lot onto the main road. They drove in silence for a while as Jenn surfed through the radio.

"I know something you don't know," Kevin teased in a sing-song voice.

Jenn turned the radio down and looked at him. "Oh really, that would be a first. Do tell." Kevin shook his head and stared straight ahead. Jenn pulled her hand from his and gently poked his shoulder. "Do not do that. Give up the information." He jokingly grabbed his shoulder, acting like Jenn had hurt him. She rolled her eyes and rubbed the spot where she had poked him. He grabbed her hand and kissed it. She tilted her head and stared at him, "Come on."

He continued to stare straight ahead but glanced toward her when she began to glare. "OK, but you cannot say anything to Riley. I mean it. Curt will kill me if she finds out."

Jenn had a nervous feeling in her stomach. "Nothing bad, right. This is a good thing, right?" she asked nervously.

"All good, nothing bad. He didn't tell me his entire plan but … he's proposing sometime over break." Kevin glanced back at Jenn with a huge smile.

Jenn let her jaw drop before letting out a squeal of delight. She was bad at keeping secrets, but she knew how important this was for Riley. She and Riley had talked about getting engaged. They had both been with their boyfriends for three years and thought that was adequate time for dating before becoming engaged.

"Oh, this is going to eat me alive until she calls me to tell me," Jenn said. They talked for the rest of the car ride about how they thought he would propose. Kevin thought he would do something private, just Curt and Riley together somewhere decorated for Christmas. Jenn thought he would do some grand gesture, somewhere public. Without coming out and saying it, that was how she thought she would want it done. She and Kevin had never really talked about it and at that moment, she felt the slightest twinge of jealously towards Riley. Luckily, Jenn was a big believer in letting things be the way they would be. If it was meant to be, it would be. She could tell Kevin was a little uncomfortable talking about it, so she switched subjects. They talked about the break and all the hometown traditions that they would have to celebrate.

They pulled into Kevin's mom's driveway shortly before dark. He knocked on the front door and his mom opened the door. The warmth and wonderful smell of dinner hit Jenn and Kevin as she pulled them both in for hugs. Kevin took their bags down to his room as she was pulled into the living room. His mom wanted to show off the decorations before offering her a hot cider. Kevin joined them, and they sat and chatted, catching up on everything that had been going on in each other's lives. A timer buzzed from the kitchen and Kevin's mom excused herself.

"It smells wonderful, Cheryl," Jenn called.

"Thank you, Jenn. You two can wash up and come sit down." The meal and company were great. Kevin's mom was always so welcoming. She fed them way too much and soon Jenn was getting groggy.

She and Kevin excused themselves and headed down

to his room. She changed into her pajamas and climbed into bed, feeling warm and full. Kevin gave her a quick kiss before heading back to the kitchen. He wanted to spend some time with his mom alone. She fell asleep quickly and didn't hear him when he climbed into bed later.

Chapter 6

The rest of the time with Kevin's mom went quickly. They celebrated Christmas Eve with presents and a candlelight church service. Jenn and Kevin were saying goodbye to his mom and packing the car the next day when Jenn's phone rang. She looked to see who it was, and she smiled widely when she saw Riley's photo pop up. She giggled and showed the phone to Kevin. She calmed herself with a deep breath and pushed the talk button.

"Hi Riley, Merry Christmas! How are you?" Jenn rambled, trying not to sound too excited. She hit the speaker button, so Kevin could hear the conversation.

"Oh my god, oh my god. I need to show you something!" Riley said, her voice a little higher and faster than usual. Jenn's phone chimed, and a message popped up on screen. Jenn inhaled and opened the photo. It was a picture of Riley's hand and the most beautiful diamond ring.

Jenn squealed, "I'm so happy for you!" She turned the phone so Kevin could see, and he clapped his hands.

"Atta-boy!" was his response.

"Hi Kevin! Oh Jenn, didn't he do good?" Jenn could tell Riley had tears in her eyes.

"So good, Ri, so good. I can't wait for you to tell me

all about it. We're getting in the car now and heading home. We will get together tomorrow, OK?" She and Riley exchanged goodbyes and she hung up.

She turned to Kevin and smiled. "Thank god, I didn't want to hold that secret in any longer."

They got in the car and headed back on the road and towards Jenn's hometown. Kevin and Jenn made a bet about the proposal and shook on it. Jenn thought he proposed Christmas Eve in front of family. Kevin thought he proposed Christmas Eve when they were alone. The stakes weren't high, the bet was only that they would buy each other's drinks while celebrating tomorrow.

There were several cars in Jenn's parent's driveway when they pulled up. Her brother and sister had gotten there first. Jenn loved her busy family Christmas, but the quiet Christmas Eve with Kevin's mom had also been nice. She walked inside and was greeted by her brother's daughter running towards her with her arms open for a hug. She and Kevin hugged everyone and joined the group in the living room. Jenn's sister handed her a drink and then handed over her baby nephew. They sat and talked, catching up on each other's lives. Jenn's mom bustled in and out of the kitchen until it was time to eat.

They gathered around the large dining room table before saying grace and eating. The sounds of silverware clinking, and the smells of roast turkey filled the air. With their plates almost empty, the conversation slowed as everyone settled into the post-turkey haze.

"Hey Mom, did you hear the news yet?" Jenn asked, sitting up with excitement. Her mom shook her head and Jenn glanced around the table. Her entire family was at full attention and she wavered slightly. She felt a panicked sensation in her chest as she realized her family thought she would be telling them about her engagement. She cleared her throat, "Riley and Curt are engaged!" Her mom and sister's faces turned for only a moment before recovering with smiles.

"That is such great news!" her mom replied. Jenn pulled her phone out and showed them all the picture Riley had sent. Each one made a little comment on the ring and said how happy they were for her.

Jenn's brother, who never had a filter, finally said what everyone was probably thinking. "So, Kevin, I take it Jenn will be getting one of those soon, too?" Jenn shot him a look and was scared to look back at Kevin. When she finally did, she noticed his ears were pink.

"Well, I can't steal Curt's thunder now, can I?" He looked back at Jenn and smiled. That answer seemed to placate Jenn's family and the conversation changed to school and family life. Jenn glanced a few times at Kevin, trying to read his expression. He was too good at hiding his emotions. After clearing the table, everyone headed into the living room for presents.

Jenn caught up with Kevin and grabbed his hand. "I'm so sorry, my brother is such an idiot."

Kevin kissed her forehead, "No worries. It was a fair question. Just not one I'm ready to answer quite yet." They walked together into the living room and sat down together on the couch. The rest of the evening was so busy that Jenn didn't get an opportunity to think about what Kevin had said. His tension had disappeared as he laughed and talked with the family.

The party stopped when Jenn's niece started dozing off on her dad's lap. Jenn's brother and sister gathered their presents and headed out the door. After many goodbyes and hugs, Jenn and Kevin headed to the guest room. Unlike at Kevin's house, Jenn's mom did not let them stay in the same room.

She sat on the guest room bed and waited for Kevin to finish in the bathroom. He entered the room and went to his bag, looking for something. Jenn's stomach tensed as she watched him. She let her mind wander to what she thought he was looking for. Kevin stood up and slowly turned toward her. He was holding a small envelope. Jenn did not realize she had been holding her breath as she exhaled.

"I got you a little something. I know we said no big gifts, but this made me think of you." Jenn took the envelope from him and slowly peeled it open. Inside were two plane tickets to Scotland.

Jenn gasped slightly and looked quickly up at Kevin. "Are you kidding me?"

He laughed and sat down next to her. "I figured we needed a celebratory trip for after graduation. You always talk about wanting to travel and I know Scotland is at the top of the list." Jenn squealed and pulled him into a tight hug. She had tears in her eyes.

"Thank you. Thank you so, so much." Kevin wiped her eyes and gave her a soft kiss on the lips.

"You are very, very welcome." She pulled him in to another kiss, this one lasting slightly longer.

"I should get to my room. Merry Christmas, Kevin, I love you." She held onto his hand until she was too far away, and it slid free.

"I love you too, Jenn." She softly closed the door behind her and stood for a moment with her back against it. She hugged the envelope to her chest and sighed deeply. She made her way to her room and closed the door behind her before flopping onto the bed. She fumbled for her phone and dialed Riley's number. She answered after two rings.

"Merry Christmas again. How did your family take the news?" Jenn asked.

"Well, apparently my fiancé is a true gentleman and

had asked their permission, so they all knew," Riley replied. "Ah, fiancé, that's so weird to say." Jenn laughed.

"Kevin bought us plane tickets to Scotland for after graduation." She heard Riley make a high-pitched noise.

"Oh my gosh, that's in the top five places that you wanted to travel to!" Jenn nodded in agreement before realizing she was on the phone and Riley couldn't see her.

"I know! He was digging in his bag when we were alone and I half-thought he was going to pull out a ring." Jenn hadn't wanted to admit it before, but she was momentarily disappointed when he didn't.

"That would have been so awesome, we could have wedding-planned together!" Riley said. They chatted briefly about plans for the following days before saying goodnight. Jenn hung up and jumped when she heard a door open and close. She put her ear to the door to try to eavesdrop, but all she could here was mumbling. She assumed her parents were chatting in the kitchen before heading to bed themselves. She climbed into bed and flipped out her light. She started to run over ideas for the trip in her head as she drifted off to sleep.

Chapter 7

The next day, she and Kevin drove to a small bar called Doc's to meet Curt and Riley. The newly engaged couple was already sitting in a corner booth when Jenn and Kevin walked in. Jenn jogged over and pulled Riley into a jumping hug, both squealing with excitement. Kevin shook Curt's hand and gave him a clap on the back. "Congrats, man." Riley and Jenn continued to talk in their fast, high-pitched tone while examining the ring. Kevin and Curt gently guided them to the booth and poured out two more beers.

"Tell me everything. Where? When? How?" Jenn asked with intensity. Curt and Kevin laughed, but Riley replied with enthusiasm.

"You know the small bridge in the park where they have all of the Christmas lights hung? Christmas Eve, there. Just me and him. He was down on one knee in the snow and everything. It was like a dream." Jenn sat back and placed her hands on her heart.

She smiled at Curt. "Well done, my friend. Well done." She turned to Kevin. "Looks like the tab is on me tonight." Curt and Riley exchanged confused looks. "Oh, we guessed how you did it. He thought private and romantic. I thought more public, with family or something." Kevin put his hands up in victory.

"Oh, no public. It was perfect, and I wanted it just between us," Riley said, sliding next to Curt. He placed his arm around her shoulder and pulled her next to him.

"Sorry, Jenn. I don't do public displays like that. I'd be terrified she would say no!" Curt said, as Riley playfully smacked his knee.

"Like I would say no to you. I would have accepted regardless of where we were." They shared a quick kiss.

Kevin tapped Jenn on the shoulder to get her attention, "Hey, I'm going to need that drink." She rolled her eyes, scooted out of the booth and headed up to the bar. When she returned, Kevin was talking animatedly about something. He stopped as she approached and took the drink from Jenn's hand.

"So, Scotland? That's exciting," Riley said, seemingly changing the conversation that they were just having.

Jenn looked at Kevin and then back at Riley. "Yeah, another perfect gift. What were you all talking about?" Kevin and Curt glanced at each other and back at Jenn.

"Just plans for how to survive the last semester of college and getting on with the real world," Kevin said without a flinch. Jenn clicked her tongue and took a sip of her drink.

They talked about their break and the time with family. Riley's mom already had bridal magazines ready for her, and Curt's mom showed them pictures of possible venues in the area. Jenn showed them the beautiful bracelet Kevin's mom had given her and brought up how her brother embarrassed Kevin after she told them about Riley's engagement.

Kevin cleared his throat, "I was not embarrassed, I just don't like someone else trying to tell me what I should or shouldn't be doing." His ears were slightly pink again and Jenn knew she had struck a nerve.

"I didn't mean anything by it, I'm sorry. I was embarrassed. I brought it on though, bringing up Riley's engagement. I think my mom and sister thought I was going to announce our engage…." She stopped. "I'm sorry, I know you don't want to discuss this." He shook his head. The four of them sat in awkward silence for a moment, which was broken by a waitress asking if she could get them something to eat. They ordered some appetizers and the conversation slowly started back up. The boys discussed the upcoming baseball season, and Riley started talking wedding details.

"I think I want a fall wedding, dark colors to match the changing leaves." Jenn sat and nodded, throwing in her opinion on flowers and cakes when asked. "And of course, you'll be my maid of honor!" Jenn clapped her hands before pulling Riley into another hug.

"Yes, I'd be happy to!" Jenn squealed as she turned to Kevin, who was smiling again.

"Oh, he locked me in as best man before he even asked. So, Riley, you see who is first in his mind." Riley lightly kicked Kevin in the shin before bursting into laughter. The mood lightened more as the food and more drinks arrived.

By the end of the evening, they were filled with greasy food and a touch too much alcohol. Riley called her mom to come pick them up since none of them could safely drive. They told the bartender that they would be back to get their cars in the morning. Riley climbed into the front seat of her mom's car and Jenn was sandwiched between the guys in the backseat. They drove mostly in silence on the way home, Riley's mom asking about everyone's Christmas break and talking about the engagement. Jenn's head was starting to hurt as they pulled up outside of her parent's house. She thanked Riley's mom for the ride and said goodnight.

She and Kevin walked side by side to the front door in silence. Jenn took some deep breaths, trying to calm the throbbing in her head.

She fumbled for her keys and Kevin grabbed her hand. "Listen, I feel like you have questions that you're holding back because you don't want to upset me."

She turned to face him, not sure if she should

answer. Yes, the alcohol gave her a little more confidence than she usually had, so now would be an ideal time to get it off her chest. She wasn't sure she could handle the answers, though. "Is now really the time for this? Drunk conversations are not always good conversations."

He took a deep breath and kicked some snow off the front porch. "I know, but I feel this looming above us. It feels heavy. So, free pass. Ask whatever you want, and I will honestly answer." Jenn turned away for a moment and rubbed her temples. She did not feel that it was the right time. The alcohol, however, was interested in his answers and had a little more control over Jenn's brain in that moment.

She turned back to face him. "OK, fine. You keep acting like being engaged to me is upsetting to you." He started to respond, but she put up her hand to stop him. "Please don't interrupt, I have to say this. Am I jealous that Riley is engaged, and I am not? Yes, yes, I am. Do I want to be engaged to you? Yes, yes, I do. I'm not saying right now, but I would like to know if that is something that I can hope for." She paused and thought about what to say next. She could see Kevin fidgeting, waiting for his turn to reply. "I want it Kevin, I do. You are the first boy I've ever felt this way about. We've been together for three years and you are one of my best friends. I want to stay with you for as long as you'll have me. I hope that is a long time. I want the beautiful ring. I want the big proposal. I want it all, and I want it with you." She took a deep breath and looked up at him. He had a crooked smile on his face.

He took a deep breath. "Jenn, I never said that I didn't want to be engaged. I never once said that that wasn't my end goal. I just don't want to be pressured into when that needs to be. I don't feel like there is a time limit on this. If you're going to be together forever, then what is the rush? I love you more than any girl I've ever dated. I've never even had thoughts of this before. I just need everything to be perfect because I only plan on doing it once." He didn't break eye contact at all and pulled Jenn into his chest. She relaxed and leaned into him, letting his warmth surround her. She looked up at him and pulled his lips down to hers. They stood on the front steps kissing for several minutes before they decided to go inside.

Jenn lead him down the hall to the guest room and kissed him goodnight. "Thank you for the explanation. It will be tucked in the back of my mind until the time is right." She turned and walked towards her room, hearing the door close quietly behind her.

Her headache was improving, but she grabbed ibuprofen from the medicine cabinet before climbing into bed. Jenn was happy in that moment and the excitement of heading back to school to start her last semester was palpable. She knew that her near future included graduating college, a trip to Europe and God willing, a proposal. She fell asleep with nothing but happiness in her mind.

Present

Chapter 8

Jenn heard her phone chiming and startled awake. She glanced at the clock on her bedside table. It read 5:30. She fumbled for the phone and turned the screen on. It took her eyes a moment to adjust to the bright screen. One new text appeared, and it was from Mike. She rubbed her eyes and opened it.

Sorry if I woke you, just wanted to know when I could call. No hurry. Reply when you can.

Jenn smiled and set the phone down. She stretched her arms over her head, listening to her shoulders and back pop. She rolled out of bed and headed to the bathroom. It was always funny being on a third shift schedule. Sometimes she was disoriented waking up in the evening. Tonight, however, her head was clear. She was surprisingly excited to see Mike again, which made her incredibly nervous. She grabbed a cup of coffee from the kitchen before settling on the couch to call him. She took two big gulps before working up the courage to hit the dial button.

It rang three times before he answered. "I thought I was supposed to call you," he said with a small laugh.

"I'm one of those modern women who doesn't follow the rules," Jenn replied with a smile.

"So, does this mean that you are free tonight? Or am I supposed to let you ask me out?" Mike was funny and charming. Jenn loved his sarcasm.

"Yes, I am free, but I'm going to let you do the asking. You can't get off the hook that easily." Mike laughed out loud.

"Fair enough. Jenn, would you like to get some dinner with me tonight?" She felt her stomach flip and her throat tighten. Why was she so nervous? It was just dinner.

She took a deep breath, "Yes, Mike, I would love to." They chatted briefly before deciding on a place to meet. She wasn't ready to drive together because she needed an escape route in case things went wrong. They agreed to meet at 7:30 at a small mom and pop restaurant downtown. Jenn started to get ready, so she could get on the bus with plenty of time to spare. She hated to be late. It took her a good half hour to pick out an outfit since she was so nervous. She messed with her hair and makeup for another 15 minutes before grabbing her purse and heading out the door. She got on the bus at the corner and pulled out her phone.

She sent a quick text to Riley, *Heading out to dinner with Mike. I'll call you after.*

She barely set the phone down when it chimed with a new message. Riley replied with a smiley face emoji and good luck. Jenn leaned back in her seat and looked out the window. She had never been to the restaurant that he suggested. This made her both nervous and excited.

"First date jitters?" A sweet voiced sounded from the seats across the aisle. Jenn turned to an older woman. She smiled at Jenn and Jenn couldn't help but smile back.

"Am I that obvious?"

The woman winked, "Well, he's a lucky guy. You remember that." She continued knitting a small hat in her lap. Jenn looked back towards the window and felt her nerves settle. The bus rolled to a stop near the restaurant and Jenn stood to get off.

"Thank you," she told the woman before getting off the bus. She glanced at her watch and saw that she had 15 minutes to spare. She decided to walk a little to ease her mind. The breeze was cool, and she pulled her jacket tightly around herself. There were several small shops along the street and Jenn window-shopped. She was looking at a clothing display in one window when someone tapped her shoulder. She jumped and turned around in a defensive pose.

Mike stepped back and put his hands up, "I'm sorry. Didn't mean to startle you." She lowered her hands slowly and relaxed. He laughed nervously.

"I'm sorry, too many self-defense classes," she replied. She stepped forward and gave him an awkward hug. "Good to see you again."

He stepped back and smiled. "OK, now the awkward part is over. You can relax, and we can have some good food." He held out his hand, which she accepted, and he guided her to the restaurant. He opened the front door for her, and a small bell rang. The woman at the hostess table looked up and smiled. She stood and walked over to Mike, giving him a huge hug.

"Oh, Michael. It is good to see you," she said in a thick Italian accent. "Who is this beautiful young lady?" She reached out and took Jenn's hand, squeezing it.

"Mira, this is Jenn. Jenn, this is my Aunt Mira." Jenn shook her hand before being pulled into a hug as well. After she let go of Jenn, Mira led them over to a small round table near the back of the restaurant. She walked over to the bar and grabbed two glasses of wine, placed them on the table and walked away towards the kitchen.

"Aunt Mira, huh?" Jenn smiled.

Mike chuckled, "Yeah, she and my uncle opened this place years ago. Best Italian food in the city and not just because I'm biased." Jenn looked around. The restaurant was small and quaint, modestly decorated and with low lighting. She loved it. It felt very personal and inviting. She and Mike chatted for a bit before his aunt returned with a bowl of salad and bread. Jenn thanked her and then turned to Mike as she walked away.

"No menus?" she asked. He had a smirk on his face.

"No menus. At least not when I'm here. Trust me, she's a wizard. You won't be disappointed." This made Jenn nervous, but she was already feeling too many nerves at that moment to worry about the food. They ate salad and shared the bread while they learned more about each other. "A nurse, really? That's a hard job." Mike said with a little awe in his voice. Jenn blushed. She had never thought of it as hard. It was just her calling.

"Being a middle school teacher has to be harder," she said.

He shrugged, "Never thought of it. I just love it and think it is what I am meant to be." She smiled at his reply. The conversation flowed easily as they talked about school and family. They compared likes and dislikes. Mike was different from the other men that she had met. Either that or she just hadn't cared to know more about them. Mira came back around with two plates of food. She instructed them to share and left two extra plates. They thanked her and stared down at the huge plates.

"I can't eat all that!" Jenn whispered.

"Of course not. Leftovers from this place are as good as the meal itself," Mike said, grabbing a spoon to push food onto his plate. Jenn followed suit and soon there was silence punctuated only by Jenn's sighs.

"This is the best food I have ever eaten," she said.

Mike finished his bite and smiled, "Told you so." They continued to eat, sharing food off each plate. When Jenn felt her stomach expanding dangerously, she set down her utensils and leaned back. Mike was still taking a few bites but stopped when he noticed that she was done.

"Don't stop on account of me" she said. He motioned to his aunt and she came over to the table.

"Two boxes, please. Oh, and bring my favorite for her to take home." Mira beamed at him and headed back to the kitchen. Jenn leaned forward and held out her hand. Mike placed his in hers and smiled.

"This was lovely, thank you. I don't think I'll have to eat for the rest of the week." He squeezed her hand and nodded. Mira returned with two large takeout boxes and one small rectangle box. Jenn looked at Mike questioningly.

"Trust me, you'll want that later" was all he would say. Jenn thanked Mira again and received another tight hug. Mike kissed her cheek and picked up the boxes before heading to the door. He helped her slip on her jacket on and held the door open. She walked out and paused, waiting for him to catch up. "So," he said.

She turned to face him, "So," she replied. They sat in silence for a moment, staring at each other. "OK, so we're back to awkward," she said with a giggle.

"Well, we kind of did this backward so I'm at a loss

for what comes next," Mike said nervously. She blushed and looked at her feet.

"Fun fact. This is my first date in about five years," she said, slowly glancing up at him.

His mouth was slightly open. "No way. You are way too good looking to not have dated anyone in five years."

Jenn fidgeted with her purse. "That's a story for another time. So, what happens now?"

Mike shrugged and took her hand. "What do you want to happen now?" Jenn looked down at their hands and thought about it. What did she want? It had been so long since she was at this point. "OK, now I'm really nervous," Mike whispered.

Jenn laughed. "Well, this may sound odd seeing as we have already slept together, but can we take this slow?" He didn't flinch, and the smile stayed on his face, which was a relief to Jenn.

"Of course, we can. I'm happy that I've made it this far. I haven't been on a date in a while either." Jenn let out a sigh of relief. She turned, still holding his hand, and started walking toward the bus stop. "We'll save our sob stories for the next date." She smiled at the fact that she was wanting a next date.

They walked in silence until they reached the bus

stop. "Thank you for making this easy on me. I didn't know what to expect or how I would handle it," she said quietly.

He put his arm around her shoulder, pulling her into a side hug. "You're easy to talk to. And easy to look at, so that's a plus." She chuckled and leaned her head against his shoulder. The bus turned the corner and pulled towards the stop. Mike handed her the box of leftovers and the small box.

She started to turn towards the bus and stopped. "Thank you again. I'll let you call first next time." She stepped back towards him and leaned in to kiss his cheek. His cologne wafted towards her and she felt a warm sensation in her legs. She looked up at him and leaned in for a kiss on his lips, which he accepted. Everything was silent for a moment until the bus driver opened the doors. Jenn pulled away and smiled, said goodnight and stepped onto the bus. She watched out the window as the bus pulled away. Mike stood silently before shaking his head, touching his lips and turning to walk back down toward the restaurant.

A single tear rolled down her cheek as the bus pulled away. She was relieved that the night had gone so smoothly. She was proud of the way she handled everything and glad that she didn't have a panic attack. It had been several years since she had one, but new things were always hard on her. She checked the time and it was almost 10.

She texted Riley since it was late. *Date went so well,*

he's calling in a few days for another date.

She put the phone back in her purse and leaned her head on the window. She felt calm in that moment and also excited, wondering what would happen next.

Her phone started to ring as the bus pulled up near her apartment building. It was Riley. She waited until she was off the bus to answer. "Hey, I didn't want to wake anyone." She walked across the lobby and up the stairs to her apartment.

"Not asleep, I was just reading a magazine while Curt finishes something in the office." Riley was on maternity leave and Curt was picking up extra hours to make ends meet. "So, tell me everything."

Jenn sat down on the couch and told her about the family restaurant, the good food and drink and that kiss goodnight. "I tried not to kiss him, but his cologne made my knees weak."

Riley was silent for a while and Jenn wondered if she had dozed off. "Not to sound rude, but I'm surprised you're home at this time, and alone."

Jenn gave a dramatic gasp and laughed. "Yeah, me too. But I told him we had started out backwards and I wanted to move slow." Jenn could imagine Riley's motherly expression in that moment.

"Well, I'm proud of you, kid. That was a huge first step. How are you feeling?"

Jenn thought about it for a moment before answering. "You know, I was nervous. It was awkward at times, but I'm glad I did it. I'm looking forward to the next step."

Riley exhaled loudly. Jenn assumed it was a breath of relief. They chatted briefly about the kids before saying goodnight. Jenn promised to come by the house for dinner soon. She hung up the phone and flipped the TV on. Her phone chimed again as she was surfed through the channels. It was a text from Mike.

I hope you made it home okay. Thanks for a memorable first date.

She couldn't help but smile. She quickly replied.

One of my top first dates ever.

He responded after a few minutes.

Well, that means I must do better each date. Challenge accepted.

She smiled and set her phone down. She continued to flip channels for a few minutes before she came across an older movie she liked. She picked up her phone and started another text, this one for Jake.

I made it through, and a second date is looking

possible!

It took him a little while to reply since he was at work.

Hallelujah, there is a higher power.

Jenn smirked at his reply. She wanted to talk to him, but she knew he was working.

I'll call you tomorrow, okay?

He texted back a thumbs-up and she set the phone down. Jenn went back to flipping channels absent-mindedly. She gave up after a few moments and switched over to Netflix. Another vice that came with third shift work was the ability to stay up late and binge watch her favorite shows. It was also a source of comfort for.

A few years back, Jenn had been in and out of the hospital. She sought solace in romantic TV shows, books and movies. You could say she was lost in them for a while. When the world around her was dark and painful, she disappeared into perfect romances with happy endings. It made her believe in love, or rather what she wished love would be. Jenn was still waiting on a man who could rival those fictional characters, but in the back of her mind he was still out there. Riley used to joke with her that she was too much of a dreamer, but Jenn believed that she deserved something more. She thought she had it at one time. She thought it was true love, but that's the thing. *Those stories are not real*, she thought. She settled in, starting her favorite TV show for the hundredth time.

Chapter 9

The phone rang, making her sit upright quickly. She blinked a few times, allowing her eyes to focus. The TV was still on and sunlight was streaming through the curtains. She glanced down at her watch and saw that it was 7 in the morning. The phone continued to ring as she shook her head. She pushed the talk button and cleared her throat. "Hello?" Her voice sound hoarse.

"Good morning, sunshine." It was Jake. He must have just finished with his shift.

"Easy for you to say. I fell asleep sitting up and now my neck is stiff." She stretched and rubbed behind her neck.

"Well, I still have too much energy. Was wondering if you wanted to grab some breakfast or something? I could come and pick you up." Jake sounded like he had drunk too many cups of coffee. Jenn laughed and stood up from the couch, stretching more.

"Sure, give me fifteen to make myself presentable." Jenn hung up the phone and went to wash up in the bathroom. She threw on a pair of jeans and a T-shirt, then combed her hair back into a ponytail. She was brushing her teeth when she heard a knock. She rinsed her mouth and went to open the door.

Jake gave her a quick hug. She grabbed her purse and followed him out of the apartment. They chatted about the weather and where they were going to get breakfast. Jake drove toward a small diner two blocks away, one that they enjoyed at least twice a month. The waitress nodded as they entered, and they slid into a booth in back. Jake picked up the menu, but Jenn always ordered the same thing.

"So, tell me all about the date," he said. Jenn put her chin in her hands and looked out the window.

"Well, we had dinner at a little Italian restaurant that I'd never even heard about. Then, it turns out that his aunt and uncle own it! Great food though."

Jake smirked. "Throwing family at you on the first date? Brave soul."

Jenn kicked at him under the table. "Be nice, it was very welcoming. It made it more comfortable. I have some food left over. I'll send you home with a sample, so you know what I'm talking about." The waitress walked up to the table and took their order. She placed a pot of coffee between them and smiled. They thanked her and poured two cups.

Jake started talking about a new machine that they had at work, and the tests it could run. He was so passionate about helping others. Jenn loved that about him. The waitress retuned with their food after a bit and they ate in silence.

82

"Hey Jenn, do you remember Kelly?" Jake asked between bites.

Jenn nodded, chewing her food and swallowing quickly so she could answer. "The tech? Blonde?"

Jake nodded and blushed slightly. "I finally asked her out," he added, not looking up.

She was silent for a moment, but then replied with a slightly high pitch in her voice. "That's great. I'm happy for you. It's about time you get some action. I mean, a good-looking guy like you. Single? It's a shame." She took a big bite of food and looked out the window again.

"Yeah, I mean. I figured there was no reason not to. Right?" He finally caught her eye and they stared at each other for a moment.

Jenn shook her head. "Right. No reason." They both looked back down at their plates.

Jenn didn't know why she had a tightness in her chest at that moment, but she took a few deep breaths and it went away. Things were always complicated with Jake. She was very protective of him. After all, he was her best friend.

Jake steered the conversation back to Jenn's date. "I think I'll go out with him again. He is really nice." She pushed the last piece of food around her plate before setting her fork down. Jake started to yawn so they decided to finish up and pay. Jenn tried to pay for her portion, but Jake insisted on picking up the tab. She thanked him and headed out to his car.

"I hope that I didn't come across wrong when I told you about Kelly," he said as they walked.

"What do you mean?" she asked as they stopped outside his car.

Jake sighed. "I just always feel so protective of you after everything that has happened. I don't want you to go through that again. It was terrifying and heartbreaking to be a part of. I guess I feel like I come across as jealous sometimes. I'm not, I promise. I just know you deserve so much more than you think." He reached out and took her hand. They stood in silence for a minute just holding hands.

Jenn sniffed and pulled him into a tight hug. "Thank you. I don't know if I ever really thanked you for everything you've done and do for me. God knows you shouldn't have stuck around, especially when I dragged you into my mess." Jake kissed the top of her head.

"Drag me through anything, doll, it would be worth every minute." She stepped back and smiled, wiping a tear from her eye. He opened the passenger door and she climbed inside. They drove back to her apartment in silence, listening to the radio.

Jake stopped out front and Jenn hopped out.

"Thanks for having breakfast with me. Let me know how your date goes." He waved as she walked inside. She stood at the door and watched him drive away.

Jenn knew that Jake was a good man and that she was lucky to have him around. He had been tangled up in her mess five years ago and it was entirely Jenn's fault. He never faltered though. Jenn was truly grateful for him.

Chapter 10

Jenn was sitting in the kitchen, reading a book when her phone began to ring. She glanced at it and saw it was Riley. "Hey, what's up?"

Riley sounded flustered. "Oh, hi. I was wondering if you were busy. Curt just left, and I need some adult conversation."

Jenn set the book down and stood up. "I'll be there shortly." She headed out to the parking garage that was attached to her apartment. Her blue compact car sat in its assigned parking space.

Riley lived just outside the city limits so taking the bus wasn't an option. Jenn got in her car and drove slowly onto the busy street in front of her apartment. She loved living downtown, but she did not like driving. She did love Riley though and swore she would always be there for her, especially since Riley was there for her when it mattered most. She turned on the radio and drove the 10 minutes to Riley's house.

She pulled into the driveway and could see Riley pacing in the kitchen, bouncing a crying baby. Curt and Riley had two children, a boy who was two and a newborn girl. They would be celebrating their fifth wedding anniversary in a few weeks.

Jenn parked the car and walked up to the door, knocking softly before opening it. She was met with the sounds of a wailing baby and cartoons echoing in the front hall. "Riley? I'm here."

Riley walked into the front hallway, still bouncing the baby. She looked disheveled, her hair in a messy bun of top of her head and a mystery stain on the front of her shirt. "Oh, honey. Give her to me." Jenn reached out for the baby and Riley gladly handed her over. Jenn started to softly sing to her and stroke her head. The wailing eased up, and she stopped after a few moments.

Jenn walked with the baby into the living room. Toys were scattered over the floor, and a blonde toddler sat in front of the TV, enthralled with the dancing animals and music on the screen. Jenn leaned down and patted his head, but he did not move.

She looked at Riley and shrugged. "Now, you get upstairs and shower. Change your clothes. I will make some coffee." Riley smiled and turned, walking quickly upstairs. Jenn walked a few laps around the rooms downstairs while shushing and rocking the baby. She liked the feel of Riley's home. She and Curt put a lot of work into it. Jenn paused to look at the family photos on the wall.

She came to a large glass case filled with pictures in the corner of the dining room. She knew what photos they were, but she looked at them every time. Riley and Curt were in the center, looking at each other with a gaze of true love. It was their wedding photo. Around that photo were a few of their favorites from the wedding.

Jenn's heart raced a little as she looked from photo to photo. She knew that she could just stop looking, but she never did. There were several of her, wearing her burgundy bridesmaid dress. Smiling and laughing with Riley and her other friends. Then there were several photos of him.

Jenn stopped rocking the baby for a moment and just stared. She didn't blame them for having the pictures out as they were free to decorate however they chose. It wasn't their fault that her relationship imploded after their wedding. It was his fault.

She felt her cheeks get warm and her heart began to pound in her ears. She closed her eyes and turned away, rocking the baby again. She hummed to herself to calm down. She walked back to the living room and gently placed the baby into her swing. She turned the swing on and began to pick up the scattered toys.

After the room was picked up, she headed to the kitchen to start a fresh pot of coffee. It was still brewing when Riley came downstairs. She looked better and more relaxed. "Thank you for that, I was about to explode."

Jenn poured a cup of coffee and handed it to Riley. They took the cups back to the living room and sat down on the couch. Riley looked at her kids, "I love them, but man do I miss talking with adults all day." Jenn laughed and sipped her coffee. The warmth in her face was almost gone and her heartrate was almost back to normal. Riley looked at her and sighed, "You need to stop looking at those pictures."

Jenn shrugged. "I want to remember how happy you were that day. It was an amazing wedding. What I saw of the reception was great. This feeling has nothing to do with you or Curt. I don't want to associate this feeling with your wedding."

Riley patted Jenn's knee. "No need to ruin nice coffee talk with garbage from the past. Tell me about your date." Jenn smiled and gave the details. She talked about the restaurant and the conversation and how Mike was a gentleman when she asked to take things slow. "Well, sounds like you had success. I'm proud of and happy for you," Riley said. They chatted for a while before the baby woke up, hungry.

"I need to catch a quick nap before work tonight. You OK?" Jenn asked, standing up.

"I'm great, thanks for coming by. I'll talk to you this weekend. I'd like to meet this Mike sometime." Riley picked up the baby and began bouncing again. Jenn smiled, leaned in and kissed Riley's cheek. She kissed the baby's head and mussed the toddler's hair before heading out of the house.

She drove back towards her apartment with her radio on a little louder than normal. It always took her a while to come down from the anger associated with her ex. She didn't like that it affected her so much, but it did. Years of therapy hadn't stopped it, so it was part of her for now.

She parked the car and made her way into the apartment building, stopping to grab the mail and tossing it on the kitchen table. She settled into a chair and turned her phone on. She noticed she had a missed call and a voicemail. She smiled as she listened to the voicemail. It had been Mike checking in. She sent him a quick text letting him know that she was taking a quick rest before work, but she would call tomorrow evening. She plugged her phone in and went to take a shower. She had only two hours before she'd have to be up for work, but if she didn't sleep, tonight would be a disaster.

She brushed her teeth and climbed into bed. She lay there for a while, letting her head rush over everything that had happened since last night. Her thoughts were mostly positive, which is something that didn't happen often. The feeling that the pages had finally turned on a dark chapter of her life was refreshing. She smiled as she drifted asleep, praying that this feeling would continue.

6.5 years ago

Chapter 11

The last semester of nursing school was extremely busy for Jenn. She had clinicals twice a week, lectures every other day, and she had to work on the weekends. She also had picked up some shifts at her work-study job after class to make some extra cash. All of that, plus trying to be at all of Kevin's baseball games kept her running from sunrise to sundown, and sometimes after that. Most nights she collapsed into bed after finishing homework.

Kevin was as supportive as he could be. He was busy with baseball and had no problem going out with his teammates if she was too tired. Jenn thrived in chaos, though, and she was getting almost all A's and had been asked to join the Nursing Honor Society.

With the extra cash she was making, she was also planning her trip to Scotland and looking into apartments in St. Louis after graduation. She and Kevin had discussed where they wanted to go after graduation, but she had never officially asked him to come to St Louis with her. She planned on talking to him about it soon.

His baseball season was ending and heading into post-season tournament play, and Jenn was helping the other baseball girlfriends prepare for Senior Night. Since Christmas, Jenn and Kevin's relationship had been so in sync. Neither had mentioned their previous conversation about being engaged, and Jenn hadn't had time to think about it with everything else going on.

Riley and Curt were practically married already. They had decided that they wanted to get married in November the following year in St. Louis. This would give them time to settle into a routine and find work after graduating before planning the wedding. Jenn and Riley still wrote notes out whenever an idea popped into their heads. Burgundy and gold were the colors of the wedding.

Riley wanted to get married in a local church and Curt agreed to this if he could pick the reception site. He and Kevin had been looking online for ideas. It was a bonding experience for the four of them, and they had never been closer. The guys on the baseball team gave Curt a hard time for proposing, but Kevin was always quick to defend him. That made Jenn happy since she knew he would always have her back as well.

Senior Night fell on the last Friday night game before post-season started. Jenn and Riley met with the coach to go over plans since he oversaw sending out emails to invite the families of all the seniors. There were six players graduating. Jenn was putting together gifts for them, and Riley was helping gather information about each one, so they could have something personal to say during announcements. They also had shirts made for each parent with their son's number on the back. They did all their work in the coach's office so the players wouldn't see what they were up to. He was impressed by their commitment and let them work after hours most nights.

They were locking up the office on the night before the game when they overheard someone talking in the hall.

"I can't believe that, they seem so happy," a male voice said with a hint of anger.

"I'm just telling you what I was told. They said they saw it happen," another voice said, and the girls listened to two sets of footsteps heading down the stairs.

Riley and Jenn looked at each other and shrugged. "Didn't realize guys gossiped like that. I wonder who they were talking about?" Jenn mumbled. Riley shrugged again and picked up the box of gifts. Jenn grabbed the bag of shirts and headed down the stairs.

After packing the boxes in Riley's car, they headed back to their apartment. It was late when they got home, and Curt and Kevin were dozing in front of the TV, waiting for the girls. They woke up when Jenn closed the front door.

"About time, did you guys finish up?" Kevin asked, rubbing his eyes.

"You'll have to wait and see tomorrow," Jenn said and kissed him lightly on the lips. She said goodnight to Curt and Riley before pulling Kevin toward their bedroom. After getting ready for bed, she crawled under the covers next to Kevin. He was already falling asleep, so she laid her head on his chest. "Tomorrow is going to be great," she whispered.

"I think it will be," he muttered before starting to snore quietly. She kissed his cheek and rolled over to turn out the light.

Chapter 12

They had class in the morning before meeting with parents to go over the events for that night. Classes ended at 1 and the parents' meeting was at 4, three hours before the start of the game. Jenn loved schedules, so the number of events that day did not bother her. Friday classes were not as busy, and she was mostly done with the coursework aside from her senior paper.

She and Riley met with the parents on campus to hand out their shirts and give a short explanation of what to expect.

"You'll take the gift and give it to your son, and they'll have flowers for the moms. We'll say a little about each of them and then take pictures. After everyone is announced, we'll have a group photo." Everyone nodded and murmured in agreement. Riley and Jenn thanked everyone and headed home to get ready for the game.

Kevin and Curt were already at the fields when the girls got home. Jenn made them something to eat while Riley changed. She came out wearing a grey shirt that had Curt's number on back. Jenn laughed, "When did you get that?" Riley did a spin to show off.

"I ordered them when we ordered the parent's shirts." She tossed a shirt at Jenn, who caught it and held it up in front of her. She hugged Riley and checked her watch. "We better head over soon." They ate their sandwiches quickly and headed out to the car.

The parking lot was nearly full when they pulled in. The lights were already on at the field and music echoed across the parking lot. Jenn adjusted the box in her arms and followed Riley to the press box. They placed the boxes inside and made their way to the stands. The team was warming up. Kevin looked up from stretching and waved. Jenn spotted Kevin's mom and walked over to sit with her.

"Hi Cheryl," she said as they hugged. Riley walked over with Curt's parents and sat down next to Jenn. Jenn looked around at the stands and noticed how full they were. The night was clear and warm. It could not have been more perfect for Senior Night. Riley distracted Jenn by tugging on her sleeve to get her attention.

"How much longer until they call for the parents?" she asked. Jenn looked at her watch and back at the field.

The team had started to make their way to the dugout, and the group of six seniors hung out near the fence. A voice cracked over the intercom calling the senior parents out to the field. Cheryl squeezed Jenn's hand and followed Curt's parents down the bleachers. Riley scooted closer to Jenn and took her hand. Jenn thought she seemed overly excited about the game, but she *had* been giddier since the engagement.

The seniors lined up with their parents and the ceremony began. Each player walked with their parents from home plate to the pitcher's mound while the announcer read off the script Riley and Jenn had prepared. It was going so well. Riley beamed with pride as Curt walked out. Kevin was last to go. He walked arm in arm with his mom, giving her a kiss on the cheek once they reached the pitcher's mound. The announcer concluded the ceremony and the families posed for a group photo.

Everyone started to clear the field when the announcer came back on over the loudspeaker. "Coach also wanted to thank the two young ladies that helped put this ceremony together. Could we have Jenn and Riley out onto the field?" Jenn looked at Riley with confusion. Riley shrugged and pulled her up and down the stands. They walked out towards Coach, who was standing on the pitcher's mound.

He gave them both hugs before saying anything. "You girls have done so much for this team, whether it be working concessions, taking tickets, cleaning up after games, you name it. And thank you for keeping your boys focused and helping them be the best they can." The coach handed them each a bouquet of flowers. "I know flowers don't really cover all the hard work you've put in, so the team decided to do something special for you." He motioned for the girls to turn around.

Jenn looked at Riley, who looked nervous before

turning around. She jumped, covering her mouth to keep from screaming. Kevin was down on one knee holding out a small black box.

"Oh my god," she stuttered.

"Jenn, you are my best friend and my soul mate. You have made these past three years the best years of my life. I would be the luckiest man in the world if you let me continue on this path with you." He opened the box and pulled out the ring. "I want to spend the rest of my life trying to make you as happy as you make me. Will you marry me?"

Tears ran down Jenn's face as she silently sobbed. She couldn't answer at first because she couldn't catch her breath. She lowered her hands and held out her left hand, shaking her head yes. Kevin slipped the ring onto her finger and stood up. He picked her up in a hug and kissed her. The crowd erupted into cheers as the team ran out onto the field and surrounded them. They all clapped Kevin on the back as Riley pulled Jenn into a tight hug. The commotion finally died down and the team made its way back to the dugout.

Riley and Jenn walked off the field and into a crowd of people congratulating her. She looked over the crowd and saw Kevin's mom standing with her parents. She pushed through the crowd and ran over to them. "Mom, Dad? When did you get here?"

Her mom smiled and wiped her eyes. "Kevin told us

what he was planning at Christmas, when he asked our permission to ask you." Jenn's jaw dropped.

She hugged her mom and dad then turned to Cheryl. "Did you know, too?"

She smiled, "Of course. We've been talking every week, preparing for this. I gave him my grandmother's ring on Christmas Eve." She held up Jenn's hand to admire the ring. Jenn looked down at her hand in awe. The announcer came over the loudspeaker to call the start of the game. Jenn's parents and Kevin's mom made their way to the stands.

Jenn turned to find Riley and saw her standing near the snack counter with their old friend Jake. She walked over and gave him a hug. "What are you doing here?" she said as she squeezed him.

"I finished my exams for the week and Riley told me that there was something happening tonight that I shouldn't miss."

Jenn turned to Riley, "You knew? You're horrible at keeping secrets."

Riley shrugged and blushed. "Guess I did OK with this one." Jenn linked arms with Jake and Riley and headed to the stands. It reminded her of high school when they did the same thing for all the football games.

They cheered for the baseball team in between catching up with everything going on in each other's lives. Jake's college was about an hour away, so he came down about once a month to visit.

Kevin hit a walk off single in the bottom of the ninth inning to win the game, topping off the perfect evening. Their parents all headed back to their hotels after the game ended. Jake, Riley and Jenn hung out behind the stands waiting for Kevin and Curt to get changed. It felt like a good time to go celebrate.

Chapter 12

Curt and Kevin came out of the locker room 20 minutes later. Jenn ran to Kevin and jumped into his arms as he dropped his bag. She hugged him tightly before pulling her head back and kissing him.

"Ugh, get a room," Riley joked. Kevin set Jenn down and walked over to Riley to give her a hug.

"Thanks for helping me out and keeping my secret. Hey, Jake. Didn't know you were coming tonight." Kevin shook Jake's hand.

"I was promised a good show, and boy, did I get one. That was impressive. I would have been terrified," Jake said, pointing to the field.

Kevin nodded, "It was nerve-racking, but I've been practicing for weeks." They walked to the parking lot while discussing where to celebrate. Kevin and Curt wanted to head to the pub down the road where most of the team would be. Riley started to object but thought better of it. It was Kevin's night, he could choose. Curt had driven, so he and Kevin headed out together. Jenn, Riley and Jake jumped in Riley's car and followed.

"Ugh, I have to hang with the old married couples. What a drag," Jake joked as they pulled into the pub's parking lot.

"Well, maybe we'll have to go and find you a wife," Jenn teased.

Kevin and Curt were already inside with most of the baseball team. The team was toasting Kevin and had bought him two shots. "Uh-oh, I'm going to have a handful tonight," Jenn muttered. She motioned for Jake and Riley to go take a seat in a booth while she ordered a pitcher of beer.

Kevin snuck up and hugged her from behind, "Why hello, my fiancé." His breath already smelled like rubbing alcohol. She turned and gave him a kiss. He squeezed her shoulder and headed back over to his teammates. Jenn was used to the after-game celebrations, which usually ended up with Kevin passed out and Jenn having to take care of him. She carried the pitcher and three glasses over to the booth.

"Wow, he's not going to last an hour at that pace," Jake commented as he poured himself a glass of beer.

"But it won't stop him from trying," Jenn muttered, taking a sip from her glass.

Riley cleared her throat and raised her glass. "To Jenn, for having tamed the boy that I thought was untamable." Jenn laughed and clinked her glass to Riley's and Jake's.

The three finished off the first pitcher quickly and

Jake went to grab another. Every once and a while, Kevin and Curt stopped at the booth to say hi. They both were fading into a drunken stupor as the night came to an end. Riley decided to drive Curt's car home and Jenn poured Kevin into the front seat of Riley's car. Jake climbed in back and they drove home. Kevin was muttering incoherently before dozing off against the car window.

"I hope he wakes up, because I can't carry him inside," Jenn laughed. She looked in the rearview mirror at Jake, but he didn't crack a smile. "You OK?" she asked.

"Yeah, yeah. Only tired. Riley said I could crash on your couch for the night. Is that alright?" Jake asked.

"Sure, no problem. I might hang out with you. Kevin snores so loud when he is drunk." Kevin snorted at this moment, as if supporting Jenn's statement. They pulled into the parking lot of the apartments and Jenn helped Kevin out of the car. Jake stood on his other side for support.

"You know, Jake, I used to be worried about you and Jenn. She always talks about you. I was a little jealous at first. But now you can't have her," Kevin slurred his words. Jenn blushed and they kept walking. Riley had gotten Curt inside without issue as he handled alcohol better than Kevin. Jenn took Kevin to their room and got him settled before returning to the living room. Jake sat on the couch with his head in his hands. Jenn sat down next to him.

"Are you sure you're OK?" she asked again as she

107

leaned into him. To her surprise, he scooted away.

"I don't know Jenn. I mean, I want to say something, but I don't want to because I've been drinking." He rubbed his temples before sitting up and turning to face her. "I know you love him, and I know you think he's your soulmate, but I have a bad feeling about this. I don't trust him. I've known too many guys like that to think that he is the right person for you. You deserve so much more, Jenn. You are a spectacular woman and you deserve the world."

Jenn leaned back and crossed her arms around her. She didn't know how to respond. Jake had been her friend for years and he knew her better than anyone, except Riley. He had known Kevin for about three years and had never mentioned any of this before tonight. "Why are you saying this now?" she whispered without looking at him.

Jake moved back towards her and placed his hand on her knee. "Jenn, I want what's best for you. I feel so protective of you, I just don't want to see you hurt." Jenn nodded slowly and looked at him.

She uncrossed her arms and looked down to her hand where the diamond ring was. She felt her chest tighten and had to take several deep breaths. Then she started to feel her ears burn, irritated that he waited until this moment to say anything. Her inner voice was angry.

She looked back at Jake, feeling the anger in her stomach. "I have been thinking about it. For the past three

108

years. Why would you wait until tonight to bring up your concerns? That is terrible timing, don't you think? Are you jealous?" she asked in a shaky voice, regretting instantly the last question.

Jake moved away again. "Jealous of what? Of my friend making a huge mistake?" He absentmindedly ran his hands through his hair. "Yeah, I should be so lucky to make such a terrible mistake." He stood and started pacing in front of the couch. "Excuse me for caring, excuse me for being worried about one of my best friends." He stopped in front of her and stared. "Why are you getting angry? Could it be that deep down you agree?"

Jenn let out a frustrated sound and stood as well, facing him and not breaking eye contact. "If you didn't like Kevin, you should have said something years ago. It's preposterous that you wait until the night he proposes to object."

Jake did not stand down. His shoulders moved up and down quickly as he tried to calm himself. "It's never too late to change your mind."

Jenn felt the tears filling her eyes and blinked. One tear ran down her cheek, "It is too late. Goodnight, Jake," she said as she turned and walked to her bedroom.

She closed the door and leaned her back against it. More tears rolled down her face and she softly banged her head on the door. She hoped the alcohol had much to do with their argument. She didn't want to be mad at Jake. He was just being a good friend. She crawled into bed and faced away from Kevin, staring at the wall. She hoped that this would blow over by morning. With her mind racing it took several hours for her to fall into a restless sleep.

Chapter 13

The next morning, she woke up with a splitting headache. Jenn rarely drank alcohol, so her hangovers tended to be intense. Kevin was still snoring loudly next to her as she sat upright on the edge of the bed. Her head spun for a second as a wave of nausea rushed over her. Taking a few deep breaths, she stood and walked out of the room. The bright lights in the hall blinded her momentarily and she had to blink to adjust.

She stumbled to the bathroom and then out to the kitchen where Riley sat with two cups of coffee. She slid one to Jenn and smiled, "Well, don't you just look lovely this morning."

Jenn ran her hand through her hair, realizing that it was sticking up in every direction. "I do what I can," she mumbled. She sat across from Riley and took a large gulp of coffee. She closed her eyes and inhaled deeply, trying to properly wake up. The clock on the wall read 9. Jenn glanced to the living room and noticed the couch was empty.

She looked back at Riley, who gave a knowing shrug. "He said you guys fought last night and he wanted to go for a walk this morning to clear his head." Jenn looked down at her coffee, feeling slightly guilty. Riley tapped her fingers on her coffee cup and didn't look away from Jenn, who was trying to avoid eye contact.

"What?" Jenn asked with a small voice, finally meeting Riley's gaze.

"You fought? What does that even mean? You two never fight."

Jenn took a few swallows of coffee before clearing her throat. "He told me that he thinks this engagement is a mistake. I stupidly told him he was jealous, which I know is not true, but he just made me so mad."

Riley nodded her head slowly before setting down her coffee. "He is, you know that" was her only response.

Jenn set her cup down and looked at Riley as if she was speaking a foreign language. "He is not. What would he even be jealous of?" Riley chuffed. Jenn just stared, waiting for an answer that was apparently so obvious to Riley.

"Really, Jenn? You know he's always had a thing for you. I bet in the back of his head he thought that someday you two would be together. Now, he's watching that idea slip away. Of course he's upset."

Jenn continued to stare, not knowing how to answer. She never thought of it. Jake was always there for her, but as a friend. He never gave any indication that he felt otherwise until the outburst last night. He was a great guy and treated her like a best friend.

She was baffled. "No way. We decided a long time ago that we were friends. Just friends."

Riley rolled her eyes. "Maybe *you* decided, and he agreed because it was better than not having you in his life?" Riley stood and put her empty cup into the sink just as Curt came stumbling into the kitchen. He grabbed a cup of coffee, gave Riley a quick kiss and joined Jenn at the table. Riley started making breakfast for everyone as Jenn stared off into space.

"Earth to Jenn, are you OK?" Curt asked. She nodded, forcing a smile. Curt and Riley started chatting and Jenn's mind wandered. She honestly did not know if Riley was right.

She was startled from her thoughts as the front door opened. Jake walked in and paused for a moment when he noticed everyone in the kitchen had turned toward him.

"Sorry, I was just walking a little. I'm going to be heading out soon." He walked over to the couch and picked up his bag. He collected his belongings from the floor when Jenn walked over to him.

"Hey, can we talk for a second?" she asked, motioning to the door. Jake shrugged and pulled his bag over his shoulder. He followed her out the door. She walked a few feet from the door and turned.

They both said "I'm sorry" at the same time,

followed by nervous laughter.

Jenn sighed and leaned against the wall. "I didn't mean to get so defensive with you. Your opinion means a lot to me. You are my best friend and I was just wanting your approval, too. I'm sorry I said you were jealous."

He smiled slightly and leaned against the wall as well. "I'm sorry I attacked you like that. Too much beer didn't help my filter. I am happy for you, I am. I guess I was just taken aback because Kevin never struck me as the commitment type. But if you are happy, I will be by your side the whole way." He held his arms out and motioned for a hug. Jenn slid into his arms and they hugged in silence for a moment.

"I needed that, thank you. Maybe I was mad because I was having doubts about Kevin. But this shows that I was wrong. Now we can all move forward. I wouldn't want to do that without you." She leaned up and gave him a quick kiss on the cheek.

He placed his hand on her shoulder and stood for a moment, not breaking eye contact before adjusting the bag on his shoulder. "I better get going. I have to study for my last exam before graduation. I'll see you in a couple of weeks and good luck with graduation." He blew her a kiss before turning and walking towards the stairs. Jenn stood for a moment and collected her thoughts. She walked back to the apartment and went inside. Kevin had joined Riley and

Curt in the kitchen and all three were eating.

"Did he leave?" Riley asked. Jenn nodded and joined them. Kevin looked worse for the wear, but the breakfast was helping. They chatted about the day before and their upcoming finals. Once they had fully recovered, they spent the rest of the weekend studying.

Chapter 14

The last week of school was filled with studying, testing and more coffee than any person should ever drink. Graduation took place the following Sunday. Their graduation and Jake's were the same day, but they texted each other throughout the ceremony and agreed to celebrate when they were back home.

Jenn spent the month after graduating studying for her nursing licensure test. She took the official test on a Thursday morning. The results would not be posted until the following Sunday. She and Riley sat in front of her email and waited. Jenn held her breath as she clicked on the email icon, letting out a sigh as she read. She had passed the test and was officially a registered nurse.

The Monday after learning she had received her license, she and Kevin were on a plane to Europe. They had planned to spend two weeks backpacking across Scotland. They flew into Edinburgh and were staying at the local university which converted to a bed and breakfast during summer break.

They took several days to explore Edinburgh before heading out to other parts of Scotland by train. They enjoyed the local food and people, staying at hostels and taking in all the culture. It was a great way to wind down after the last semester of school. Jenn was sad to board the plane two weeks later and head home.

Jenn and Riley went to St. Louis together after returning from the trip. Jenn went apartment-hunting downtown while Riley looked for a small home to rent outside of the city. Kevin and Curt stayed at school for a month to help with the baseball camps.

After looking at numerous apartments and homes, Jenn and Riley each paid a deposit and began to move in. Kevin and Curt joined them in St. Louis after finishing up at school. It took several days to move everything in.

Jenn and Riley had applied for jobs early in summer and had interviewed at different locations. Jenn received the call that she had been hired at a rehab facility downtown a few days after moving into her apartment. She would start training in early August. Riley was hired as a kindergarten teacher at a small private school downtown a few weeks after she applied for the job. The school year started in early September.

Kevin and Curt had graduated with business degrees and neither one had a definite idea about what type of job they wanted. Together, they decided to apply at a temp agency and take different types of jobs until they figured it out.

Everything settled in as they entered the fall. Jenn loved her new job and Kevin found several temp jobs that he liked. Riley was excited to be a full-fledged teacher and

118

dove into work with gusto. Curt liked his first temp job and was hired on full time after several weeks.

Riley and Jenn continued to plan Riley's wedding and had all the major details squared away nine months before the big day. They had found a church and venue. Riley picked out her dress and invitations were ready to be sent out.

Jenn felt like everything was falling into place and she was happy and satisfied. It seemed like nothing could go wrong. She looked forward to the future and hoped everything would stay exactly as it was. If only it had.

Present

Chapter 15

Jenn worked that night alone due to low patient population, which made the night longer. By morning she was happy to get out of there. She stopped at a corner coffee cart and grabbed a cup before getting on the bus to head home. She sent a quick text to Mike to check in and ask about catching a movie that evening. He texted back quickly and promised to call her after he was done at school. She smiled and sipped the coffee while staring out the bus window.

The bus slowed as it came to her corner and she stood up and walked towards the front. She was saying goodbye to the bus driver as her phone started to buzz. She stepped onto the sidewalk before pulling it out of her bag. It was Jake. "Hello?" she answered.

"Hey, how's it going?"

"Just getting off my bus. What's up?" she asked as she walked toward her apartment.

"Oh, nothing. Just checking in, you know." Jenn dug into her bag looking for her keys while trying to balance the phone on her shoulder. "Here, let me get that for you." A voice sounded from behind her. She jumped and turned, coming face to face with Jake.

She smacked his shoulder and laughed. "You know I'm trained in martial arts, right? That could have ended badly for you." He smiled and picked up her phone, which had dropped to the ground.

"Can I come up and have a cup of coffee?" Jake asked. Jenn smiled and motioned for him to follow her inside. He sat down at the kitchen table while she started the coffee. They chatted about work and other trivial things while the coffee brewed. She poured two cups and sat down across the table from him.

"So, when's your date with Kelly happening?" Jenn asked, taking a sip from her cup. Jake paused before taking a sip himself. "Don't tell me you chickened out."

He smirked. "No, she said she'd look at her schedule and text me." Jenn nodded. She was happy that he was dating. Jake always was so busy with work and studying for his med school exams. "We'll have to see how this goes. Anyway, I'm still pushing to take my entrance exams soon, so I have to focus." Jenn reached out and squeezed his hand.

"You're going to do great. You are the smartest guy I know. Hell, you saved my life." She trailed off and looked away. Jake looked down into his cup.

They never really talked about the darkest time in Jenn's life, but they were all present for it. Jake was overprotective of her because he really did save her life.

He cleared his throat and changed the subject. "So, next date with Mike?"

She blushed again. "He's calling me tonight and we're going to see a movie."

Jake leaned back in his chair and stared at her. "You really like him, don't you?" She nodded shyly. Jake clicked his tongue and fidgeted with his cup. "Well, I'm glad. Now, I need to meet this guy, so I can use my radar on him." Jenn met his gaze and gave a half smile. Jake had been the only one to see the bad in her ex. If only she would have listened to him then.

"Yeah, make sure I listen to you this time," she said quietly. She sipped her coffee, avoiding his stare.

There was always a thin line between Jenn wanting to talk about her past and not wanting to relive it. Everyone said it would take time to get over it. She had heard that from therapists, family and friends. She had a hard time listening to them, but it seemed easier with Jake. Maybe because he was there at the ultimate low point. She was grateful that he stuck around after that.

"Be sure you do" was his response. He smiled and stood to put his cup in the sink. "Well, I should let you get your beauty sleep before your hot date tonight," he said as he walked towards the door. Jenn followed and gave him a tighter than usual hug before he left. She fought back the urge to ask him to stay longer.

The door clicked behind him and Jenn stood there for a moment before realizing she was crying. These moments happened, though less frequently than before. Jenn had an excellent memory for both the good and the bad things that had happened to her. When she went to the bad, she needed to vent. She hated leaning on her friends or family for that, so she usually went for a run or exercised.

She quickly changed out of her scrubs and grabbed her headphones. She headed out the door and took off jogging down the street. The music and adrenaline washed over her as she ran. Before she realized it, 45 minutes had passed, and she had instinctively ended back at her apartment. She grabbed some water before lying down on the couch.

Chapter 16

Jenn woke up to the phone ringing. She sat up and looked around, momentarily confused. She had fallen asleep, fully clothed, on the couch. She stood up and stretched before walking to the kitchen to find her phone. It had stopped ringing by the time she found it and she clicked on the missed call icon. It was Mike, and now he probably thought she was ignoring him.

Jenn took a minute to wake up and drink something before calling him back. He answered after a few rings, "Thought you had changed your mind."

She chuckled, "No, sorry. I passed out on the couch after I went for a run." She paced in the kitchen while they planned their date. The run had calmed Jenn's earlier nerves, but they began to creep back in as she talked to Mike. These were the good nerves, though.

They agreed on a movie and a time, planning to meet at the theatre in two hours. Jenn quickly showered and changed before grabbing something to eat. It was drizzling, so she grabbed an umbrella. She walked to the theater, just a few blocks away.

Mike was standing outside the box office when she finally arrived. He was holding a small bouquet of flowers and blushed slightly as she approached. She thanked him and took them. They stood awkwardly for a few moments, like two high schoolers on a first date.

"I got the tickets already. Do you want to head inside?" Mike held the door open for her and they walked to the snack bar. Mike insisted on getting Jenn something, so she ordered a small popcorn. They made their way inside theater and took their seats.

The movie wasn't new, so the theatre was almost empty. Jenn preferred it that way as she wasn't too fond of crowds. She had agreed to an action movie, even though her favorite movies were all romantic and unrealistic. She rarely made a guy sit through those and she had yet to find a guy willing to do so.

After finishing her popcorn, she rested her arm on the armrest next to Mike. He laid his arm next to hers before slowly reaching over and taking her hand. His hand was warm and soft. She felt the unfamiliar feeling of butterflies in her stomach. Jenn smiled and relaxed back into her chair. She could see Mike smiling out of the corner of her eye.

The movie was decent, though not really her taste. Mike seemed to enjoy it. "Wow, those special effects were outstanding," he said as they left the theatre hand in hand. They continued to walk and talk, still holding hands.

Jenn was happy. Conversation was easy with Mike and she was comfortable with him. She felt a little bit of her shell cracking away.

They decided to grab some ice cream before ending the night. After ordering, they sat outside and talked for a while longer.

"So, tell me more about yourself. I know you're a nurse and I know you haven't dated in a while. What else is there to Jenn?" Mike asked. Jenn inhaled, not sure if she wanted to tell her sob story.

She looked up at Mike and paused. He seemed interested, but she did not want to scare him off. "I don't think you're ready for the real Jenn yet. How about some highlights?" He leaned back and motioned for her to continue. "OK, well. Here you go. Highlights. Hmm, I grew up in a small town in Illinois. I have two best friends from high school that live in the city, Riley and Jake. I don't have a lot of other friends, kind of a loner. I played collegiate volleyball and still play recreationally when I can. I like to run and I'm a blue belt in tae kwon do." She paused and took a deep breath before continuing. "And the reason I don't date is that I was almost married before a guy destroyed me." She finished talking and stared at her ice cream. She was almost afraid to look up at Mike.

When she finally did, he was looking back with a small smile. "You made it seem like there was something worse than that. I thought maybe you had a tail or something." She giggled nervously. "You can relax, Jenn." She let her shoulders relax and leaned back. He laughed slightly before taking a bite of ice cream. "Thank you for the highlights. I hope you eventually feel comfortable enough to tell me the whole story. But for now, I will take what I can get."

Jenn was grateful that she didn't have to go deeper. She was not ready for that. "OK, your turn."

Mike cleared his throat like he was ready to tell a long story. "I'm boring. I grew up here. The only time I've been away was college. I play beer league softball with a group of teachers every Sunday but was never good enough to play any sport in college. I'm a die-hard Cubs fan which never goes well in this city. I hate running, sorry. I love movies and have an extensive collection. Oh, and I play guitar." He took a deep, dramatic breath like he had just run a mile.

Jenn laughed and held out her hand. "Well, nice to meet you Mike." He smiled and took her hand and shook it. They sat for a moment holding hands across the table before Mike cleared his throat and she let go.

"Do you want me to walk you home?" he asked as he took the last bite of his ice cream.

Jenn checked her watch. It was 9, which was early for her but not early for someone who had to teach in the morning. "Sure, that would be nice."

They stood and threw away their empty ice cream cups before heading toward Jenn's apartment. Mike gently took Jenn's hand as they walked and talked. When they reached her apartment, she stopped and turned to face Mike. "Did you want to come up?" He looked up at the building and back at Jenn.

He fidgeted, as if struggling to make an important decision. "God, you don't know how much. But I'm going to say no this time," he finally answered.

Jenn was a little disappointed but glad at the same time. She knew it was worth the wait and wanted this to be more than just physical. "You do know by being a gentleman, you're making it harder on me," she said quietly.

"Making what harder?" he asked with a quizzical look on his face.

"Me not pulling you inside this building and not letting you leave." She met his gaze and he frowned slightly.

"Believe me, it's not so easy for me either." They stood there, locked in place not breaking eye contact. Jenn moved first, stepping slowly towards Mike. She raised her arms slowly and looped them around his neck. He responded by hooking his arms around her waist and pulling her toward him. They stopped with their faces so close that she could count his eyelashes. She closed her eyes as she met his lips, kissing softly at first before leaning in for a deeper kiss. He turned her and pushed her gently against the wall, letting his hand slip under the back of her shirt. She gasped slightly at his touch and ran her hands into the back of his hair.

For a moment, she forgot that they were outside and people walking by could see what they were doing. Mike pulled away, breathing hard. Jenn let her arms fall so he could step backwards. "Yeah, not making that easier," he mumbled. She blushed and ran her hand through her hair. She calmed her breathing and reached into her bag to grab her keys.

"So, this was fun," she said, fanning her face. Mike chuckled. "You feel up to meeting my friends this weekend?" Jenn asked.

He thought about it briefly. "You must like me if you want them to approve of me."

"Am I that obvious?"

Mike leaned in for one last small kiss, "I will call you Saturday and you tell me where to meet you." Jenn nodded and kissed him back. He turned to walk away, giving a small wave before heading around the corner.

Jenn stood for a moment with her back against the wall. She put her hand to her heart and felt it beating rapidly. She then touched her lips, which were tingling. She hadn't felt this feeling since … well, it had been a while.

She turned and went into her apartment building. She tossed her bag on the counter before flopping onto the couch. Her mind was racing, but she was also tired. She needed to text both Riley and Jake, so they could plan their weekend. Maybe she could talk Riley into having everyone over for a barbecue or something. She decided to call Riley first. It went to voicemail, which meant she had her phone silenced to avoid upsetting the baby. Jenn left a short message about her date and that she wanted to introduce her to Mike. She then texted Jake since he was at work. He didn't respond, but she knew that he was just starting his shift. Jenn relaxed back into the couch and sighed.

This felt promising. For once, she didn't have that fear in her chest that often came with any idea of romance. She picked up a book and started to read from where she left off. Her eyes grew heavy after a few chapters and she forced herself up and into the bedroom. The day had finally caught up to her as she changed into pajamas and slipped under the covers. Her mind was calm, and she fell asleep easily for the first time in months.

5 years ago

Chapter 17

Jenn stood in front of her kitchen table, looking over a large poster board with a drawing of Riley's reception venue on it. Small round tables were marked with a seating arrangement. She crossed her arms as she looked from name card to name card, making sure they were all in order. She nodded in satisfaction and collected the cards together in order, placing them in a large box. Kevin entered the room and sighed, "Man, will I be glad when this weekend is over."

Jenn huffed. "You do realize we'll be doing this again in six months for our wedding, right?"

He pulled a carton of milk out of the fridge and took a long sip. "Hopefully, Riley will take her duty as matron of honor as seriously as you do. I feel like between work and this that we barely have time for each other."

Jenn walked behind him and hugged him around the waist. "I'm sorry, but it will get better. I just want this to be perfect for her."

Kevin turned and leaned down for a kiss. "I know, I just miss you."

Jenn pouted and kissed him again. "Maybe after the wedding we can rent a hotel room and have some fun?"

Kevin perked up and smiled. "Deal." He kissed her

again and headed out the door to work. Jenn turned back to the table. She picked up her "to do" list and checked off the place cards. The next tasks on the list were centerpieces and favors. Riley was coming over after she got off work to help with that so Jenn thought she would take a break.

She grabbed a cup of coffee and sat on the couch, turning the TV on to watch the morning news. She was meeting Jake in an hour to pick up the groomsmen's tuxes and Riley's dress. Jenn's dress was finished and hanging in her closet. She tended to finish things early because she could not handle being late or rushed.

Tomorrow, she and Riley would talk to the florist and the caterer to put the finishing touches on everything. Friday would be the rehearsal dinner. Jenn had spoken to Riley's family last night and they planned on driving into town Friday. Riley's mom had been in and out of town to help with planning, but Jenn liked to be organized so everyone was confident in putting her in charge of the details. She had taken the rest of the week and weekend off work to focus on the wedding. It also helped her figure out what things she did and didn't want for her wedding.

She and Kevin had set a date and picked a venue, but she hadn't narrowed down the other details. Luckily, she had contacts with florists, caterer's, DJs and photographers from helping Riley.

After flipping channels for a while, Jenn turned the

TV off and decided to head out to meet Jake. He had been made an honorary bridesmaid and was an usher. They had to stop at the tux shop, the seamstress, and then Jenn wanted Jake's opinion on a wedding gift. That was Jenn's only procrastination because she wanted it to be perfect. She grabbed her bag and texted Jake that she was leaving the apartment now. It was a cool, but sunny day so Jenn wanted to walk a little.

She made it to the tux shop in 15 minutes and Jake was waiting in front, leaning on his car. He smiled as she approached, and they linked arms before entering the store. Curt had asked only two people to be groomsmen, his brother and Kevin. Jake also had to wear the tux as an usher. He got his tux and grabbed Curt's to save time. They carried two tuxes each out to the car and laid them over the backseat.

The seamstress was on the edge of town. Riley had insisted on an older woman who did her work from home, and Jenn obliged because it was her dress and her wedding. Jenn figured a dress shop could do just as well, but it wasn't her say.

A middle-aged woman answered the door with a warm smile, leading the two of them into a room set up for her work. "Here it is," she said dramatically as she unzipped the dress bag to show them. Jenn sighed as she looked at the dress. It was beautiful. Jake squeezed her arm and smiled. "Oh, should the groom be seeing the dress?" the woman asked.

Jenn chuckled, "Not the groom, he's her best friend. I'm the maid of honor."

The woman nodded, "Sorry, my mistake. I shouldn't assume." Jenn looked at Jake, who didn't meet her eye. He was blushing slightly. She nudged him, and he looked up and shrugged.

"Well, thank you for doing this. I'm sure she will look fantastic this weekend." Jenn carefully carried the dress out to Jake's car and hung it from the hook above the back door. "So, when's your wedding?" Jenn joked, trying to break the tension she felt from Jake.

He smiled and started the car. "Oh, it will take me a while to plan. I have some big ideas," he joked as they drove back towards Jenn's apartment. She wanted to drop off the tuxes and dress before doing anything else.

After they were safely in her closet, she and Jake headed back out. "I have no idea what to get Riley and Curt," Jenn muttered. Jake was silent as he drove down the street.

He pulled up in front of a small shop that Jenn wouldn't have noticed if Jake hadn't pointed it out. "This guy is amazing. He can make a personalized painting for them. I think they would love something to hang in their new house."

Jenn entered the store and was amazed by all the

beautiful artwork lining the walls. An older man stood behind a desk and introduced himself. He and Jenn spoke for a while, walking together and looking at different pictures. Jenn stopped in front of a painting of a tree. She pointed at it and Jake nodded. She gave the man information about Riley and Curt, including their wedding date, and paid a surprisingly small fee. The man thanked them and told her to pick up the painting Saturday morning.

"Oh my gosh, Jake. Thank you for showing me that. They will love it!" Jenn exclaimed. He smiled, and they got back in the car.

They picked up some lunch before heading back to Jenn's apartment and starting on the wedding tasks. Riley would be there in a couple of hours. She had taken the next two days off before the weekend to finalize everything.

A few hours later, Riley, Jenn and Jake sat on the living room floor making favors while listening to music, drinking wine and talking. Curt and Kevin showed up later that evening and they were able to finish all the tasks.

Jenn ordered take out and they gathered around the TV to watch a movie and relax.

"You are a lifesaver, Jenn," Riley said with a slight slur from drinking too much wine. Jenn gave her a thumbs up and continued to eat her dinner.

"Yeah, you've got a job to re-create the level of

commitment when helping with her wedding," Curt joked.

Riley giggled, "I will be the best matron of honor ever."

After the movie, Riley and Jenn picked up the living room, and Jake helped Curt carry the tuxes and the dress out to the cars. "Don't you peek," Riley teased.

Jenn rolled her eyes, "No more wine for you." Riley blushed and grabbed a glass of water.

When he returned, Curt took Riley by the hand, "I'll take this one home. I'll drop her back here tomorrow and she can get her car back." Jenn blew Riley a kiss as she walked out with Curt.

Jake gave Jenn a hug and headed out after them but turned before he made it to the door. "I'll be at work tomorrow but call me on Friday if you need any last-minute help." Jenn smiled and gave a small wave.

She returned to the living room where Kevin was dozed on the couch. "Hey, I put your tux in your closet. You have shoes, right?" Kevin mumbled yes and nodded.

Jenn sighed and pulled him off the couch and into the bedroom. He crawled into bed without complaint and Jenn changed into her pajamas before opening her laptop to work on her wedding toast. It took her about an hour to be satisfied with it. She stretched her arms above her head and closed the laptop. She was extremely excited for the next few days but fell asleep easily due to her exhaustion.

Chapter 18

Riley got to the apartment surprisingly early the next day and with only a slight hangover. Jenn poured her a cup of coffee as they went over the day's tasks. Most of the list involved going to each wedding vendor and paying off the remaining balances. Riley and Curt had also finalized the song list for the DJ, so they had to drop that off.

Jenn made a schedule for Saturday and copied one for each vendor, so everyone was on the same page, and everything would go smoothly.

The errands took most of the day, and the girls were worn out by the time they got back to Jenn's apartment. They made a quick lunch before packing all the favors and centerpieces into boxes and loading them into Riley's car. They dropped them off at the reception hall and spoke with the manager about coming back tomorrow to set up. The girls looked around. "Just imagine, you're going to be a wife at this time Saturday evening," Jenn said to Riley.

Riley had tears in her eyes and Jenn put her arm around her. "It's not nerves, I'm just so happy. I know that everything will be perfect because I have the greatest partner ever. You, not Curt … but don't tell him I said that." Jenn smirked and nodded.

Riley dropped Jenn off at her apartment and headed

home. Kevin was sitting at the kitchen table with a beer when she entered the apartment.

She kissed his cheek and grabbed a glass of water. "Everything is squared away for Saturday. It's going to be amazing." Kevin nodded and continued to look at his phone.

Jenn paused before opening the fridge and pulling out things to start dinner. She cooked in silence and placed a plate in front of Kevin. He finally looked up and thanked her.

They chatted about the day, with Jenn doing most of the talking about the wedding. Kevin seemed slightly annoyed by all the wedding talk, so she turned the conversation to his day and the World Series. He perked up at that and talked animatedly about the last game he watched. Jenn nodded along with him, even though she had no idea what was going on in the world of baseball.

They finished dinner and she cleaned up the dishes. Kevin grabbed another beer before heading into the living room and turning on the news. Jenn sighed and went to take a shower. She and Riley had a spa day planned tomorrow before the rehearsal dinner, so she decided to turn in early.

Kevin climbed into bed after a while, smelling strongly of beer and started kissing Jenn's neck. "I'm so tired, Kevin. Can we save it for this weekend please?" Kevin huffed and rolled over, facing the wall. Jenn rolled her eyes. Sometimes, he acted like a toddler who lost a toy.

He started snoring soon after that and Jenn drifted off.

****

Jenn met Riley at the salon the next day. They had scheduled a pedicure and manicure and left feeling relaxed and ready for the evening's festivities.

Riley was planning on staying the night with Jenn after the rehearsal dinner, and Kevin was staying with Curt. Kevin had joked about a bachelor party, but Riley shot daggers with her eyes and he retracted. The girls planned on watching some classic wedding movies while doing facials.

The rehearsal and dinner went off without a hitch. After the families headed off to their homes or hotels, the wedding party went to the reception hall to set up. All the tables were in place with the table linens, so the group just had to lay out the decorations and favors. The ceremony area was already set up and the finishing touches would be added by the florist in the morning.

They worked for just over an hour before they could stand back and admire the hall. It looked perfect, and Riley again had tears in her eyes. This time Curt put his arm around her and kissed her forehead. They walked together to the parking lot before saying goodnight. "I'll see you tomorrow!" Curt called after Riley.

"I'll be the one in the white dress," she replied before blowing him a kiss.

Jake went with the girls because he was technically a bridesmaid. However, he refused to do a facial with them. They sat and watched bad romantic movies, reminiscing. Jenn gave up her bed to Riley because she needed to be well rested for the next day. Jenn and Jake stayed out in the living room, Jenn on the couch and Jake on the floor.

"I can't believe this weekend is actually here. I knew they would get married. You could tell from the moment they met," Jenn reminisced.

"That boy fell in love the first day of college," Jake said with a yawn. "What about you? When did you know Kevin was the one?"

Jenn sat for a moment, thinking. She didn't really know. He had just always been there. "He kind of grew on me. I really fought it at first, but he is persistent." She told Jake about how she told Kevin no many times before she finally agreed to date him. After that, she never looked back.

"Well, not quite as romantic as love at first sight, but there you have it," Jake muttered.

Jenn frowned. She was attracted to Kevin instantly because he was very good looking, but she couldn't really recall when she turned the page of her heart. He did give her butterflies when they kissed, and she remembers him always being kind to her. Maybe that is what a soulmate is, just knowing that person will always be there. "Whatever, all the romance things in books, movies and TV shows are unrealistic. I'm sure it may happen to someone, but not everyone."

Jake rolled onto his side. "Really Jenn? Is that coming from the person who thinks love should be like a romance novel? You live for those things."

Jenn cleared her throat, her mouth suddenly dry. "I need some water," she said quickly, standing and walking to the kitchen. She stood at the sink with both hands gripped on the counter. She had to take several deep breaths to calm herself. She heard Jake enter the kitchen, but she did not relax her grip on the sink.

"Come on, Jenn, I didn't mean anything by it. I was mostly agreeing with you about Riley and Curt. I'd kill to have what they have. I'm sorry if it came out wrong."

Jenn turned around and crossed her arms across her chest. "I'm not mad at you. I'm just worried. I know Kevin loves me and I know I love him." She took a deep breath. "But what if he isn't my one? What if I am just settling for him because he asked me first?" She began to hyperventilate.

Jake walked over and placed his hands on her shoulders. She slowed her breathing and looked up into his eyes. "You are going to marry him in six months. You wouldn't have said yes if you weren't sure. You are one of the smartest and most logical people that I know. You don't do things without thinking."

Jenn leaned forward and rested her head on his shoulder. "Thank god this isn't Riley freaking out the day before her wedding," Jenn joked.

"Hell no, she's probably sleeping in her wedding dress, so she can get married as fast as possible tomorrow!" They laughed and shared a hug.

Jenn followed Jake back into the living room and lay down on the couch. She stared at the ceiling and let her mind wander. There was no other guy, besides Jake, who knew her as well as Kevin did. She was never unsure about their relationship, but there were always small questions that nagged at her. She had an enormous amount of faith and trust that everything was the way it should be. She heard Jake's breathing slow and turn to soft snores. She smiled and rolled onto her side, forcing herself to sleep so she wouldn't have to struggle tomorrow.

Chapter 19

Riley came bouncing into the living room early the next morning, "I'm getting married today!" she yelled. Jake raised his arms in weary celebration while Jenn sat up and stretched.

"You were wrong, Jake. She's not wearing the dress," Jenn joked sleepily. Jake laughed and rolled onto his stomach. Riley skipped over, smacked his bottom and skipped over to pull Jenn off the couch.

"Coffee first, then wedding!" she squealed.

Jenn jokingly covered her ears as she followed her into the kitchen. "Don't think you need caffeine, friend." Jake slowly followed and poured himself a cup.

Riley talked a mile a minute while Jake and Jenn sipped their coffee to wake up. They had to be to the ceremony by 1 o'clock. Jenn would do Riley's makeup and hair at the apartment, and they would change right before the ceremony.

Jake ate some breakfast with them before leaving, since *he* didn't need hair and makeup done. Jenn had offered, but he politely declined with a smirk.

Jenn set up a faux salon while Riley showered. She did Riley's hair first, braiding and pinning it up into an intricate half-knot. She slipped small flowers into the back since Riley had not wanted a veil. After fussing over small imperfections, Jenn finished with what seemed like a can of hairspray. She wouldn't let Riley see until she was finished, though. She started on her makeup, giving her a natural look with dramatic lip color.

Jenn stepped back when she finished, a little tearful. Riley looked nervous, so Jenn took her in front of the bathroom mirror. Riley's eye got big and she sniffed, fanning her face. "Damn it, Jenn. Don't make me cry."

Jenn blotted her own eyes and handed a tissue to Riley. "Don't worry, it's all waterproof." They hugged tightly.

Jenn excused herself to get ready. After a quick shower, she curled her hair and pinned it half up. She paused between hair and makeup to make sure Riley ate something. She finished her makeup quickly, and they packed their dresses into the car. Riley was tense with nerves as they drove towards the venue. Jenn played music and joked to calm her down.

Riley's mom was already in the changing area when they arrived, and she started to cry when she saw the girls. "Mom, no," Riley said, fanning her eyes again.

"You two look like angels," she said, pulling them both into tight hugs.

"You look beautiful, too," Jenn said. They hung up the dresses and heard a knock on the door. The photographer wanted to get some shots of them getting ready, so they faked putting on makeup and jewelry.

Jenn and Riley stood in front of the wedding dress. "You ready?" Jenn asked, squeezing her hand. Riley nodded, but couldn't say anything. Jenn slipped the dress from the hanger and helped her friend step into it. She pulled it up into place and had her mom help tie the laces in back. They worked in silence with only the click of the camera sounding in the background.

When they finished, Riley turned, and both Jenn and the bride's mother gasped. "Perfect" was all they could say. Jenn slipped into her dress, too, a strapless burgundy gown. They posed for a few more photos before a second knock came. Jenn answered, and Jake was there, looking handsome in his tux.

"Wow, you girls are stunning. I have your dad here, Riley, and he said it's time. I'm going to take this lovely lady to her seat." He motioned to Riley's mom and she took his arm.

Riley's dad entered the room and she begged him not to say anything because she was inches from a sobbing mess. He nodded and sniffled, extending his hand to her. She linked arms with him, and Jenn handed her the bouquet before grabbing her own flowers and exiting first.

They stopped in front of a set of double doors to wait for their cue. The music started, and Jake opened the doors. Jenn walked slowly down the aisle towards Curt, Kevin and Curt's brother, Ken. Kevin winked at her and Curt smiled nervously.

The music changed, and everyone stood as Riley entered with her father. Jenn looked back at Curt, who was fighting back tears. She felt a tear rolling down her cheek. Riley stood with her father and kissed his cheek before he gave her hand to Curt. Jenn took Riley's bouquet and adjusted her dress train.

The beautiful ceremony had everyone in tears. Jenn had to give Riley a tissue halfway through because she was sobbing.

The crowd cheered loudly when they kissed, and Curt and Riley walked out with their hands in the air. Jenn linked arms with Kevin on the way out and they shared a quick kiss. All the worries from the previous night had washed away. The wedding party stood in the hallway after the ceremony to greet those in attendance and point them in the direction of the reception.

After the ceremony space emptied out, the bridal party gathered in the changing room for a moment. "Thank you all for being a part of this. It was perfect," Riley gushed.

Kevin pulled out six shot glasses and a flask. "To the happy couple!" They all took the shot and cheered, performing an awkward group hug before heading towards the reception hall. Jenn watched Curt and Riley walking hand in hand and smiled. Kevin was busy talking with Ken, so Jenn chatted with Jake.

"Did you manage to hold back the tears?" she joked.

"Oh please, you know I was weeping like a baby," he teased, and pulled out the tissues from his pocket. Jenn laughed out loud.

The DJ was waiting for them outside the reception hall to give them instructions for the big entrance. The music came on and he announced the bridal party. Jenn danced between Kevin and Ken as they made their way to the head table. Riley and Curt walked in hand in hand before Curt spun her into his arms and kissed her. The reception hall burst into cheers. After everyone was seated, Riley's dad said a prayer before dinner was served.

Since the reception was in the early evening, the menu was light. Jenn sat next to Riley, and Kevin sat next to Curt. The wait staff kept their wine glasses filled, and Jenn had to pace herself so she could give her speech without slurring. Kevin, however, did not.

He went first and made a short and funny speech about his and Curt's time as roommates and teammates. He had the crowd laughing and gave Curt a tight hug when he finished. Jenn's speech was a little longer, but she had to fit in over 10 years of friendship, including becoming best friends, being volleyball teammates and going to college together. Jenn was pleased at the emotional reactions to her speech. She and Riley hugged tightly before Jenn raised a glass and everyone cheered.

The DJ announced the cake cutting and dances next. Everyone moved to the dance floor and the liquor flowed from the open bar. Riley and Curt were in the center of the dance floor letting loose. Jenn had to help Riley bustle her dress in back so she wouldn't trip over it.

When Jenn realized her maid of honor duties were done, she let loose as well. She and Kevin danced to a few songs before he excused himself to the bathroom. Jake joined her on the dance floor and brought her a shot. They clicked glasses together before drinking and cheering.

Chapter 20

The crowd started to thin out after a few hours and Jenn felt the room starting to spin. She made her way out of the reception hall to get some fresh air and to use the bathroom. She had just walked out of the hall when she heard soft giggling coming from the coat check area.

The alcohol enhanced her curiosity, so she made her way over to see who was fooling around. Sliding along the wall she peeked around the corner of the door. Her stomach dropped as she stood, staring and shocked.

Kevin had a brunette woman pressed against the back wall and was kissing her neck as she giggled. Neither of them noticed Jenn standing in the doorway.

She felt a wave of nausea roll over her. Spinning around, she took off running to the bathroom. The vomit came just before she reached the toilet. Tears rolled down her face as she wiped it from the floor. She covered her mouth and screamed, punching the wall of the bathroom stall. The alcohol dulled the pain and she hit the wall several more times.

After minutes of sitting on the bathroom floor, she gathered herself up enough to stand and wash her face and hands. She stared at herself in the mirror, her eyes bloodshot and her cheeks red. Her chest tightened, and she was breathing heavily. She had to go back to the reception to grab her purse, but she did not want to walk by that coat check room again.

She went outside. The cool air hit her face and she inhaled deeply. She stood still for several minutes, looking up at the clouds. The sun had just started to set.

Wiping her face, she headed in the front door and back into the reception hall. The DJ was announcing that the bar would close shortly, and a slow song was playing. Jenn headed straight to the bar and ordered two shots. Curt and Riley danced alone in the center of the dance floor.

Jenn jumped when someone touched her shoulder. "Hey, are you OK?" Jake asked, handing her a tissue from his pocket. She laughed and took both shots. He raised his eyebrow but didn't push her to answer.

Turning to face the dance floor, she wiped her eyes and cheeks. Jake stood next to her in silence.

After several tense minutes she answered. "I need to leave."

Jake looked confused. "Do you want to talk to Riley? Where's Kevin?"

Jenn bit her bottom lip hard and tasted blood. "I need to leave, now." Her cheeks were burning.

"OK. Let me go talk to Riley and you grab your

stuff." Jake quickly walked toward Riley and Curt, meeting them as they came off the dance floor. Jake whispered in Riley's ear and she looked over at Jenn without a smile. Jenn met her gaze, shook her head and turned towards the back door of the hall.

She grabbed her purse and coat from the changing room and walked out of the building and into the parking lot. She stood next to Jake's car with her arms folded across her chest.

She gagged as another wave of nausea hit her and she leaned over in case she was going to vomit again. There was a crunch of gravel behind her as Jake came jogging out of the door. He didn't say anything but placed his hand on her back and offered her a bottle of water.

"Thank you" was all she could mutter.

Jake opened the car door and she climbed in. He sat in the driver's seat looking nervous, still unsure of what was going on. Jenn burst into tears and she put her hands over her face. Jake reached for her but pulled his hand back and let her cry for a few moments. She hated crying, so her crying spells were usually short.

Once she calmed her breathing, she finally looked at him. "I need a drink," she said in a flat tone.

He didn't break eye contact but raised his eyebrow again. "You sure about that?" She nodded, and he sighed.

He pulled out of the parking lot and they drove in silence. Jenn's phone started chiming and buzzing as soon as they pulled away. The first was a message from Riley.

What the hell happened? Followed by, *I hope you are okay.*

Jenn stared at the phone for a moment because there were also two missed calls and a message from Kevin.

His read. *Riley told me you left crying. What is going on?*

She gripped the phone tightly and fought the urge to throw it out the car window. She erased Kevin's message and responded to Riley.

Not okay. I will call you tomorrow. She hit send and then turned off her phone.

She could tell that Jake was watching her from the side. She took a drink of water before speaking. "You were right," she said softly. He turned for a moment to look at her. Tears rolled silently down her cheeks now. He reached over and took her hand.

They drove in silence, holding hands, until they found a small bar near Jake's apartment.

Jenn realized they must have looked out of place at the small, dark bar, she in her formal dress and he in his tux. They settled into a booth near the back, and Jake headed to the bar to order some drinks. He handed her a vodka tonic and sat down across from her. Jenn downed the drink before he had taken a drink of his. Jake whistled softly and went back towards the bar. He returned with a bottle of beer and four shots. He set two in front of her and two next to him.

Jenn stared at the drinks for a moment before looking up at him. He had a cautious look on his face but continued to not push her.

She blinked, and two more tears fell. She wiped her nose with the tissue in her hand and sighed. "I hate men," she muttered as she took both shots. Jake fidgeted with his shot glass before downing one.

He cleared his throat. "Care to elaborate so I can know what the hell is happening?"

Jenn put down the beer bottle and her chin started to quiver. Between sobs, she told Jake what she had walked in on. His face remained blank, but his ears were getting red. Jenn finished talking and picked up her beer and guzzled it. Jake looked down at the table and was gripping his beer bottle tightly. Jenn closed her eyes and took several deep breaths.

When she opened her eyes, Jake was sitting closer to her. "I am so sorry," he said as he pulled her into a hug. They sat hugging without saying anything for several minutes. Jake pulled away first and took her face in his hands. "You do not deserve any of this. You are the best person I know. I can't believe he would throw that away. What a moron." She didn't respond. She just stayed still and watched him. Her chest began to tighten again, and she sat back.

Jake went back up to the bar and Jenn watched him closely. She took more deep breaths and calmed herself by the time he came back. She didn't break her gaze as he sat down next to her again.

He handed her another beer and gave her a quizzical look. She looked down at the bottle and took a drink. Her head was swimming from the alcohol, but she had a warmth building in her chest that she couldn't explain.

After taking another long drink she looked back at Jake. She studied his face, from his hazel eyes to his dimples. She had never looked at him like this. He watched her carefully, not knowing what else to do. She slid towards him slowly, pushing the bottle along the table. He didn't look away. The tension was thick between them and Jenn's heart began to beat fast.

Jake started to say something as Jenn leaned forward to kiss him. He froze for a moment before pulling his head back. "What are you doing?" he gasped, trying to catch his breath.

"You told me once that I think too much. Right now, I'm not thinking." She stared without blinking and watched emotions flash across Jake's face. His eyes were wide open and his mouth was opening and closing, as if he was trying to find an argument.

Jenn smiled and leaned in slowly, meeting his lips softly this time. Jake didn't react at first, but then he began to kiss her back. She looped her arms around his neck, and he slid his arms down her back. The kiss became deeper and Jenn felt her stomach flutter.

After several minutes she pulled away. "Do you want to get out of here?" she asked breathlessly. Jake stared for a moment before nodding. He took her hand and led her out to his car.

They drove in silence to his apartment. She walked in before him and waited for the door to click shut before turning around and kissing him again. She pushed him against the door, and he pushed the jacket off her shoulders. She did the same with his and began to unbutton his shirt.

They moved slowly from the door and stumbled towards the bedroom. He unzipped her dress and let it fall to the ground. He stopped momentarily to admire her before picking her up and laying her on the bed. Jenn fumbled with his belt and pushed his pants onto the ground.

Jake stopped after they were fully naked, and he held himself over her on the bed. "Are you sure about this?"

The alcohol made Jenn feel warm and her brain fuzzy. All she knew at that moment was that she wanted

Jake, in every way she could have him. She nodded, and he leaned down to kiss her again. His kisses were deep, but soft. Jenn moaned in pleasure as he touched her. The haziness of the night overtook her mind, and everything went blank.

Chapter 21

The next thing she remembered was the sun shining in her eyes as she tried to open them. Her mouth tasted awful and it felt like she was chewing cotton. Her eyes were crusted with old makeup. She tried to sit up, but her head was pounding, and a wave of nausea rushed over her. She stood quickly and stumbled into the bathroom. She stared at herself in the mirror. Her hair was sticking out at different angles and makeup was smeared around her eyes and lips. She leaned over the sink to splash cold water on her face and to take a drink. Looking around the bathroom, she tried to remember what had happened.

She turned back towards the bedroom and saw Jake sleeping with a sheet wrapped around his leg. *Oh my god, what did I do?* Her inner voice was screaming.

Flashes of last night ran through her head. She slid her back down the wall and sat on the floor in the bathroom. She covered her face with her hands as she remembered. Kevin kissing another girl. Leaving with Jake. A lot of alcohol. Kissing Jake. She banged the back of her head into the wall behind her.

She sat for a while before standing and looking for her cellphone. Powering back on, she sat at the kitchen table. As soon as the home screen opened there were at least 20 missed calls and messages. They were a mixture of

Riley's and Kevin's.

Jenn felt a rock hit the pit of her stomach. She flipped through the messages. Concern from Riley and annoyance from Kevin. The voicemails were the same. She rubbed her eyes and set the phone down.

A door clicked closed behind her and she heard the sink running. She bit her lip nervously. What was she going to say to Jake?

He slowly made his way to the kitchen and began to make a pot of coffee in silence. He poured two cups before joining her at the table.

He didn't meet her gaze. "Well, that was certainly interesting."

Jenn smiled at his awkwardness. It was endearing. "Yeah, we don't have to talk about it. Thank you for coming to my rescue last night." Jenn took a sip of the coffee and Jake finally looked at her.

He smiled. "So, no talking about it?"

She shook her head. "I've got some other things that I need to deal with today. Maybe some other time."

He nodded, and they drank the coffee in silence. She gathered up her things and borrowed some old sweats from Jake.

"Call me later if you need to," he said as they awkwardly hugged goodbye. She smiled and headed out the door.

Jenn made her way to the bus stop before deciding to walk back to her apartment. Her head still hurt, and she couldn't stop tears from silently falling down her face. Luckily, the streets were not busy on a Sunday morning because she was certain that she looked horrible.

The apartment building came into view and she stopped, trying to muster up the courage to go inside where Kevin was probably waiting. Her phone had chimed several times since she left Jake's apartment, but she didn't have the energy to look at it.

To the left of the apartment building was a little alley. Jenn headed there instead. She stopped once she was out of sight from the sidewalk and sat down against the wall. She cried silently as her head rushed through all the events that had occurred the night before. The feeling of guilt mixed with anger and sadness.

She pulled out her phone with shaking hands and sent a text to Riley.

I'm going to need to come by in a bit, sorry to bother you on the day after your wedding.

The phone began to ring shortly after that, and Jenn cautiously answered. "Jenn, what the hell happened? You had me freaked out. Kevin was frantic," Riley stated. Jenn chuffed and shook her head.

"Yeah, I'm sure he was," she mumbled. "I don't want to talk about this now. I have to go deal with something and then I'm coming over. Is that OK?" Jenn sounded a little harsher than she had wanted to, but she was too drained to care.

Riley paused before answering. "Yeah, no problem. We'll be home all day." Jenn thanked her and hung up the phone. She steadied her breathing and wiped her face before standing and heading towards her apartment. She didn't know what she was going to say, but she knew it was not going to go well.

Present

Chapter 22

Jenn had been officially dating Mike for two months before she felt comfortable enough to tell him more details about her past. He had proven himself trustworthy. Her friends approved, and her family was thrilled she was dating again. Mike had become a fixture in her everyday life. They spoke daily and went out together several times a week. She had even joined his Sunday softball league.

Jake had mentioned to her during one of their coffee dates that she should open up to Mike. "He needs to know what happened. It's part of who you are, and you shouldn't hide that from him."

Jenn sipped her coffee and looked down at the table. "I don't want to tell him all of it yet. It would just scare him away."

She looked up at Jake and he smiled. "Well, then he doesn't deserve you if he's scared of your past. I'm still here and I had a front row seat to it."

She leaned back in her chair and frowned at him. "I guess I just have to try harder to get rid of you." He stuck out his tongue and she returned the gesture. They finished up their coffee and headed out to the bus stop. "Shame you have to date someone with such a boring past," Jenn joked.

Jake smiled and shrugged. "I know. Kelly never did anything wild like you."

Jenn was glad that they could joke about the things that had happened. She found that humor was her best coping mechanism.

The bus rolled up to the stop and she hugged Jake. "I'll talk to him tonight." Jake nodded, and she climbed onto the bus.

She and Mike had planned a night in with bad movies and takeout. The bus ride was used as a quiet time to prepare what she would tell him. She would not be telling him about her hospitalization yet. That was the only thing for certain.

Once home, she threw a load of laundry in and took a long shower. After two months of dating, she still had not spent the night with Mike. It seemed like a big step for her, even though they had slept together before they were dating. Excess alcohol would not be involved with her next "first" time with him.

Jenn had a personality of excess. She tended to drink too much when she did drink. Her therapist always told her to avoid alcohol after what had happened, and she listened most of the time. After tossing the clothes into the dryer, Jenn decided to get a few hours of sleep before Mike came over.

She was straightening up her living room when he knocked. She opened the door and he came inside, his arms full of paper bags. She took them and walked to the kitchen. "You do know there are only two people here, right?" she teased.

Mike smiled and kissed her softly. "I know, but I couldn't decide. Plus, leftovers." He reached into her cabinet and pulled out two plates. Jenn laid out the containers and grabbed silverware.

After loading their plates, they settled onto the couch and turned on the TV. They discussed several options before she put on a classic '80s teen movie. The clink of silverware was punctuated by laughter. Jenn had a habit of quoting along with movies, but she resisted until Mike started doing it, too. Both of their stomachs ached from laughing when the movie ended.

Jenn picked up the empty plates and took them into the kitchen. She grabbed a couple of beers from the fridge, figuring that a little alcohol would help the conversation that she wanted to have. She returned to the couch and handed Mike the second beer before taking a long drink of hers. Mike held the bottle without drinking and looked at Jenn with questioning eyes.

She sighed and set down the bottle. "My friends tell me that I should tell you more about myself. They said that you just know the surface Jenn." She didn't look up while she spoke, her heart beating slightly faster.

Mike set down his beer and rearranged himself so that his full attention was on her. "Is that something *you* want, too?" he asked quietly. She nodded slowly.

She pulled her eyes away from the table and looked at him. He looked nervous and it made her smile for a moment. "You look like I'm going to tell you about a murder I committed or something."

He relaxed his shoulders and smiled. "So, no murders. Got it."

She rubbed his knee and sighed. "I just want you to understand my feelings about relationships and my trust issues. I haven't had any issues in these last few months with us, but I want you to know why I do when I do. Trust me, I will." He squinted and nodded slightly.

Jenn inhaled deeply before jumping into her story. Mike sat and listened, nodding every once in a while, but never interrupting. When she began to talk about Riley and Curt's wedding, she paused and had to take several deep breaths before continuing. She tried not to cry, but the tears naturally came. Mike handed her tissues as she finished talking and placed a hand on her knee.

He sat silent for a moment, making sure she didn't have more to say. Jenn met his eyes and shrugged. "That's me. Just a broken little teapot." She forced a weak smile before leaning back and exhaling.

"Why were you afraid to tell me that? That story just shows that your ex is a complete idiot who did a very horrible thing." Mike's ears turned pink. "Plus, I've been there. My college girlfriend broke my heart and it took me a long time to want to date again." Jenn let her shoulders relax as the weight was lifted. She was glad that she told him part of her story. She left out what happened after she left the wedding, and she left out her hospitalization.

"Yes, he did," she muttered.

"Well, I'm flattered that I am the person you chose to trust after all of that happened." Mike slid closer to her and put his arm around her waist. "Thank you for that. I hope that I can make up for all of the bad things you have been put through."

She smiled and raised her hand, placing it on his face. "I'm not asking you for any miracles, just don't go and break my heart."

He smiled and leaned down to kiss her. She returned the kiss and leaned into him. Without thinking about it, she climbed onto his lap and began to kiss with more urgency. He ran his hands under her shirt and up her back, causing her to shiver. She pulled back from the kiss and stared at him, breathing deeply. Standing slowly, she turned and walked towards the bedroom.

Mike sat on the couch breathing deeply, his cheeks red. She turned around as she reached the doorway and smiled. Trying to be seductive, she slowly pulled her shirt over her head and nodded toward the bedroom. Mike stood up quickly and nearly tripped on the coffee table. Jenn chuckled and walked into the bedroom.

He met up with her at the end of the bed, pulling her into another kiss. He ran his hands down her sides as she unbuttoned his shirt. She let her fingers brush his chest lightly as she pushed his shirt away. Mike's hands reached around her, and he pulled her legs around him. Slowly, he lowered her onto the bed and began to kiss down her neck before stopping near her waist. She ran her hands into his hair, pulling gently. Mike pulled her pants off before working on his own. Jenn sat and admired his body before pulling him back on top of her.

The chemistry between them was palpable, and Jenn imagined that this was what happened in every great movie or book.

After, Jenn lay with her head on Mike's chest, listening to his heartbeat. His chest was slippery with sweat, but Jenn was content where she rested. They both were breathing deeply, waiting for the adrenaline to subside.

"No offense, but I don't remember that from our one-night stand," she teased.

His chest rose as he laughed. "Different set of

moves for a girlfriend," he said before trailing off.

Jenn pushed herself up, so she could see his face. He looked as if he just said a filthy word. "You can relax, Mike." She patted his chest before lying down again.

He chuckled. "Sorry, haven't used that word in a long time." They lay in silence for a while, Jenn's head rising and lowering with each of Mike's breaths. He cleared his throat and ran his hand through her hair, "So, should we have this conversation, or have we had enough big moments tonight?" Jenn did not answer at first. Her mind started to race, and she took several deep breaths.

She pushed herself up onto her arm and wrapped the sheet around herself. "I'm almost at my limit, but I think we should figure this out."

She rolled over, taking the sheet with her and leaving Mike lying naked on the bed. He dramatically covered up with a pillow as she giggled and walked out of the bedroom. She was sitting on the couch, drinking her beer when he caught up to her.

He grabbed his beer and joined her on the couch. "So?" She drank the last bit of beer and set down the bottle. "I think it's safe to say that I am, in fact, your girlfriend," she said quickly. "That being said, I haven't been in a relationship in a long time and I'm still trying to figure this out. I haven't wanted this in a long time because I was scared. You are the first man that has calmed that fear." She ran her fingers along his hairline before resting her hand on his shoulder.

He smiled and kissed her. "We can figure it out together. All I know is that you are unlike any woman I have ever met, and I want to know more about you. I will go as slow or as fast as you want, as long as we are going together." Jenn felt a tightness in her chest, but this time it was good. "I really like you, Jenn." He took both of her hands and squeezed gently.

"I really like you, too, Mike." She pulled him into another kiss, which started out soft and became more aggressive after a few minutes.

She pushed him over on the couch and pulled the sheet from around her. She climbed on top of him and resumed kissing him deeply. Mike moaned as she took control of him. He didn't last long the second time, and they collapsed on the couch, breathing rapidly.

"You are something," he panted, trying to slow his breathing.

"Well, this something is going to hop in the shower if you want to join." Jenn stood from the couch and walked slowly towards the bathroom, making sure to over-exaggerate her hip movement.

Mike jumped up from the couch to follow. After taking a long shower together, Jenn offered Mike one of her spare toothbrushes, so he could stay over.

"I would love to, but I have to work in the morning and I don't have any clothes here." She blushed and nodded her head. Mike put his hand under her chin and made her look him in the eye. "I didn't say I didn't want to. We can work this out. Maybe I could leave some stuff here, just in case?"

This made Jenn blush more and she mumbled "OK". She followed him to the bedroom and sat on the bed while he got dressed.

"I know you work this weekend, but what about next week some time? Or you can come by my place?" Jenn nodded as she watched him dressing, admiring his back muscles. He caught her staring and laughed. She shook her head and laughed, too. Jenn grabbed her robe and slipped it on, following him to the door. He pulled her into a tight hug once they reached the door. She pulled away and kissed him softly. "I'll call or text tomorrow, OK?" Mike promised.

"Of course, have a good Friday at school," Jenn said. She watched him as he walked down the hall before closing and latching the door. She did a small happy dance before racing to her phone to text Riley. *I'm a girlfriend again, Ri!* Jenn looked at the clock and realized it was late. Hoping she didn't wake Riley, she plugged her phone in and headed back to her bedroom to straighten her bed. She was genuinely happy at that moment.

Mike was a good guy, great in bed and very handsome. At that moment, she saw no reasons to doubt this new relationship, which was odd because Jenn tended to be a pessimist. She picked up the beer bottles and empty takeout containers, throwing them away.

After the leftovers were put in the refrigerator, Jenn grabbed a glass of water and went back to the bedroom. She climbed under the covers and could still feel the heat from Mike. Sighing deeply, she pulled out her tablet and started reading a news story. She hadn't had much sleep that day, so she quickly started to doze. She turned off her tablet and light, rolling over and falling asleep before she had time to overthink anything.

5 Years Ago

Chapter 23

Jenn stood in front of her apartment door, trying to figure out what she would do or say when she saw Kevin. She really wanted to walk in, get her things and leave, but she doubted that would happen. She and Kevin were both stubborn and always had to have the last word in an argument, so she figured this would end badly for one of them. She slowly pulled her key out and opened the door.

He was sitting at the kitchen table and stood up as she entered. "Where the hell have you been? I've been calling and texting all night and all morning. You could have at least let me know you were OK." His face was red, and his hair was a mess. It looked as if he hadn't slept. She wanted to laugh at the situation, but she was so angry.

She dropped her purse and walked past him towards the bedroom. "Seriously, Jenn? You have to talk to me. I have no fucking idea what is happening here. You disappeared from your best friend's wedding and show up the next morning wearing some guy's clothes?" He grumbled and looked her over. "I'll assume those are Jake's and he took you home because you were too drunk. I would have taken you home, you know. Riley said you were crying. What happened?"

Jenn pulled a bag out of her closet and started tossing random clothes in it. Kevin had followed her and stood silently, watching. She could tell his anger level was simmering just below the surface and he was trying not to explode. She smiled to herself, secretly wanting him to.

She carried the bag to the bathroom and threw her personal items inside. Kevin followed her and stood in the doorway, blocking her so she couldn't leave. Jenn turned to face him and met his gaze. Both their faces were red, though Kevin had no idea why Jenn was so mad.

"Please move, Kevin," she said softly.

He stood his ground. "I'm not moving, and you are not leaving until you explain what is happening." Jenn wanted to run at him and knock him out of the way, but she took a few deep breaths to compose herself before putting her bag down.

She took a small step toward Kevin and stopped, still not looking away.

"How was your evening, Kevin? Did you have a good time at the reception, Kevin?" she taunted him.

He raised his eyebrows. "You were there with me, what are you talking about?"

Jenn took another small step towards him. "Are you sure about that, Kevin? You didn't step away for a moment, did you, Kevin?"

Jenn watched a wave of realization wash over his

face. He dropped his arms from the door, and she picked up her bag and pushed past him. She was almost to the door when he grabbed her shoulder.

"Get your hands off of me," she said through gritted teeth as she turned around. He stepped back as she stepped towards him. She dropped her bag and stopped in the center of the kitchen. "You gave up your right to touch me ever again when you decided to touch her. Do you understand me? You don't get to talk to me, you don't get to see me. You can get your shit out of my apartment by next week or I will burn everything that is left behind." She pulled the ring off her finger and laid it on the counter. "I hope she was worth it, you stupid asshole."

She turned quickly, grabbed her bag and purse and slammed the door behind her. She paused for a moment, thinking that he might come after her.

She shook her head and realized she did not want him to follow. Walking quickly, she made it to her car and threw the bags inside before breaking down. She sat with her head on the steering wheel, sobbing loudly. The energy it took to hold the breakdown in until she left the apartment was enormous. She started her car once she calmed down and headed towards Riley's house.

186

Chapter 24

Riley was sitting on the front porch swing when Jenn pulled into the driveway. She stood and walked towards the car, pulling Jenn into a tight hug as soon as she stepped out. "Kevin called Curt after you left. What a douche." Jenn chuckled as she cried. Riley took her hand and led her onto the porch, sitting down with her on the swing. "Are you OK?"

Jenn shrugged and wiped her nose on her jacket sleeve. "As I can be, I guess." She fidgeted with her finger where the ring once sat.

Riley looked at her hand and then tapped on the window. Curt looked up from the couch and Riley made a motion at her coffee cup. Curt stood and disappeared into the kitchen. "I'd get you a real drink, but I assumed you had enough for a lifetime." Jenn smiled feebly.

Curt walked outside and handed her a warm cup. "Jenn, I am so sorry. He's my friend, but I won't even defend him this time." She took a sip of coffee and thanked Curt. He stood awkwardly as the girls cradled their drinks in silence.

Riley spoke first. "I would have never guessed he would do something like that. You two were always so happy, you hardly fought. What was going through his mind?"

Jenn shrugged. "I guess I wasn't giving him what he needed. I was so engrossed in work and your wedding, maybe he felt neglected. I'm sure his drinking didn't help." Jenn tried to see this from his point of view, but she couldn't.

"What do you think, babe?" Riley asked Curt. He looked away quickly and began fidgeting. Riley's eyes narrowed. "What?"

He looked slowly from Jenn to Riley before speaking. "I caught him before." Both girls gasped, and he put up his hands defensively. "Years ago when we were still in college. Before you were engaged. I called him out on it, and he swore he would stop. I never told you because I believed him, and I thought it would hurt you more to know."

Jenn set her cup down and stood. "College?" She muttered through gritted teeth. "*College?*" Curt looked worried that she would charge at him. Riley pulled on Jenn's hand and she sat back down.

Curt exhaled in relief and sat down in a patio chair. "I thought he was being sincere, and when he proposed, I figured there was nothing to worry about and no reason to throw gas on the fire." Riley clicked her tongue, her eyes still narrow. "Oh, come on." Curt pleaded, "There was no way to tell you without her finding out. Kevin is my friend and I had to back him up."

Jenn rolled her shoulders back. "So, that's the only

time?" she asked.

Curt paused and shrugged. "I asked him about it from time to time and he always denied it. I had nothing to prove otherwise."

Riley started to get angry. "Did you suspect?"

She stared intently at Curt. "I didn't have any proof."

Jenn put her head in her hands. "Well, aren't I just a clueless little idiot." Her hands were shaking.

Riley placed a hand on her shoulder. "He fooled us all. I don't even know what to think." Jenn sat up and sniffed. "I'm going to say nothing because that's what he deserves." The three sat in silence for a moment.

"Curt, I need to talk to Riley without you here, please," Jenn said, breaking the tension. Curt nodded and walked back inside. Jenn turned to Riley, who looked like she was waiting for an explosion. "I did something stupid last night," Jenn muttered, her cheeks flushing.

"More stupid than Kevin?" Jenn chuckled slightly, and it broke the tension.

She paused. "I slept with Jake." She couldn't look up at Riley, but she felt her gaze.

It took several minutes for Riley to respond. "Like, slept over, or like, slept with slept with?"

Jenn fiddled with her watch, not knowing the best response. "I guess both?" She finally looked up at Riley and her mouth was hanging open.

"You did not have sex with Jake. Tell me you did not do it." Jenn blushed, and Riley smacked her leg. "Jenn, you have got to be kidding me. How was that the appropriate response to what happened?"

Jenn shrugged, still trying to figure out the answer to that question herself. "I was drunk, he was there taking care of me. I don't know, I messed up." She covered her face with her hands. "Then I left this morning without even talking to him about it. But it's out there, can't take it back now."

Riley whistled softly. "Yeah, you screwed that up."

Jenn looked at her and was offended. "At least it wasn't a random guy. It was Jake, our Jake."

Riley shook her head. "No, he screwed up too." Jenn crossed her arms across her stomach and leaned back. "Jenn, you know he has feelings for you. How do you think this is going to help that?"

Jenn didn't know the answer to that. She hoped nothing would change and that they could chalk it up to too much alcohol and bad decision making. "I don't know, I wish I could erase last night, but I can't. I'll just have to deal with it. But some other time. I'm so tired and I'm starving."

Riley stood, and Jenn followed her. They sat in the kitchen to eat and talk more.

After a while, Curt joined them. "I really am sorry, Jenn. I should have said something." She wasn't mad at Curt as she would have done the same thing if the situation was reversed.

"I understand your point of view, but it doesn't stop the situation from being so shitty." Jenn squeezed Curt's hand and smiled. "Thank you, guys, for taking me in. This is the worst timing and I know you have a honeymoon to get to. I promise I will be fine. I'm just not going back there until he is gone." Jenn's cheeks flushed again, and she took a deep breath.

"We'll be back in two weeks and we can help you with whatever you need," Riley added. The conversation switched to the honeymoon, and Jenn tried to ignore the lump in her stomach.

She settled into the spare bedroom and lay in the bed, staring at the ceiling fan. Thoughts kept flying through her mind, alternating between anger and sadness. Flashes from the night before came every time she closed her eyes. She was angry and ashamed, a trickle of guilt sneaking into her mind.

Jenn hated that she cared too much about hurting others, even when they hurt her. She didn't know what she was thinking when she turned to Jake. Did she think it would hurt Kevin? It probably hurt Jake more. All she knew was that she was never going to sleep that night.

Tossing and turning for several hours, she gave up and turned on her phone. There was one message from Kevin and two from Jake. Her heart sank. She pushed the read button on Kevin's message.

"Jenn, I'm so sorry. I was drunk, and I didn't know what I was doing. Please talk to me."

She sighed and wanted to reply, since she now knew that it wasn't the first occurrence. She hit delete and opened Jake's messages.

"I don't really know what that was last night, but I hope you are OK. Call me soon, okay?"

There was a lump in her throat and her guilt intensified. Jake was such a good guy and she pulled him into a mess that he didn't deserve.

She also didn't want to admit to herself how it made her feel. Jenn would never say out loud that she had feelings for Jake, but last night threw a question mark into the situation. It wasn't something she wanted to figure out at that moment. She messaged Jake back that she was OK and at Riley's for a while. She planned on calling him soon anyway to air out the situation. She just wasn't quite ready. Jenn looked at the clock and realized it was close to 3 a.m., so she forced herself to go to sleep.

Chapter 25

Jenn had hardly slept and gave up trying when she heard Riley and Curt shuffling around outside her door. "We didn't mean to wake you," Riley said as Jenn stumbled out of her room.

"No worries, I wasn't really sleeping. I wanted to say goodbye anyway. Thank you for letting me be here and I promise I won't trash the place." She hugged them both, and they headed out the door. She watched the car drive away and then just stood at the window.

The next few days went by in a blur. Working 12-hour shifts was nice because she didn't have to work as many days during the week. The work kept her mind occupied, even though she was exhausted. Most nights she was only able to sleep for a few hours.

She slept in on her first day off and spent most of the day drinking coffee and watching TV. The solitude was helping clear her mind.

The sun was setting as she finished a frozen dinner when she heard a car pull up in the driveway. Jenn froze and listened. She could hear footsteps on the front porch, followed by loud banging on the door. She rose slowly and pulled out her phone, ready to call 911 if she needed to. Peeking out of the front window, her heart dropped when she saw Kevin leaning with his arms on either side of the doorframe.

"What do you want?" she called.

"Jenn, we need to talk about this. Please let me in." Kevin sounded calm, but his voice had a little slur to it which made Jenn think he had been drinking.

"I thought I said I was done talking to you," she said.

He hit the door and his voice became a little louder. "Bullshit, let me in. You're not even giving me a chance."

She laughed to herself as the anger started to rise in her chest. "Never said I wanted to give anything a chance."

He hit the door again. "I'm going to keep yelling and hitting this door until you open it or the door breaks. Your choice."

Jenn sighed and reached for the handle since she knew he wasn't bluffing. She sent a quick text to Jake, letting him know that Kevin was there and drunk. She said she would call if she needed help. Jenn slowly opened the door but stood in the way, so he couldn't enter.

"What do you want?" she asked again. He took a step forward and Jenn flinched, giving him the opportunity to push the door open and walk in.

He walked to the living room and sat down on the

couch. He didn't speak at first but sat and wrung his hands. Jenn could tell he was working out what to say. She stood at the doorway of the living room with her arms crossed.

"I just needed to talk to you. To explain," Kevin finally said, not looking up at Jenn.

"Explain away, don't think it will help though," she said, stepping into the room. He looked up at her and his eyes were red, either from anger or from tears. Jenn felt sorry for him, but only for a moment.

"I had too much to drink that night. That girl caught me at a vulnerable moment." He put his hands over his face.

"A vulnerable moment, really?" Jenn muttered. Kevin looked up at her. Jenn's moment of sympathy was gone, and her anger was coming back in full force. "I'm curious, Kevin, how many of these moments have there been?"

He looked shocked and then anger came across his face. "What are you accusing me of now?"

Jenn shook her head. "Not accusing. I know what you have done, so I'm just asking for a moment of honesty."

Kevin leaned back and cleared his throat. "Look, I don't know what you think you know, but you're wrong."

Jenn sat down in an easy chair and looked at him intently. "So, you're telling me that this is the first slip you have made?" She didn't break eye contact, and Kevin did his best to maintain his.

"I've never ..." he started. She smiled and shook her head. He frowned. "What did Curt tell you?"

She looked away and laughed. "Are you going to blame Curt for this now? Come on, I'd like to hear the excuses." Jenn looked back at Kevin and he leaned his head back against the couch with his eyes closed.

He finally sat up and looked at her. "OK, when we first were dating, I was not faithful. I was nineteen and in college, I didn't know any better. I changed when I realized that you were the one for me. Come on, I proposed. We have a wedding day set." He grasped for anything that would justify his actions.

"You sure about that? So, I could check in your emails or on your social media and I would find nothing? Maybe I'll go talk to your work friends. That girl you were with the other night, she looked familiar. She works with you, right?" Jenn was starting to feel like a police interrogator. Kevin shook his head and looked terrified at the thought of Jenn digging for more information.

He sighed and lowered his head. "You're right. I'm sorry." He seemed genuinely upset, but then the excuses started. "I've been so stressed at work and you've been so busy. I've been lonely. I never meant to do anything, but you know what happens when I drink. Those girls didn't

196

mean anything to me. I love you. I'm an idiot and it will never happen again." He kept talking as if he thought something he said would make the situation better.

Jenn realized that she had been digging her nails into her palm and stretched her hands out. She finally cut him off, "You know that there is no excuse for what you did, right?" She kept her voice steady, but her hands were shaking, and her heart was beating fast. "You can blame alcohol, blame the girls or even blame me. The final and only blame lies with you, Kevin. You are the one that made the decision to ruin what we had."

She stood suddenly and started to pace. "Ugh, I should have listened to my friends and I should have trusted my gut instinct. I knew when I first met you that you were a player. I should have trusted myself. I should have listened to Jake when he told me that you weren't right for me."

Kevin stood up as well. "What the hell did Jake say about me? That punk only wants to step in between us because he wants you." Kevin's shoulders moved up and down quickly as he took shallow breaths.

For some reason, this angered Jenn even more, and she took a step towards Kevin. "He's the only one that saw you for what you are, a cheating asshole!" she yelled.

Kevin didn't back down. "If you didn't spend so much time at work and with him then maybe I wouldn't have had to find another person to take interest in me!" he yelled back.

Jenn's eye widened. "Are you serious right now? Did you just blame me for your cheating?"

Kevin looked smug, like he was happy that he struck a nerve. "Well, a satisfied man doesn't cheat. I know that's a fact."

Jenn took another step towards him. "I have to work, and I enjoy working. I have bills to pay. I spend a lot of time with Jake because I've known him most of my life and he's always there for me. He was there for me the other night when you ripped out my heart." They stood about two feet apart, breathing heavily and not breaking eye contact.

"I bet he loved swooping in to save the day," Kevin muttered.

Jenn clenched her jaw. "He wouldn't have had to if you could keep your damn hands to yourself." She was oddly calm and furious at the same moment. The tension was thick between them and neither one wavered.

Jenn jumped when the front door opened, and Jake walked in. This made Kevin tense up. "And here he is again, Jenn. Swooping in to save the day."

Jake walked slowly in and put his hand up to show he wasn't coming to start anything. "Listen, Kevin. I was just making sure everything was OK. Jenn said you were here, and she was afraid you had been drinking." He kept his voice calm and walked over toward Jenn.

"It's really none of your business, Jake. This is between me and her," Kevin said through gritted teeth.

Jake nodded. "I understand that, but it's not really your business how I choose to protect my friends." He moved another step closer to Jenn.

Kevin looked from Jenn to Jake. "Always your lap dog, huh? What, are you happy now that this happened so that you can have her?" Jake's cheeks flushed, and Jenn clenched her teeth.

"You don't get to talk to him like that. He's just being a good friend. This is what someone does if they care about someone else. They take care of them and they are loyal. They don't go around sleeping with anything that breathes." Jenn's voice was getting louder. Jake placed his hand on her shoulder to calm her. Kevin stared at Jake's hand, his eyes squinting.

It was silent for a moment before Kevin let loose. "How do I know that you haven't been cheating on me? Huh? You're always with him and I know that he's had a thing for you for years. I never worried because I didn't think you thought of him like that, but maybe I should have. There are two sides to every story, what's yours, Jenn?"

Jenn started to protest but Jake cut her off. "Kevin,

it was one time and it was a mistake. She had already decided you two were over and she was drunk and confused. I should have stopped her, but I didn't. It didn't mean anything."

Kevin's eyes widened as he looked back and forth between Jenn and Jake. Jenn noticed his hand ball into a fist, but she didn't react quickly enough.

Kevin lunged towards Jake and landed a solid punch to his nose. Jake stumbled backwards, and Kevin knocked Jenn out of the way. Jake shook his head and was able to block the second punch before landing a punch into Kevin's ribs. Both men stepped back, breathing rapidly. Blood dripped from Jake's nose.

Kevin moved toward Jake again, and Jenn stepped in between them. "Kevin, you need to leave. Now."

Kevin lowered his arms slowly. "Jenn, I'm sorry. I love you. You can't do this."

Jenn stood with her arms raised in a defensive stance. "*I* didn't do this, you did. Now you need to leave." Kevin looked at her and at Jake before backing away towards the door.

Jenn kept herself between Kevin and Jake until he had closed the door behind him. She rushed towards the door and locked it, looking out the small window until Kevin drove away.

Once he was gone, she sighed and relaxed her shoulders before turning to check on Jake. "Oh my god, I am so sorry." She handed him some tissue and sat him down on the couch.

"I'm sorry I didn't react faster. He's got one hell of a punch," Jake said with a laugh. Jenn sat next to him and grabbed more tissue. There was not much blood, but Jake's nose was swelling.

"You should get that looked at," Jenn suggested.

Jake seemed to ignore her suggestion. "Are you OK? I tried to get here as fast as I could."

Jenn nodded. "I'm fine, you didn't really need to rush here, but thank you." Jenn suddenly felt a slight awkwardness around Jake. "Jake, I'm sorry about the other night. You're right, it was a mistake and I'm sorry that I dragged you into this mess."

Jake didn't meet her eyes. He didn't speak while he patted the tissue to his nose. He stood and walked into the kitchen as Jenn stared after him. She suddenly felt embarrassment and a strong feeling of guilt.

Jake returned with ice wrapped in a towel and sat down, leaning back and setting the towel on his nose. They sat in silence for a moment before Jake spoke in a quiet voice. "This situation is really messed up, Jenn." She looked at him, not sure how to respond. He still had his eyes closed and head tilted back. She cleared her throat and shifted positions, feeling uncomfortable.

After several more minutes of awkward silence, Jake sat up and removed the ice. He turned to face her, a faint red rim around each eye as if he was trying not cry. "I can't do this anymore," he muttered, looking down at the ice pack.

This statement brought a lump to Jenn's throat. "Do what?" was all she could say.

Jake sniffed and took a deep breath. "This, between us. I can't. It's killing me." Jenn went to reach for his hand, but he pulled away. He stood from the couch and walked over to the window, looking out.

"Jake, you're scaring me. What are you talking about?" She could see his shoulders and head drop.

He turned around to face her and a tear fell from his eye. "God, I don't want to do this now, but I can't deal with the mess that's in my head."

Jenn stood and walked towards him. He put up his hand when she came close and she stopped. "Please, don't. I can't." Jake was breathing deeply, trying to stop himself from breaking down.

Jenn crossed her arms over her chest, but she stood facing him. "Jake, please tell me what is happening. What did I do? What can I do to help?"

Jake finally met her eyes and paused. "Ten years, Jenn. We've been best friends for ten years. I've been there for you. I've looked out for you. I've sat by and watched you make bad choices. I've been by your side for the good choices."

Jenn inhaled sharply and shook her head. "Oh Jake. Please don't do this now," she said quietly. He raised an eyebrow and his demeanor changed.

He began to pace again. "No, no. It's my turn. Everything has always been on your terms," he muttered as he walked back and forth in front of the couch.

Jenn slowly sat down, her eyes following him. He paced, chewing on his thumb nail.

After a few passes, he stopped and turned to face her. "This whole situation sucks, you realize that. Right?" Jenn nodded, her cheeks flushing. "You can't not realize how I feel," he said in almost a whisper. Jenn's eyes widened. She wanted to stop him from saying more. "Ten years, Jenn. Do you know what it's like to care about someone for that long with no reciprocation?" The feeling of guilt and the tightness in her chest increased. She kept her eyes wide, trying to stop the tears that were threatening. "I know that I should have stopped you last Saturday, but for god's sake, I thought maybe this would be our turning point. You could have chosen to go home with any guy, but you chose me."

Jenn opened and closed her mouth silently. She couldn't find the words. "And my god, we connected. That was one of the most mind-blowing experiences I've ever had." Jake walked forward and sat on the coffee table, facing Jenn. "You can't say that it was a mistake, that it didn't mean anything. I felt it, didn't you?" Jenn looked down at her hands and started picking at her nail.

She didn't know what she felt. A combination of anger, pain, confusion mixed with a whole lot of alcohol fueled that night. Yes, she loved Jake as a friend, that she knew. Of course, he was attractive. She wouldn't have slept with him without that attraction. But, now? This moment was not the moment to figure this out.

Jenn finally looked up at him. He looked at her with anticipation. "Jake, I don't know what you want me to say here." He seemed to deflate at the statement. "I'm sorry," she whispered.

He stood again and paced a few times. "Sorry?" he muttered. Jenn could see that he was clenching and unclenching his fists. "So that's it?" he finally asked. Jenn could feel her face warm and felt a tear run down her cheek.

"That's it?" she asked. He nodded and continued to pace. Jenn slowly stood and walked over to him, catching his arm so he would stop moving. They stood face to face in silence. "What are you wanting from me?" she asked. He didn't break eye contact but narrowed his eyes slightly.

"Dammit Jenn, all I've wanted for ten years is you," he replied, a hint of annoyance in his voice.

She lowered her hand from his arm. "No, we decided back in high school that we were better as friends." Tears were falling onto her shirt now.

Jake chuckled. "No Jenn, you decided. I went along with it because I didn't want to lose you altogether."

She stepped back. "We can't do this right now, Jake. *I* can't do this right now. My world just imploded. I'm sorry. I went to you because you're a source of comfort for me. You're my best friend. I don't want that to change." She watched a wave of anger roll across his face.

He bit his lip and exhaled sharply. "No." he whispered.

"What do you mean, no?" Jenn asked, fear building inside her chest.

He took a few deep breaths and stared at the ground. Then, he turned and started to walk towards the door. Jenn let out a small gasp and jogged after him. "Jake, what are you doing?" she asked as she reached for his arm.

He stood facing the door. She held his arm and stared at his back, waiting. "This isn't fair to me, Jenn. You must see that. I've been there for you more than any guy has ever been. I've basically been your boyfriend for ten years with none of the physical perks. I'm emotionally drained and I see now that that's not going to change. I can't ..." he trailed off and lowered his head.

Jenn's sobs intensified, but she didn't let go of his arm. He slowly turned to face her, tears in his eyes as well. "Jenn, I love ..." he started. She put her hand to his mouth to stop him. He pushed it away. "No, I love you. That's as simple as it gets. If you can't realize that and you don't want to hear it then that's your problem. I know you are not in a great place right now, but I also know you feel the same way I do even if your stubbornness won't let you admit it."

Jenn stood with her mouth open. Her eyes were wide, and tears were falling freely. Jake took a long inhale before continuing. "Until you figure out your side of this, I can't be here. I can't put myself in the fire day after day. It's killing me and it's not fair. I want you to work through this whatever way you have to, but I can't be a part of it."

Jenn squeezed a little tighter on his arm as he tried to pull away. "Jake, I can't. I need you."

He looked sad but pushed her hand away. "I know, but not the way I need you." Her hand fell limply at her side as she started to hyperventilate. He wiped his eyes and turned to the door.

As he opened it, Jenn muttered, "Please." Jake paused without turning before walking out and getting in his car. Jenn stared blankly as he drove away.

After he was gone, she collapsed onto her knees and began to sob uncontrollably. She was alone. Her fiancé was gone. Her best friend was gone. The complete emptiness of the moment overtook her.

She didn't know how long she sat there before realizing she was cold and stood to close the door. Everything around her felt constricting and unwelcoming. She rubbed her arms and walked from room to room, not knowing what to do.

She eventually came to rest in front of Riley's wine collection. She slowly reached for a bottle and pulled it off the shelf. Grabbing a bottle opener, she made her way back to the couch before opening the wine and taking a long drink. Half the bottle was gone before she realized it and the pain in her chest was lessening. After finishing one bottle, she stumbled to grab another. She needed the pain to stop.

Thus began the downward spiral that would change her life.

Present

Chapter 26

Jenn had to meet with her doctor and therapist every six months for a checkup. It had been a little over four years since her hospitalization, and the checkups became less frequent as she improved. She had been doing well, but she was always nervous when it came to doctors. As a nurse, she should be used to them, but she wasn't. It was different as a patient, the vulnerability.

Sitting in the exam room, Jenn flipped through a magazine. Her primary doctor did blood work, a urine test and a general checkup to make sure she was healthy with no lasting damage from her attempted suicide. They'd already drawn her blood and taken her urine sample, so Jenn just had to talk to the doctor for a few minutes and she'd be done for another six months.

He came into the room after about 10 minutes and did his assessment. "So, no new side effects from your medications?" he asked.

Jenn shook her head, "Not that I've noticed. Appetite's good, no more tired than any other third shift worker." She smiled.

The doctor gave her a forced smile. "And you've stayed clear of alcohol and non-prescribed medications?" He kept eye contact, trying to get response.

She thought about it. "No pills. I've had a beer or two when I'm with my friends, but that's it."

He frowned. "Jenn, you need to be careful. It only takes one slip."

Jenn returned his frown. "Doctor, I'm not an addict. I had a few bad months and one really bad night. I'm not drinking like I was, and I'm in control now. It's been four years."

The doctor continued to frown and scribbled something into Jenn's chart. "I just want you to be careful, Jenn," he said as he laid a hand on her shoulder. She nodded, and he left the room.

Jenn exhaled and grabbed her coat. She said goodbye to the receptionist as she left the doctor's office and headed down the street to her therapist. Scheduling both appointments for the morning made it easier on her. She really liked her doctors, but the checkups were emotionally taxing. She felt like her battery was drained and most of the time she wanted to go home and sleep after.

Her therapist was a woman named Rebecca who was about five years older than she was. She worked with Jenn's doctor on a treatment regimen. Jenn checked in at the front desk and sat down in the waiting room. She took out her phone and started reading a news article. Mike had texted her earlier that morning, but Jenn had yet to tell him about this part of her life, so she didn't want to reply until she was done. Jake had also texted to wish her luck today.

It had been three months since Jenn and Mike started dating, but she still wasn't comfortable enough to admit that she had to see a shrink and take medication or to admit that she almost died four years ago. Jenn absentmindedly flipped through articles while trying to calm her racing mind. That was not a good way to enter a therapy session.

"Jenn, she's ready for you," the receptionist called, and Jenn stood and walked through the large wooden door of Rebecca's office. She was sitting behind her desk when Jenn entered, and she motioned for her to take a seat in a high-backed chair.

"So, how did the physical checkup go?" Rebecca asked as she gathered her notes.

"Healthy as a horse," Jenn joked.

Rebecca smiled and walked around the desk to sit in a chair facing Jenn. "And the medication, no problems?"

Jenn shook her head. "Doing good."

Rebecca wrote a few sentences on her notepad. "Well, it's been six months, so bring me up to speed on your life," the therapist said as she leaned back in the chair.

Jenn shrugged and leaned back. "Well, work's great. They hired a few new people, but they all are working well with us so far. Riley's good. She had her daughter four months ago. Jake is dating a new girl that works at his hospital. My mom and dad just took another trip to Mexico. My niece started playing volleyball. Um ..." Jenn trailed off. "I'm dating someone," she said quietly.

Rebecca smiled. "Dating someone?" she asked in a motherly tone.

"Yes. His name is Mike. We've been together for about three months," Jenn said, feeling self-conscious.

Rebecca's smile widened as she wrote her notes. "This is the first boyfriend since Kevin, right?"

Jenn flinched at the mention of her ex and nodded. "He is. He kind of snuck up on me. Was supposed to be a one-night stand, but he wouldn't go away."

"And your friends like him?" Rebecca asked, continuing with her notes.

"Yeah, he gets on well with them. They are more upset with me because I haven't told him about my past." Jenn looked down and picked at the armrest of the chair.

Rebecca stopped writing and looked at Jenn. "And, why do you think that is?"

Jenn bit her lip. "I told him about Kevin. Well, I told him I was crushed by a guy. I don't want him to think I am crazy."

She looked up at Rebecca, who was still staring. "Jenn, you are not crazy. You have worked through your darkest days and you are getting better every day."

Jenn chuckled. "How do I start a conversation about that? Oh, by the way, about four years ago I tried to kill myself and now I have to take a medication every day, so I don't live in a perpetual state of anxiety and depression?"

Rebecca looked taken aback for a moment before writing a note and continuing. "I'd word it differently," she replied. Jenn laughed out loud and Rebecca smiled. "Jenn, the point is … this incident is part of you and who you are. It shaped who you are today. There is no shame in what happened, and you should be proud that you made it through."

Jenn nodded. She knew that Rebecca was right. "It's just a lot to take in for some people. Jake and Riley are used to me and my tics. I've been trying to hide those things from Mike, so he doesn't run away."

Rebecca nodded and wrote another note. "The thing is, Jenn, if you want him to stick around, he needs to know you. All of you."

Jenn nodded and smiled. "Nothing like a big talk with my new boyfriend about my ex-fiancé to help with the anxiety," she joked.

Rebecca laughed quietly. "Well, when you put it like

that." The 30-minute session was just about over. Rebecca wrote a few final notes down. "Jenn, do you want to schedule an extra session in May?"

Jenn paused and frowned. "You know, I think I'll be OK this year." She hated the month of May as it had too many bad memories and associations. Most years she took an extra session on her "dark day" to help her through, but this year she had her friends and Mike. That would be enough.

"I would talk to Mike about this before May or else he's not going to be able to help you," Rebecca suggested.

"I will, I promise," Jenn replied and shook Rebecca's hand after standing.

"I'll see you in six months then. Please call if you change your mind," Rebecca added. Jenn nodded and headed out the door. She waved at the receptionist before stepping out into the sunshine. Jenn was frazzled and decided to take a walk to clear her mind. Her mind went back over everything from that morning and her anxiety began to build. She wasn't sure that skipping her extra appointment in May was a good idea, but she also knew she would never get better if she didn't try to do this on her own.

After grabbing a coffee, she walked in the direction of her apartment. Her mind wandered as she walked, trying to figure out the best way to broach the subject of her hospitalization with Mike. After 20 minutes of walking, she decided that it could wait a little longer. She knew it would have to happen eventually, but she wasn't ready yet. As she finished her walk and approached her apartment, her cellphone rang. It was Mike.

"Hey, what's up?" she said as she opened the apartment door.

"Just checking in. Wanted to know if I could see you later?" Mike asked. Jenn felt like the universe was tempting her and telling her to talk to him, but she shook it off.

"Sure, do you want to come here for dinner and then watch something on TV?" she asked. Mike agreed, and they chatted briefly before hanging up. Jenn tidied up the apartment and decided to take a quick nap to recharge her brain.

She was just settling into the couch when her phone rang again. She picked it up and saw that it was Jake. "Hey Jake, what's going on?" she asked with a yawn.

"Sorry, did I wake you?"

"No, was just going to lay down for a bit. Had a busy morning," Jenn said as she stretched her arms above her head.

"I bet. I was just checking in. Everything go OK?" he asked.

Jenn nodded and then remembered that he couldn't

see her. "Yeah, great. Rebecca thinks I should confess all of my sins to Mike."

Jake laughed. "I would agree, but I wouldn't start the conversation like that."

Jenn smiled. "I won't, I promise. She also said I don't need an extra appointment in May," Jenn said, not telling the entire truth.

Jake paused for a moment. "Is that a good idea?"

"I'm fine, I have you guys and Mike. I will be OK." she said, trying to sound reassuring.

Jake clicked his tongue. "Well, I guess she is the professional." Jenn agreed. They chatted for a couple of minutes before Jenn said that she was tired and needed a quick nap. They said their goodbyes and hung up. Jenn settled back into the couch and drifted off quickly.

She slept several hours before a text from Riley woke her. She was also checking in on Jenn after her checkups. She gave Riley the same rundown that she gave Jake, getting the same response. Jenn once again promised to tell Mike the whole truth when she was ready.

Mike came over shortly after he got off work and brought dinner. He and Jenn had started staying at each other's apartments a few times a week.

They ate and watched TV until Mike started to doze

off. Jenn smiled as he snored softly on the couch before gently shaking him awake and telling him to get to bed. He was already settled into the bed when Jenn finished up in the bathroom. She smiled at how comfortable he looked lying in her bed. She felt a flutter in her stomach as she crawled next to him and leaned over, brushing his hair off his forehead. Mike opened his eyes and kissed her, and she climbed on top of him.

She pulled back suddenly and looked at him. "I need to tell you something," she said.

A flash of worry went across Mike's face, "OK, go ahead."

Jenn inhaled. "I take a medication daily to help with an anxiety disorder." She closed her eyes and waited for a response, hoping it would not be a bad one.

Mike laughed softly. "Jenn, you can open your eyes and breathe. There is nothing wrong with that."

Jenn exhaled loudly and lowered her head to his chest. "I just don't want you to think I'm crazy."

His chest bounced as he chuckled again. "Anxiety happens, and it doesn't make you crazy. Plus, I'm pretty sure that's not a term we're supposed to use." Jenn looked up at him and smiled. She returned to kissing him and ran her hand down his side. He shuddered slightly. He gently pulled her nightgown over her head and started kissing her neck and chest. She let a small moan escape before rolling over, so he was on top of her. He stopped momentarily and smiled at her. "Plus, I like you the way you are. So, if that's a little crazy, I'll take it." He returned to kissing her.

Jenn lay with her head on his chest after they made love, listening to his heart racing. She smiled to herself. She didn't know what she was afraid of, since Mike was a genuinely good guy. His breathing was slowing as he started to drift off to sleep. Jenn yawned and moved her head back over to her pillow. She watched him sleep. For the first time in a long time, she was feeling confident about a relationship. Jenn smiled at the thought of this working out. Her fears remained below the surface, but she was able to ignore them for the first time in a long time. She was happy. With that thought, she fell asleep.

4.5 years ago

Chapter 27

When Riley returned from her honeymoon, she walked into a mess of epic proportions. Jenn hadn't eaten much or slept much in the weeks after her blowout with Kevin and Jake. She mustered up the energy to make it to work when she was scheduled, but other than that she sat on the couch and drank.

A week after the fight she returned to an almost empty apartment. Kevin had left a note, apologizing again. She crushed it and threw it away. In a moment of anger, she kicked a hole in her living room wall.

Jenn had left Riley a voicemail the night of the fight, so Riley came straight over when she returned. She looked at the mess around the apartment and the hole in the wall with her mouth hanging open. She sat with Jenn as she cried and drank, not really knowing how to respond. Jenn had started drinking a lot to dull the voices in her head and she was emotionally and physically exhausted.

Her apartment felt empty, and she felt alone most of the time. She hadn't spoken to anyone until Riley came home. She had texted Jake, but he ignored her which made her hurt more. Riley told her to give it time, that everything would work itself out. Jenn wasn't so sure this time. She usually was an optimist, but this situation wasn't promising.

Jenn decided to head to her parents' home for Christmas to get some distance from everything, but she returned feeling even more alone. Her mother was upset that the wedding was off, and her brother only talked about kicking Kevin's ass. Jenn put on a happy face, but all she wanted to do was to get home and drink. Her mind was her own worst enemy. She alternated between extreme anger and extreme guilt, with a mixture of sadness. She never drank when she had to work, but she was in a perpetual tipsy state in between.

After a month of being alone, she started to crave physical attention, so she went to bars and picked up random guys. It never went further than sex because she emotionally felt nothing. She would typically kick them out afterward and cry herself to sleep.

Riley was in and out, checking up on her but not stopping her. Curt would stop in, too, but he was uncomfortable with spending too much time with her because Jenn would start talking about Kevin with him. When that started, Curt stopped coming with Riley.

During the downward spiral, Riley discovered that she was pregnant. Jenn was thrilled, but that added an extra layer to her feelings. "I thought I'd get pregnant right after our wedding," she mumbled to Riley a few weeks after she found out.

Riley patted her shoulder because she didn't know

how to respond. She had tried all of the common responses. "Jenn, there are other guys. Jenn, this is a good thing. You wouldn't have wanted to find out after the wedding, right? Jake will come around eventually. Give it time." Give it time was the most common response she got from Riley, her sister and her mom. Yet time went on and Jenn's feelings stayed the same.

Somehow, she managed to hide this situation from her bosses, but her best work friend Nicole knew. She took the angry side when talking to Jenn about it. "He's a douchebag. You are so much better off. Live for you right now, don't worry about them." Jenn would nod and go about her work, but she just wanted to be anywhere but there.

****

When spring came around, Jenn's mood sank even further. She approached what would have been her wedding date, and the new symptom of anxiety came into play. Jenn took what would have been her wedding week off work to process the situation. She had cancelled all the wedding things she had paid for but lost a good sum of money in the process. As the weekend approached, her calendar kept notifying her of the previously scheduled wedding events.

She called her mom on Friday night crying and talked to her for several hours. It did little to calm her, though. Her mom offered to come visit her, but Jenn declined.

On Saturday morning, she decided to take a walk to clear her head. She poured coffee into a travel mug and added a splash of liquor.

She walked for several hours before ending up inside of a drugstore. She stood in front of the pharmacy section, looking quickly through all the boxes before buying some cold medication.

The pharmacist smiled at her as she paid for it. "Tough luck, spring colds are the worst."

Jenn smiled, "I know, right?" She thanked him and headed back to her apartment.

Once home, she grabbed a full bottle of wine and a full bottle of vodka. She set them on the coffee table in the living room next to her drugstore bag. She went to wash her hands and stood in front of the mirror, staring at herself. She had let her hair color fade and grow out. She wasn't wearing any makeup and she had lost about 15 pounds from her already thin frame. She looked sick, and she had dark circles around her eyes. She didn't even recognize the person looking back at her.

Instinctively, she reached up to touch her face and make sure that this was real. A wave of nausea rushed over her and she turned to vomit into the toilet. After the nausea passed, she got a drink of water and headed back into the living room.

She sat cross-legged on the floor in front of the coffee table, lining up the bottles of alcohol and the pack of medication. When everything was lined up properly, she paused and looked at what was in front of her. Her mind was racing, and her heart beat rapidly. Her mind went to Kevin and then to Jake. She felt the anger, guilt and loss. Then she felt the sadness, the overwhelming sadness of everything that had happened.

She picked up her phone and texted Jake.

I'm so sorry and I love you, was all she wrote.

She didn't expect an answer. She hadn't heard from or seen him for six months.

She slowly opened the cold medicine and punched two pills out. They sat in her hand and she gazed at them for a few moments before throwing them in her mouth. She unscrewed the bottle of vodka and took a large drink. Her body cringed at the taste, but her mind kept racing. She poured some out into a cup with ice and began drinking.

The familiar numbness of her lips and nose started after a half hour. Jenn smiled as her thoughts started slowing. She popped two more pills from the packet and swallowed them with another gulp of vodka. Tears started rolling down her face as she finished the glass.

She picked up her phone and called Riley, putting on the speaker phone and setting the phone on the table so she could pour another glass.

"Hi Jenn, are you OK?" Riley sounded tentative.

"Did you know that you'd be standing next to me in your blue bridesmaid dress right now? Did you know that? Right now. I'd be moments away from getting married." Jenn was slurring heavily at this point.

"Jenn, where are you?" Riley's tone went from nervous to scared.

"I'm at home. By myself. Not at my wedding, where I should be. My mom says that time heals all. Time's a bitch," Jenn mumbled.

She poured out more vodka and spilled a little on the table. "Whoops, hands are a little shaky. Bad bartender." Jenn giggled. "Hey Riley, you know I love you. You're like a sister to me. I'm sorry that you never got to be my matron of honor. You would have done so well."

Riley covered the mouthpiece of the phone and said something to Curt. "Is that Curt? Hi Curt. I'm sorry your friend screwed me over. I really did love him before he turned into such a piece of shit." Jenn heard muffled conversation between Riley and Curt.

She took another drink of vodka and started to pop

out two more pills. "Hey Riley, did you know that some medication is childproof? Like, it's really hard to get out of the container."

Riley stopped talking to Curt. "Jenn, what medication? Jenn? Stop what you are doing, and I will be there in ten minutes. Please, Jenn." Riley sounded like she had started crying and Jenn could hear Curt talking to someone in the background.

"Hey Ri, it's OK. It doesn't hurt so bad anymore. Hey, can you tell Jake that I love him too? I'm sorry he won't talk to me, I really fucked that up. I should have just married him." Jenn's vision tunneled for a moment and she shook her head.

"Jenn, Curt's talking to Jake right now. He's going to come see you too. Please stop what you're doing. I'm getting in the car now." Riley sounded panicked.

Jenn nodded her head and reached for her phone. "Riley, I'm tired and my stomach hurts. I'm going to lay down for a bit."

Jenn fumbled with the phone as Riley yelled, "No, please don't hang up, Jenn!" Jenn hit the end call button and tossed the phone onto the couch. Seconds later it started ringing and ringing, but Jenn sat still and finished her glass of vodka.

Her head was spinning, and her heart was beating

fast. Her vision was becoming foggy, but she shook her head and it would clear briefly.

She didn't know how much time had passed before she heard banging on her door. She couldn't stand up. Her vision was tunneling again as she tried to call out to whoever was banging, but she couldn't.

There was a loud crash and Jenn jumped. She turned her head slowly and saw Jake running into the apartment. "Jenn, what the hell did you do?" he yelled, looking around the room at the empty vodka bottle and the empty medication card.

"There you are, I knew you'd come back," Jenn mumbled before everything went black.

Chapter 28

The next thing Jenn remembered was blinking slowly awake and staring at a bright light above her. Her throat was on fire and her chest felt as if someone had hit her with a car. She tried to focus and look around the room, but her neck was stiff. She turned slowly to the right and saw Jake sleeping in a chair, wearing his scrubs. She tried to smile and say his name, but her voice was hoarse. She looked down at her arms and saw two IVs running. She raised her hand and felt something attached to her nose.

She was trying to process what was happening when a young nurse stepped into the room. "Oh good, you're awake. I'll go get the doctor." She turned and walked out, and Jenn looked back at Jake. He was sitting up now and staring at her, his eyes red and bloodshot. She tried to smile at him, but he had a cold look on his face.

She frowned and looked back to the door as the doctor entered. "Well, Jenn, I'm glad to see you are awake. How do you feel?" Jenn tried to clear her throat and then pointed to a cup of water. Jake stood and handed it to her.

She took a sip and tried to talk, but it came out as a whisper. "Sore, my throat really hurts." She looked back at Jake, who was avoiding eye contact.

"Your throat will be sore for a few days. We had to

pump your stomach. You're sore because we had to revive you," the doctor said, matter-of-factly.

Jenn's mouth fell open. "Revive me?" She looked back at Jake, who kept staring at the door.

"Yes, before the EMTs got to your apartment your friend had to start CPR after you stopped breathing." Tears rolled down her face as she touched her chest. It hurt when she pressed, and she tried to remember what had happened.

"I don't remember. I was on the phone with Riley and then Jake was there. Then it was dark." She looked back at Jake, who was now looking at her with tears in his eyes.

"Yeah, you collapsed after I came in. I called 911 on the way over, but you came around quickly," he said quietly. She tried to reach out for him, but he stepped back.

"Well, you're lucky to have a friend like Jake," the doctor said as he wrote a note in her chart. He turned and walked out of the room.

Jenn stared after him before turning back to Jake. He looked down at his shoes, and she was afraid to ask him what had happened. He pulled a tissue out of his pocket and blew his nose.

"I have to get back to work. I was just taking my lunch." He stood and started to leave.

"Jake, please," Jenn called, and he stopped.

He stared at her for a moment before walking to the end of her bed. "That was, literally, the stupidest thing you could have ever done," he muttered.

She wiped her nose with a tissue and nodded. "I don't know what I was thinking."

Jake nodded several times. "You weren't." They looked at each other for a few moments in silence.

"Thank you for saving me," she whispered.

He gave a half smile, but it was strained. "I really have to get back. Get some rest and I'll come back in a few hours when my shift is over. Oh, and call Riley in the morning, she is really worried about you." Jake patted her foot and walked out the door. Jenn repositioned herself in bed and closed her eyes.

The next few hours were restless as several nurses and doctors checked in on her.

When morning came, she was finally awake enough to inventory what had happened and what was going on with her body. While she was unconscious, they had started two IVs, inserted a tube into her nose and placed a catheter.

She was very shaky, and her throat still hurt. There were bruises on her chest and it caused her anxiety to flare when she looked at them.

Jenn couldn't find her cellphone, so she used the room phone to call and speak with Riley. She answered quickly. "Jenn?" Her voice was shaking.

"It's me," Jenn replied.

"Oh, thank god. What the hell is going on in your head? I can't tell you what has been going through mine!" Riley said quickly and slightly louder than she should have.

"I'm OK. Just feel like a truck hit me."

She could hear Riley exhale loudly. "Walking into a room where your best friend is receiving CPR is not on my list for anything."

Jenn suddenly felt ashamed. "I'm so sorry, Riley." She started to cry again.

She could hear Riley sniffle. "It's OK, Jenn. I'm just happy you are here. We'll be up to see you later today." A doctor walked into the room and Jenn quickly said goodbye to Riley.

"How are you feeling today, Jenn?" he asked.

"Still very sore and very embarrassed."

He nodded and wrote a note in the chart. "Well, now that you are more stable, we can start removing some of these lines. Then we can recheck your blood work tomorrow before you move." Jenn looked at the doctor with a raised eyebrow. He flipped to another page in the chart. "I'll have the nurses run over the details and answer your questions." He nodded and left the room.

Jenn sat in silence, not understanding what the doctor had just said. She assumed once she was stable that they would let her go home.

A tech brought in a breakfast tray and Jenn tried to eat, but her throat still hurt. While she was picking at her food, Jake came back and sat in the chair next to her bed. He didn't talk at first and just sat quietly as she tried to drink her coffee.

"That stuff is terrible, good luck," he finally said. He didn't look at her but stared straight ahead at the TV. She smiled and looked at him, wishing he would look back.

"So, no one will tell me what's going on? They mentioned a move?" Jenn asked.

Jake shifted in his chair. "Your mom is on her way down and should be here later today," he said. Jenn felt annoyed. Even Jake was avoiding the question.

"She's coming to take me home?" she asked. Jake reached for the TV remote and pushed the power button before turning to face Jenn.

"Jenn, you tried to kill yourself. You're not going home for a while," he said, very matter-of-factly. Jenn felt tears coming to her eyes again.

She sniffed, "How long?"

He fidgeted in the chair again. "That's up to the doctors. Once they believe you're not a threat to yourself they reevaluate you. I wouldn't rush it, though."

Jenn grabbed a tissue and blotted her eyes. "I have to talk to my work. Where is my cellphone?"

Jake looked to the door and back to Jenn. "No cellphone for 72 hours. You're on a psych hold. And I spoke to your work yesterday after you came in."

Jenn looked out the window. "Yesterday? What day is it?" she glanced around the room, looking for some hint.

"It's Monday. You were unconscious for a day," Jake replied. Jenn's breathing became shallow and her heart was beating fast. Jake looked at the vitals monitor and back at Jenn. He reached up and touched her hand. She focused on him and took several deep breaths. The beep from the monitor slowed. They sat holding hands without speaking. Jenn's chest was heavy, and tears rolled down her cheeks.

"I didn't really want to die," Jenn whispered after a long while.

Jake bit his lip and pulled his hand back. "If I wouldn't have gotten there when I did …" he said quietly. A tear rolled down his cheek and he sniffed.

She wanted to reach for him, but her IVs hindered much movement. He cleared his throat and stood from the chair. "Well, I need to get going. I'll be back at work tonight, so I'll stop by on my break." He stood still, not looking at her.

"Jake. I don't know what to say here."

He shook his head and sighed. "Just get better. I don't know what I'd do if you weren't around," he said without looking at her.

"I'm forever in your debt, that's all I know. Thank you. I love you," she said, before regretting the last part. They hadn't spoken since he confessed his feelings for her, and she didn't reciprocate. She felt the love now, though. The tension between them was thick and it panicked her, but she felt love for him more now than ever. He adjusted his shoulders and looked at her.

"I love you, too," he whispered before walking out of the door. She watched him go down the hall and felt a flutter in her stomach. Her mind was jumbled, but she couldn't help questioning her feelings for Jake. She wanted her cellphone. It was a lifeline to her.

Chapter 29

Jenn rested on and off during the morning before her mom arrived after lunch. She was crying before she even entered the room and hugged Jenn tighter than was comfortable. "I'm OK, Mom. I promise," Jenn repeated while her mom sobbed into her shoulder.

Once she calmed down, she went to speak to the doctor while Jenn pushed her food around the lunch tray. She had no appetite and her throat was still raw.

A nurse came in with her mom after almost an hour to speak with Jenn. She nodded as the nurse explained the treatment plan and told her about the unit she would be on. Jenn's head started to hurt before the nurse finished talking, but she nodded and signed a form along with her mom. "So, at least two weeks?" she asked after she signed the paperwork.

"They will reevaluate your situation week by week, but I wouldn't rush it. Emotional recovery is much more difficult than physical." Jenn nodded, and the nurse left.

Jenn's mom adjusted her pillow and poured a glass of water. "You need to drink," she said with a wobble in her voice.

Jenn took her hand and squeezed. "Thank you for

being here, Mommy." They both started to silently cry and hugged each other tightly.

The rest of the day involved a lot of nurses coming in the room to remove various lines from Jenn. First, the nose tube was removed followed by her catheter. One IV was removed that night and the other had to stay in until after she had blood work drawn in the morning.

Riley came to visit and stayed for a short while. Jenn kicked them both out at 9 because she needed some quiet. She tried to sleep but her mind kept her awake. She stared out the window and listened to the beep of the monitors, the glow of the IV pump filling the room with a soft blue light.

She fell asleep after several hours and woke up when the sun came up and hit her eyes. She blinked slowly and rolled over. A cup of coffee was sitting on her table with a small note from Jake.

You were sleeping so soundly. I'll stop by later.

She smiled and took the cup. It was still warm, so he couldn't have been gone for too long. She took a sip and sighed. It was outside coffee. Jenn adjusted herself into a sitting position in bed and savored her drink.

A young tech came in with a breakfast tray and she thanked him. She tried to eat, but her stomach was unsettled, and her throat was still a little sore.

Her mom showed up at about 10 and the doctor came in with her transfer orders shortly after. The techs insisted on taking her in a wheelchair.

She was checked into her new room and several nurses came in to assess her. People were in and out for the rest of the day. Doctors, therapists and techs all introduced themselves and Jenn's head began throbbing.

Her mom left shortly after dinner was served, promising to stop by in the morning. She was heading home tomorrow afternoon.

Jenn's new room was much quieter than the ICU. She stood and stretched, her chest and neck still sore from the other night. Someone knocked lightly on the door and she turned to find Jake standing in the doorway.

"Figured you could use a break from the hospital food," he said, holding out a milkshake. She smiled and took the cup. Jake came into the room and looked around. "Sweet new digs."

She chuckled. "Needs some decorations." Jenn sat on her bed and Jake sat on a chair nearby.

"You need to eat that. I can see all of your bones," Jake said.

She looked down at her arms and nodded in agreement. "Guess I didn't take such good care of myself these past six months." Jake's cheeks flushed, and Jenn felt guilty for saying what she said. "No, Jake. That wasn't a dig at you."

He nodded and sighed. "I didn't help the situation."

Jenn opened the shake and took a sip. "It was my own mess and I'm the only one to blame. I know better, and none of this should have happened. It was a domino effect and I was the last domino that got knocked off the table." She took another gulp and set the cup down.

Jake met her gaze. "I'm sorry for walking out like that. It just hit me hard and I handled it poorly. I should have stayed and dealt with my feeling instead of running. Then I could have watched out for you."

Jenn shrugged. "Who knows if that would have stopped anything from happening? Don't burden yourself with my crap, it's not yours to carry." They sat in silence without breaking eye contact. "I missed you. A lot," she said softly. He stood and sat next to her on the bed. She leaned her head into his shoulder as he wrapped one arm around her. A feeling of warmth spread across her chest and she smiled.

"I regret our fight, but I don't take back anything I said. I do apologize for letting you go through that alone," Jake said while rubbing his hand on her shoulder.

Jenn pushed up and turned to face him. "I never meant to lead you on in any way and I'm so sorry if it seemed like that's what I was doing. You are my best friend and I love you dearly. My head is just so screwed up." She put her hands over her face and shook her head.

"Jenn, I don't expect you to figure any of this out right now. It wouldn't be the time for it anyway. Just know that I am always here, in whatever capacity you need me to be." Jake pulled her hands down, so she would look at him. "I'm not giving up on you. Ever." She smiled, and a tear rolled down her cheek.

A moment passed where Jenn wanted to lean in for a kiss, but he cut her off. "Well, I have to get to work and you have a busy day tomorrow. I'll check back in when I can, OK?" Jake said as he stood from the bed and headed out the door.

Jenn watched him go before lying back. She didn't know how she felt about him. The emotions were jumbled in with everything else that had happened. She shook her head and climbed into bed.

Chapter 30

The next week passed without much incident. Jenn had therapy sessions several times a day, activities at least once a day, and three meals. The doctor was concerned about her eating habits as well as her emotional state, so she was closely monitored for both.

Riley and Jake were in and out, as well as a few people from her work. Her director of nursing came in and helped her with paperwork for her time off and promised her job would be waiting for her when she completed her treatment. Everyone was being so kind but treating her like a fragile china doll. It was both comforting and irritating.

Jenn started to feel better and kept herself busy so she wouldn't have time to get lost in her thoughts. She found some solace in the library on her unit and began to read romance novels. Jenn found them a little far-fetched, but she enjoyed them. Her love life was obviously a mess, but the people in the books had it all. When she wasn't reading, she discovered several TV shows depicting what she thought were ideal relationships. It's all she thought about. Jenn made a promise to herself that the next man in her life would have to be like one of the men in these books or TV shows. She deserved that after what she went through.

Her therapist took her romantic ideas as a phase and did not discourage them. She felt that Jenn needed positives in her life and if that made her happy, she was OK with it. Riley thought the idea was preposterous but went along with it because she was afraid of disagreeing with Jenn in her current state. Jake didn't have any comments about it, but the topic of love and relationships tended to make him uncomfortable.

"That's an interesting way to look at relationships, Jenn. You deserve something like that, though," he said one day while visiting. Jenn had put her emotions toward Jake in the back of her mind. She still felt very strongly towards him, but she couldn't discern if the feelings were because she loved him or if they were related to the fact that he saved her life. Their relationship was no longer awkward, though. They put the past behind them and focused on now.

After two weeks in treatment, Jenn's doctor felt that she was well enough to go home and start outpatient therapy. She had put on some weight and started a new medication regimen. Her mom would be coming down to stay with her for a few days. The doctor wanted her to have a few outpatient sessions before being cleared to return to work.

She left the facility with her mom on a Friday. Her apartment smelled strongly of cleaning products when she got home, and everything was spotless and the hole in her wall was repaired. "Mom, did you sanitize my apartment?" Jenn laughed.

"Doctor told me to make sure there was nothing here

from that night. I also had to throw out all alcohol and medication. I did stock your fridge, though." Jenn stood in her living room, staring at the floor where she sat that night. She tried to imagine Jake performing CPR on her and the thought made her shudder.

She excused herself to the bathroom and stood in front of the mirror, breathing deeply. She fumbled with her medication bottle and pulled out a pill before swallowing it without water. She was taking an anti-depressant daily that was supposed to helped with her anxiety.

Jenn didn't want her mom to see her nervousness, so for the next several days she put on a brave face. After her mom was convinced that she was OK, she headed home and left Jenn alone for the first time in about a month. Jenn sat on her couch in the silence and let it rush over her. The entirety of what she went through hit her suddenly and she panicked. Fumbling for her phone, she called Jake.

He answered quickly. "You OK?" he asked.

"The silence just kind of hit me," Jenn replied, "Haven't been alone for a while. I think I'm just now realizing what happened." She sniffed and wiped her nose.

Jake was silent for a moment. "Do you need me to come over?" he asked quietly. Jenn thought about it. She wanted Jake here, but she still couldn't figure out what she wanted from him. The emotions were a jumble. She didn't want to hurt him more than she already had.

She cleared her throat, "No, I'm OK. I know you have to work tonight so I'll call and talk to Riley a little."

Jake sighed. "Just text me tonight if you need anything, I can stop by tomorrow on my way home. Be safe, *please*." Jenn thanked him and hung up the phone. She needed to talk to him about these feelings, but now was not the time. She called Riley instead.

"Hey babe, everything alright?" Riley asked, and Jenn chuckled. Riley had taken on the motherly role.

"I'm fine, I promise. Just needed to talk. I have some things in my head that need to get out." She settled onto the couch and could hear Riley talking to Curt quietly.

"Let me get in the other room and find a comfy spot. Then, I'm all yours." Jenn could hear Riley walking into another room and settling into a chair. "OK, shoot" she said.

Jenn paused and tried to put together what she wanted to say. "I don't know exactly what I'm feeling, to tell you the truth."

"About what?" Riley asked.

Jenn inhaled deeply. "Jake."

Riley sighed loudly. "Jenn, I'm going to be completely honest with you and I don't want you to get upset. Promise me that you won't get upset."

Jenn thought about it and told her to continue. "Jake is your best friend, so you have that connection. You made the mistake of sleeping with him while you were in an extremely vulnerable state, so you have that connection. Then he was gone for six months while you were spiraling out of control. A spiral that ended with him literally saving your life, so you have that connection. It would be insane if you didn't feel strongly towards him right now."

Riley took several deep breaths. "That being said, there is no possible way that you should be thinking about anything more with him right now. I love you, but you're a mess. Starting a relationship right now would be disastrous for both you and him. I know you love him, and he loves you. But, it's not the time or place for that. If it's meant to be, it will be. When the time is right."

There was silence between them for a few minutes before Jenn replied. "Damn it, why are you so right all the time? It's annoying." Riley laughed. "Fine, packing away my feelings until I can truly understand and feel them," Jenn said.

She and Riley chatted for a while about mundane things before calling it a night. She went to bed that night with a clear head for the first time in months. It felt like a turning point and Jenn was ready for it.

Present

Chapter 31

Jenn felt confident as May arrived. She and Mike had been strong for six months. She still hadn't told him the whole truth about her past, but it didn't seem to matter at this point. Work was going well, and she was happy. Jake had been dating his girlfriend Kelly for a few months, and Riley was off maternity leave and doing well.

The three of them always got together over Memorial Day weekend for a cookout. Her friends picked that weekend so she wouldn't be alone and thinking about what had happened to her. The thought had not even crossed Jenn's mind because she was staying busy between work, a relationship and her extracurricular activities.

Her feelings for Mike had continued to grow and while that gave her a little anxiety, Jenn was excited for the possibilities. She had given him a key to her apartment, and he was staying more and more frequently. Jenn met his parents recently and she had planned to take him to visit hers soon. They had not discussed any long-term relationship goals, but they were starting to get to that point.

Mike and Jenn packed a cooler and headed to Riley and Curt's house on the Saturday of Memorial Day weekend. Jenn had made several side dishes and desserts, the job that Riley had given her. Jake oversaw beverages, and Curt got to man the grill. The three of them and their significant others had really clicked, and Jenn was happier than she had been in a long time.

They set out the food and started grilling while Riley's kids played in the side yard. Riley's youngest was sitting up on her own, and her toddler was running around chasing bubbles that Jenn was blowing. Jake, Mike and Kelly sat at the picnic table and talked, while Riley took to hostess duties. Music played softly from the stereo Curt had set up in the window and a slight breeze cooled the air.

Jenn leaned back on the kids' blanket and closed her eyes, breathing in the warm air. The toddler's laughter filled the air and Jenn smiled and blew more bubbles. The baby was clapping, and Jenn helped her to stand to reach for the bubbles, too. Mike came and sat with her, taking over the bubble blowing. Watching him interact with the kids warmed Jenn's heart.

Curt called to say the food was done and everyone made their way to the table. Jenn helped the baby into her highchair and Riley sat the toddler in his booster seat. The sounds of conversation and laughter filled the air, punctuated only with the clink of silverware on plates.

"This is all so good," Kelly said. "Thanks for inviting me."

Riley smiled, "Well, you are a part of the group now. It's a side effect of dating Jake." Kelly smiled and leaned against Jake.

He reached his arm around her and pulled her into a side hug. Jenn smiled. It was nice to see him happy. He hadn't dated anyone in a long time, and she was always worried that their experience together had messed up his view on relationships. She raised her glass of iced tea and nodded towards Jake. He smiled, and they all joined in the toast. The conversation continued, interrupted only by the kids getting fussy.

Riley and Curt took them inside for the night as the sun started to set. Mike and Jake started a small fire in the firepit behind the house. Jenn talked to Kelly about joining her tae kwon do class. "It's so fun and it helps get any pent-up anger out."

Kelly smiled, "Sounds like a good outlet." Jenn nodded. She wasn't sure if Jake ever talked about their personal things with Kelly, so she wasn't sure how much Kelly knew about her.

Mike and Jake returned, looking smug after starting the fire. "Men make fire," Jake joked, and they followed him to the fire pit.

Riley and Curt came outside after a while with a baby monitor and a bottle of wine. Jenn declined, but everyone else took a glass. The night had cooled off and everyone huddled closer to the fire while talking and laughing.

Kelly whispered in Jake's ear and he cleared his throat. "I have a bit of an announcement to make." Jenn felt nervous, secretly hoping it had nothing to do with Kelly. "I got accepted into Harvard Medical School." Everyone's mouth dropped open, and Kelly beamed at Jake.

"Holy shit, Jake," Jenn finally said. It broke the tension, and everyone laughed and cheered. He talked about the acceptance letter and when he planned on leaving for the East Coast. It made Jenn a little sad that he would be leaving after summer, but she was genuinely happy for him.

Riley stood and wobbled slightly, "This calls for another bottle of wine."

Jenn stood and held out her hand. "I need to use the bathroom, so I will grab it. Plus, you're a little wobbly." She helped Riley back to her seat and patted her head. Riley giggled. Jenn made her way inside, smiling as she listened to the chatter behind her. She always knew Jake was smart.

After she finished in the bathroom, she headed into the kitchen to grab herself a soda and to look for a bottle of wine. Looking through the cabinets, she picked a random bottle.

As she walked towards the back door, an envelope caught her eye. It looked like a wedding invitation and Jenn's curiosity piqued. She walked over, set the wine bottle down and absentmindedly turned it over.

A wave of dizziness rushed over her and the invitation fell onto the ground. She began to breathe rapidly, and her vision tunneled. It took a few minutes to gain control of her breathing and her vision cleared as Riley entered the kitchen looking for her. She looked from Jenn to the envelope now lying on the floor. "Oh, shit," she muttered and rushed to pick it up. "God, Jenn, I didn't mean to leave this out on the counter."

Jenn was breathing deeply and counting to herself, trying to calm down. "Jake! I need you in the kitchen!" Jenn heard Riley yelling out the back door.

Jake came jogging in and stopped when he saw Jenn. "What the hell happened?" he asked, and Riley handed him the envelope. "Shit" was all he could say.

"Jenn, sweetheart?" He said cautiously as he made his way in front of her. She was hunched over the counter, breathing deeply. She looked up at him and burst into tears, falling forward into his arms. "I know. It's OK. We're here," he said as he stroked her hair.

They sat hugging for several minutes before Mike entered the kitchen. "What's wrong?" he said with wide eyes, looking from Jenn to Jake.

"Jenn's ex is getting married. She found the invitation," Riley said, handing the envelope to Mike.

Curt came in next, followed by Kelly. "Damn it, I thought I put that away." Curt said, grabbing the envelope and shoving it into the closest drawer. Jenn continued to sob into Jake's shoulder and Mike began to look confused.

Riley and Curt exchanged looks, "Jenn, I'm sorry. I didn't want you to find that. Especially not tonight," Curt said. Jenn shook her head and pulled away from Jake.

"I'm sorry, I shouldn't have this sort of reaction. I can't believe he's getting married. I mean, I shouldn't care, but that sucks." Her voice was shaky between sobs. Jake handed her some tissue and led her to a chair to sit. Riley handed her a glass of water. Kelly stood back and looked as confused as Mike looked. Jenn's crying broke a brief silence in the room.

Mike stepped towards her. "I'm lost. Why is everyone acting like someone just dropped a bomb?" Jenn looked up at him and saw a combination of confusion and annoyance on his face.

Riley decided to answer first. "It's not the fact that he's getting married. It's a combination of that and this weekend. You know." She looked at Mike and then at Jenn. "Jenn, he knows, right?"

Jenn lowered her head and wiped her nose. She wouldn't meet anyone's glares.

"Are you kidding me, Jenn?" Jake said softly, but through gritted teeth. Jenn began to cry harder again and shook her head.

"I couldn't," she whispered. She finally looked up at Mike, who stood with his arms crossed, as if waiting for an explanation. "I'm sorry."

"Will someone please tell me what's going on?" He looked to Jake and Riley.

Riley looked to Jake, and Jake's cheeks flushed. "Jenn, you have to tell him."

Jenn shook her head. "I can't." Riley and Curt exchanged looks and turned to walk outside, Riley taking Kelly's arm as they passed her. She looked at Riley with questioning eyes, but Riley just pulled her arm.

Jake was breathing rapidly, his anger bubbling right below the surface. "Mike, can I have a second alone with Jenn, please?"

Mike exhaled sharply. "If that means I get answers, knock yourself out," he muttered and turned to walk outside as well.

Jake paced over to the door to close it before walking back in front of Jenn. "You don't have a choice here, you know that. He has to know."

Jenn looked up at him and felt annoyed. "I always have a choice. That's what choice is." He pulled a chair and sat directly in front of her.

His cheeks were red. "Not this time. If you really

like this guy and want any sort of a future with him, he has to know what happened."

Jenn looked at the door, then back to Jake. "I don't know how to tell him. I'll scare him away." She wiped her eyes and nose.

Jake leaned back in the chair. "If that scares him away, then he doesn't deserve to be with you." Jenn gave him a questioning look and her chest tightened.

"But what if it does? I really like him, and he knows about my medication and my ex. Does he really need to know about the rest?" She could tell Jake was angry and about to explode.

"You tell him, or I will."

"What right do you have?" she said, feeling a little anger herself.

"What right, Jenn? Really? You're talking to the person who saved your life. Yes Jenn, when you tried to kill yourself, remember? I saved your life." Jake's eyes were getting red and Jenn had stopped crying.

"Yeah, I remember that. I remember that every day. That doesn't give you the right to try and control what I tell him." Their voices were getting louder by the minute. Jake stood up suddenly and Jenn flinched.

"It does matter. You chose him and now he has to

know how to protect you." Jake paused and took a deep breath.

Jenn stood slowly so she would be at his eye level. "I chose him? I chose him? You want to hash this out right now, Jake?" Her fists were clenched but she did not break eye contact. Jake stared as well, trying not to falter.

He started to say something but was interrupted when someone behind them cleared their throat. Riley was standing in the doorway and Jenn could see Mike standing behind her. He looked both sad and a little angry.

Jake looked back at Jenn, "You're right. You can make your own mistakes," he said and turned and walked past Riley. Riley looked at Jenn and mouthed "I'm sorry". She turned and walked past Mike, laying a hand on his shoulder. Jenn stared at Mike for a moment before sitting back into the chair. Mike made his way over to her and sat in the chair that Jake had been in.

"Are you OK?" he asked, placing his hand on her knee.

She chuckled. "Far from it, to be honest." He sat quietly, not moving his hand. "I don't even know where to begin."

Mike leaned back. "Tell me whatever you are comfortable with telling me."

Jenn looked up at him and inhaled deeply. "Four years ago, I tried to kill myself," she said in a weak voice.

She paused but didn't break eye contact. Mike kept a straight face, not reacting to the information. She continued. "I broke up with Kevin, had a huge fight with Jake and drank heavily for about six months. The weekend that was supposed to be my wedding, I decided to take some medication with the alcohol to stop the pain. This is the weekend, actually. That's why these guys always plan something for me to do so I can't sit home and think about it." Mike nodded but continued to keep his face neutral. "I was hospitalized for almost a month and still have to go to therapy sessions every six months. That's also why I'm on an anti-depressant." She took a deep breath and paused.

Mike sat forward and took her hand. "I'm sorry that you went through that, Jenn. Why were you afraid to tell me?" Jenn shrugged because she didn't know why.

She took another deep breath. "Jake saved my life."

Mike sat back. "Well, that explains the relationship you have." He had a crooked smile on his face. Jenn raised an eyebrow. "You two are so close. I never know if I should be worried or not. Now that I know you owe him your life ..." Mike trailed off, looking slightly relieved. Jenn forced a smile.

Mike did not need to know how she felt about Jake. She still wasn't one hundred percent sure about her feelings.

Mike held out his hand and helped Jenn up. He pulled her into a hug and kissed her. "Nothing is going to change the way that I feel about you, Jenn."

She put her hand up to his face and kissed him. "Thank you," she said as they walked hand in hand out to the backyard. Riley and Curt were sitting by the fire, cuddling. Jake and Kelly were gone.

Jenn looked at Riley and she shrugged. "He said he had to go." Jenn frowned and sat down next to Mike. "Everything good?" Riley asked, looking tentatively between Mike and Jenn.

"Yeah, everything's great," Mike replied, kissing Jenn's hand.

Jenn pulled out her phone and texted Jake, *I'm sorry and I know you're right. You always are right.* She put her phone away and rejoined the conversation.

Mike and Jenn headed home a little after 10. After getting home, Jenn checked her phone and noticed that Jake hadn't replied. She felt a stab of anger and guilt. Mike came up behind her and wrapped his arms around her. "Are you sure you're OK?"

She turned to face him. "I'm fine. I just hate fighting with Jake. We have an intense relationship. Lots of past crap. We always get through it, though." She looked at her phone.

"Call him tomorrow," Mike said, taking the phone and putting it on the counter. Jenn started to object but stopped when he kissed her. "I'm really glad that you decided to open up tonight. It's important for the future to know about the past."

Jenn smirked. "I've never heard you talk about the future."

Mike blushed and shrugged. "Maybe this intense evening has made me a little more vulnerable. Maybe it's the eighteen glasses of wine that Riley forced on me," he laughed, "Maybe it's because I'm falling in love with you." He met her eyes with an intense stare. Her heart started to beat faster, and a warmth came over her face.

"Thank you," she said before she could help herself. Then the embarrassment hit. "Sorry, bad response. Mike, I really like you. I haven't felt like this in a long time. I'm just cautious about saying that because, well, you know."

He kept a straight face. "I understand. Doesn't change how I feel, though." He leaned forward and kissed her. She relaxed and realized how utterly exhausted she was.

They headed to the bedroom and crawled into bed. Jenn cuddled into Mike's chest and listened to his heart beating. She was asleep before she knew it.

2 years ago

Chapter 32

Jenn had made great progress after her hospitalization, keeping up with her therapy sessions and medication. Her relationship with Jake was back to normal and she was the godparent to Riley and Curt's son. To keep busy, she had joined tae kwon do and started playing recreational volleyball.

The only thing missing in her life was dating. Jenn was still on the fence about dating again. Riley had tried to set her up a few times and the dates went horribly. Jenn's ideas of romance were a little far-fetched, but she also didn't want to settle for just anything. Riley thought that her expectations were ridiculous, and Jake always laughed when they talked about it. Jenn's therapist, Rebecca, however, thought it was interesting.

She made it a point at most of Jenn's therapy sessions. She was going once a month now, just to check in. At the last session they had delved into her dating life. "So, Jenn. What do you think is an appropriate amount of time before you start dating seriously again?"

Jenn sat and thought about this. "I don't think that there is a specific time frame. I think I'll know when it's time."

Rebecca nodded and wrote a note in her file. "What

about in the meantime?"

Jenn fidgeted and ran her hands through her hair. "I don't know. I have great friends to hang around with. Do I need to date? Really?"

Rebecca smiled and laughed softly. "No one needs to date, Jenn. But don't you miss the intimacy? The physical contact?"

It was Jenn's turn to laugh. "Are you asking me if I miss sex?" Rebecca didn't answer, just shrugged. "Well, sex has nothing to do with intimacy. I can get sex, that's easy. I'm more worried about the emotional side of things." Jenn adjusted her position in her chair. "I mean, I've been with men lately and I feel nothing. Well, I feel what you're supposed to feel when it comes to sex, but I don't *feel* anything." She emphasized the way she said feel and sighed. "You know what I mean."

Rebecca smiled and nodded. "And when was the last time you felt something?" Jenn sat and thought about her answer. Her chest tightened.

"The night I spent with Jake," she whispered. Rebecca nodded again and wrote something down. "Don't write that. What are you saying? Probably what Riley says." Jenn's cheeks were burning.

"And what does Riley say?" Rebecca asked in a motherly voice.

"That I'm in love with Jake and I'm too stubborn to realize it." Jenn looked at Rebecca. "You think so, too, don't you?"

Rebecca set down her pen and notepad. "I think you have a very complicated relationship with Jake, and I think you have very complicated feelings for him." Jenn sighed and nodded. "You are allowed to take whatever amount of time it takes to figure those feelings out." She paused and folded her arms.

"I also think that you can't pull him one way or another without figuring things out. It's not fair to either of you." Rebecca finished and picked her pen back up.

Jenn sat, lost in her thoughts. She was supposed to meet up with Jake that night for dinner.

Her session time was up, and she thanked Rebecca before heading home. Jenn walked home in the cool morning, the sun shining. Her thoughts were scattered, and she didn't know how to approach her relationship with Jake. She knew that a relationship with him would work because they were very compatible. However, she was a mess now, and she wasn't sure that she could take on that emotion. The last thing she wanted was to end up losing him altogether.

Jenn pulled out her phone to call Riley. "Hey, Jenn."

"Hi, just walking home from therapy and my thoughts are running rampant."

Riley laughed. "Sounds like the norm. Carry on."

Jenn chuckled to herself. "Well, Rebecca agrees with you about Jake. You both are real pains in the ass."

Riley laughed out loud. "I know I'm right. And then?" Jenn stopped walking for a moment and thought about it.

"I don't really know. I see the downside to it, and I see the upside. I know he's my person, but, man, does our timing always suck. I just want to get the past eight years out of my system. I've been a well-behaved girl for so long, it has to be my time to be wild, right?" Jenn continued walking towards her apartment.

Riley was silent for a moment. "Well, think of it this way. Do you want to jump into what I assume would be another long-term commitment? Or, do you want to take this time for yourself? Forget the guys. Figure out what you want and who you are. Be young, have fun." She inhaled deeply. "But I want you to make sure Jake understands. Don't break his heart. Let him be free so he can find himself as well."

Jenn nodded and watched her feet as she walked. "No relationship yet. I can do that. I can keep my feelings to myself." Jenn wondered if she could handle this idea. She knew she couldn't handle a relationship. "Thanks, Riley, I should probably pay you the same I pay Rebecca," Jenn joked.

Riley laughed. "I'll be expecting a check in the mail." They said their goodbyes and Jenn continued to her apartment.

Chapter 33

She and Jake were meeting at 6 to have dinner, something they did twice a week since she left the hospital. He had taken to the protector role with great enthusiasm. Jenn was nervous this time. She felt she needed to have a fair discussion about their relationship and feelings, but she feared the ramifications. The nature of her relationship with Jake had always been unstable. She was afraid that one push and the whole thing might fall over.

Jake was waiting outside the restaurant when she arrived. She met him with a kiss on the cheek before he led her inside.

Her stomach was turning a little as she sat down at their table. After ordering drinks and appetizers, they sat in silence for a few minutes. "Everything alright?" Jake finally asked, a look of concern on his face. Jenn nodded, avoiding eye contact. He reached across the table and took her hand. Her stomach tightened.

"I met with Rebecca this morning." Jenn said. Jake nodded and pulled his hand back.

"Everything is still going well, right?" he asked.

"Yes, everything's great. We were talking about my emotional state right now." She met his gaze, concern in her eyes.

"And, how is your emotional state?" he asked, leaning back in his chair.

"Scattered, I guess?" She replied but sounded unsure. He looked confused, so she continued. "I told her that I don't really feel anything right now, or that I'm choosing to not feel things. She asked about the physical side of everything and I told her, I can get that without issue. It's the emotional that I fear." Jenn stirred her drink with her straw.

Jake nodded. "What does she think of that?"

Jenn looked up at him, afraid to tell him about the rest of the conversation she had with Rebecca. "Well, she and Riley both think that a relationship right now would be disastrous." Jake sighed and looked away for a moment.

"And what do you think?" he asked quietly.

She leaned forward and reached for his hand. "Part of me doesn't want to agree, but I know they are right." He took her hand and didn't break eye contact.

"I'm going to hate myself for asking this," he muttered, and Jenn's chest tightened. "They're talking about me, aren't they?" Jenn looked down at the table, her face warm again. She didn't want to say it, but she knew the air had to be cleared.

"Jake, I don't know what to say here." She looked back at him.

"Say it, please," he replied. Jenn sniffed, tears brimming in her eyes.

She inhaled deeply. "You have no idea how much I want this to work. You are the only person that makes me feel right now. But, it's so confusing at the same time. The idea of messing everything up just stays in my mind and sends me into a panic. I can't lose you, Jake. I can't."

He didn't react, just held her hand in silence for a few moments. "I don't want to admit it, but it's the truth. No matter what we feel, this is not the time or place in your life to start this. It kills me to say that." He shook his head and looked away.

The waitress came back with their food and the tension broke between them. Jenn's heart was beating fast and her stomach fluttered rapidly. They ate for several minutes without talking.

Jake set down his silverware first. "I don't want our relationship to change."

Jenn set her silverware down as well. "I agree one hundred percent, I love our friendship."

They sat, looking at each other. "I will do my best to not let my emotions get the best of me. We will know if and when the time is right for anything more," Jake said first.

Jenn nodded. "I will not get jealous if you start dating some hot, blonde model and rub it in my face," she teased.

He smiled. "And I won't try to kick your next boyfriend's ass because I know he's not good enough for you." Jenn smiled widely. In that moment she knew that they would be alright.

"To us and our messy but wonderful relationship." They raised their glasses and clinked them together softly.

After packing up their leftovers, they left the restaurant arm in arm and walked towards Jenn's apartment. The night was cool, so Jenn huddled close to Jake as they walked. He was quiet, and it made Jenn nervous for some reason.

"Are you OK?" she asked.

Jake shrugged. "It's just hard, you know? It feels like we always miss our chance. And you have no idea how hard it is to hold back sometimes."

Jenn stopped and pulled him to face her. "I know, Jake. I just don't want to make your head as messed up as mine."

He chuckled. "It's already there, girl." They stood, looking at each other. She reached forward and took his hand, feeling a jolt of energy shoot up her arm.

"We can't, though. God, I regret saying that, but it is true," she said. Jake took a step towards her and took her other hand.

"I know, I am just terrible at waiting," he said quietly. Jenn's breathing quickened as she took a step forward, so they were inches apart. She let go of his hands and raised her arms, looping them over his shoulders and around his neck.

"Me, too, and I'm sick of not feeling anything," she whispered. Jake leaned down and kissed her softly, sending another jolt of energy through her. After a moment, Jenn pulled away. "I felt that."

Jake smiled and kissed her again, but stopped. "On that note, I need to take you home because I can tell that this is not going to end in the appropriate way." Jenn smiled and stepped back. Jake took her hand and they walked together.

When they arrived outside Jenn's apartment, she had to fight the urge to invite him inside. She could tell by Jake's expression that he was thinking the same thing.

"I'm glad we talked," Jenn said. "I wish things were different, but we just have to give it time."

Jake smiled and nodded. "I'll wait." Jenn pulled him into a tight hug and held on for several minutes.

"I really do love you, you know that, right?" she whispered in his ear. She could feel him nod.

"I love you, too, more than you know," he replied. Jenn eased her grip on him, and they stepped away from each other. She opened the apartment door and gave a little wave before heading in. Jake turned and walked away, Jenn watching his every step. Her heart was heavy, a mixture of happy and sad. She didn't know what was harder, admitting that she loved Jake or admitting that she couldn't be with him. In the end, she knew that it was the right thing to do.

Chapter 34

The next year passed without issue. Jenn and Jake stayed true to their word and built their friendship while repressing their feelings. Jake tried dating other women. Jenn wasn't thrilled with the situation, but none of the relationships seemed to stick. She didn't jump right into dating, but instead immersed herself in activity. Between tae kwon do and running in road races, she didn't have time to dwell on it.

Whenever there was a bubbling of emotions, she would work out to get rid of them. If that didn't help, she found a man for the night. After being a one-man person for most of her life, the idea of a one-night stand both terrified and excited her. There were no emotions involved, though. She didn't allow that to happen.

Jenn's feelings toward Jake would not go away. He seemed to be alright with the situation and they never really talked about it again. It wasn't until he started dating someone seriously that it really hit her hard.

Jake had asked to meet her for coffee, which was common. When she arrived at the coffee shop, he seemed nervous and a little sad. "Hi. Is everything all right?" Jenn asked nervously while sitting down.

"Oh yeah, I'm fine. Everything's great. I actually

asked you here to tell you some good news." He paused and took a sip of coffee. "I've met someone." He glanced away briefly and then met Jenn's gaze. She kept her face blank, but her stomach dropped.

"Oh. Well, that's great, Jake," she said slowly, trying to keep an even tone.

He nodded and forced a smile. "Yeah, um, we've been out on several dates now, and I'm really interested in getting to know her better. She's really nice." Jenn nodded, still not changing her expression. A million thoughts shot through her head.

"I'm happy for you," she finally said with a weak smile. Jake looked relieved. Jenn picked up her spoon and stirred her coffee slowly. She was lost in a thought when Jake touched her arm.

"Are you sure you're OK?" he asked. Jenn nodded and set her spoon aside.

"Of course, I told you to date. I didn't expect that you would be single forever. I mean, look at you." She replied before taking a long drink of coffee.

He smiled and reached for her hand. "It's new. I just wanted you to know." She smiled and squeezed his hand. "So, how is *your* love life?" he asked awkwardly.

Jenn chuckled. "What's that?" she joked. Jake

laughed as well. "No, no. Still not interested. I've got plenty to occupy my time. Plus, I have to talk it over with Rebecca tomorrow. I'll wait until she thinks I'm ready." Jake nodded.

They finished their coffee while talking about Jake's new girlfriend. Jenn held her tongue and tried to act genuinely interested, but her head was screaming at her. Jake hugged her before they walked in separate directions from the coffee shop.

She pulled out her phone and texted Riley with the information she had just received. Riley was sympathetic but realistic. Riley was also pregnant again, so her level of sympathy was a little lower than normal due to hormones. Jenn decided not to delve in too deeply with Riley and save most of her thoughts for Rebecca.

Her appointment was early the next morning, and Jenn did not sleep well during the night. She wrote several things down, so she would not forget to bring them up in her session.

Rebecca was pleasantly surprised by Jenn's enthusiasm. "I'm usually the one taking the notes, but it seems you have a lot on your mind."

Jenn shrugged and opened her notepad. "I'll start off by saying that I'm feeling fine. I haven't had any panic attacks. I'm not unhappy and I'm putting my energy into new activities." Jenn rambled as she looked over her notes.

Rebecca nodded and gestured for Jenn to continue. "OK, well, I had coffee with Jake yesterday." She started. "He informed me that he has a new girlfriend. A serious one." Jenn looked at Rebecca, who kept an even face.

"And how does this make you feel?" Rebecca asked.

Jenn nervously flipped a few pages in her notepad. "I can't be upset. I told him to date. I told him I wasn't ready to date him. I can't get angry at something I suggested. Right?" Jenn was speaking quickly, like she was trying to convince herself more than ask a question.

Rebecca nodded and wrote a note in her file. "Well, yes and no. Yes, you did tell him to date and no, you shouldn't be angry that he followed your advice. On the other hand, your situation is a little different."

Jenn nodded. "So, what do I do?" Jenn asked with genuine concern.

Rebecca folded her hands on her desk and sat in silence for a moment. Jenn's heart was beating fast. "Jenn, you have to decide when to take that next step. I can't tell you that. All I can tell you is that what you are feeling right now is stemming from jealousy."

Jenn nodded and frowned. "But, it's Jake. I still don't understand my feelings for him completely. Where are the lines, the boundaries? What if it's the idea of dating your best friend that you've pined after for so long, like in the movies? What if I decide I want to be with him and then it's not what I thought, and everything falls apart?" Jenn had to take a deep breath because her words were running over each other. "Is it better to have him as my friend or take the chance of losing him?"

Rebecca leaned back in her chair but kept eye contact. "Jenn, I know your last dating experience was not ideal, but I can say that not all of them turn out like that. That was unfortunate, but do not let it shape the rest of your relationships. If you do, you may miss out on something amazing." Jenn leaned back as well, nodding quickly.

There was a pause in the conversation, so Jenn could gather her thoughts. "I don't know still. I assume I'll know if it's meant to be. Obviously, right now is not the time so I'll have to go back to putting my energy elsewhere."

Rebecca picked up her pen and wrote a quick note. "I also want you to keep an open mind. Don't shut out the idea of someone else just because of Jake."

Jenn looked down at her notepad. She knew that Rebecca was right, but she also did not want to give up on Jake. "I will do my best. I'll let it be for now."

Rebecca nodded and wrote a quick note. "It will all work out. You just have to trust," she replied. Jenn nodded and clenched her jaw. Trust was not her strong suit, but she would do her best.

She left Rebecca's office feeling slightly more confused, but also understanding what she needed to do. She could not interject herself into Jake's personal life based purely on jealousy. If she did love him, she needed to let him be happy as well. With or without her.

So, she stayed in the background and watched Jake from afar. He did seem happy in his relationship. It was a little painful to Jenn, in that he didn't have as much time for her anymore. This led to Jenn trying more new activities and picking up more hours at work. When that didn't work, she began to spend the other nights out. With Riley pregnant, she didn't have anyone to go with.

This also led to Jenn having more time to try to follow Rebecca's advice and give other men a try. Unfortunately, no one was living up to her expectations.

****

About a month after Riley had her daughter, she went out with Jenn for a girl's night. They wanted to catch up and blow off some steam. They chatted about day to day life, motherhood and Jenn's progress with relationships.

"I don't know, Riley. I just haven't had a connection. Believe me, I've tried," Jenn said, stirring her drink.

Riley nodded. "Can't shake it, huh?" Jenn raised an eyebrow and looked at her curiously. "You know, the whole Jake thing." Riley had had a few drinks, so her filter was turned off.

Jenn was taken aback for a moment. "What whole Jake thing?"

Riley gave her a knowing look. "Come on, Jenn. You won't let yourself connect with any of these guys because in the back of your head you still have Jake."

Jenn stirred her drink absentmindedly and looked away. She hadn't thought about it. Jake had been with his girlfriend for over six months. "No, that's not true. He's happy, he has a girlfriend."

Riley stared at her.

"What?" asked Jenn.

"He didn't tell you," Riley said. Jenn stared back, waiting for an answer that she assumed she was supposed to have known. "Jake broke up with her two weeks ago."

Jenn sipped her drink and looked around. She set her drink down and looked back at Riley. "Why would he have kept that from me?" she asked.

Riley shrugged. "Probably because he loves you."

Jenn smacked Riley's arm jokingly. "He does not."

Riley chuffed. "Oh, come on, Jenn. Have you never wondered why none of his relationships last longer than a few weeks or months?"

Jenn crossed her arms and leaned back. "Tell me then, oh wise and tipsy one."

Riley rolled her eyes and set her drink on the table. "How would you feel if you were dating a guy that was clearly in love with his best friend? No one could look at the two of you together and not get jealous. You have chemistry." She picked up her drink and emptied the glass.

"All right. You've had enough. We should get going." Jenn pulled Riley's glass away and stood to pick up her coat.

A waiter approached the table with a drink and placed it in front of Jenn. "Sorry, I didn't order anything," she said. The waiter smiled and pointed over to the bar.

A man was sitting alone at the far end, wearing a dark blue suit. He gave her a small wave and smile, which she returned.

"My, my. He's cute," Riley teased.

Jenn rolled her eyes. "We were just leaving, though."

Riley stood next to Jenn and leaned into her. "No, I'm leaving. I will call Curt and you can go meet this nice man." She gave Jenn a small shove towards the bar.

Jenn turned and looked at her. "Are you positive? I can take you."

Riley shook her head and pulled out her phone. She quickly tapped out a text and hit send. "Too late now, better get moving. And don't forget your drink." Jenn watched her as she grabbed her coat and walked towards the front door. Jenn stood at the table for a moment. She ran over the information that Riley had just given her. Jake was single and kept that information from her for some reason. Now Riley was pushing her to talk to another man.

She was lost in her thoughts when she heard someone clear their throat behind her. She jumped and turned quickly, coming face to face with the nicely dressed man from the bar. "Oh, hi. Sorry. I was lost in my thoughts," she said, blushing slightly.

He smiled. "Well, hi. I'm Mike."

She smiled back and held out her hand. "Hi Mike, I'm Jenn." He took her hand and shook it, holding on a little longer than necessary. She stared at him, feeling a small flip in her stomach.

"May I join you?" he asked, and she nodded while sitting down.

He was extremely charming and easy to talk to. They talked for over an hour while having several more drinks. As her head became fuzzy with the alcohol, she forgot her thoughts about Jake. The only thought in her mind at that moment was about the person sitting in front of her.

She was nervous, which normally did not happen when she was with a guy at the bar. "Well, Jenn. It's getting late. Do you want me to help you get home?" Mike asked.

She looked at her watch and then back at him. "No. I'd rather not go home yet." She smiled suggestively. He nodded once and walked over to the bar to close his tab.

Without saying anything, he held out his hand, and they walked out of the bar together.

Present

Chapter 35

Near the beginning of August, Jenn helped Mike set up his classroom for the coming school year. They had been spending more and more time together as the months passed. Mike stayed at Jenn's most of the time and had even hinted that his apartment lease was going to be up soon. Jenn was not sure about that move, though she had taken the step of telling him that she loved him. She thought she did, at least. She wasn't one hundred percent convinced, but she knew he was a great guy and he treated her well. She didn't know what was holding her back anymore. This relationship had changed her views on relationships in general. It was, or so she thought, what a relationship should be like. All of Jenn's other relationships had been messy, with Kevin cheating and with the confusion of Jake. Mike was simple, she didn't have to guess because she knew he cared, and she trusted him. Yet, there was something in the back of her mind that always cast doubts on everything.

This was a standing topic whenever she was with Riley. "I don't know, should he give up his lease?" Jenn asked.

Riley folded some T-shirts and paused with her hands on her hips. "Do you want him to?" she asked.

Jenn shrugged nonchalantly. "I do…I think. Ugh, why does the voice in my head want to push against everything?" Jenn replied, tapping her forehead.

Riley smirked and continued folding the laundry. "What?" Jenn muttered. Riley didn't meet her eye and continued to separate the piles of clothes. "Riley, what is that condescending little smile about?"

Riley put some clothes in the closet. When she turned around, she had a serious look on her face. "I feel like I'm on repeat. You know why everything in this relationship is hard." She put her hands on her hips again, tapping her foot softly.

"I really don't. Please, inform me." Jenn leaned back on the bed.

Riley sighed and sat next to her. "I know things have been weird between you and Jake since Memorial Day. He said something that struck a nerve with you, but I don't know what." Jenn inhaled sharply. It was true, she and Jake hadn't spent as much time together since that night. He was also leaving for Boston in a few weeks. Riley leaned towards Jenn. "What did he say?"

Jenn shook her head. Riley looked disappointed. "He didn't say anything. It was just the whole situation. He's just … it's just … too much." Jenn sat up quickly on the side of the bed.

Riley sat next to her. "You've been putting up with his shit for years, what was so different this time?"

Jenn shrugged and wouldn't meet her eye. "It doesn't matter. He's with Kelly, I'm with Mike. He's moving, I'm staying. We're friends and that's it."

Riley nodded. "So, he did say something."

Jenn hesitated. "He told me that I chose Mike, and that's why he needed to know everything. Can you believe that? Like I made a choice."

Riley was quiet, and Jenn looked up at her. "Well, you did make a choice."

Jenn looked at her with a shocked expression. "What choice?"

Riley patted Jenn's knee. "Do you remember when you met Mike?" Riley asked. Jenn thought about it and nodded. "I told you that Jake had broken up with his girlfriend and hadn't told you yet. Then Mike bought you that drink. The next thing I knew, you were talking about a second date with Mike."

Jenn nodded slowly. "What does Jake have to do with that?"

Riley looked down at her hands. "He's going to kill me ..." she muttered. Jenn reached for Riley's hand and squeezed. "Fine, I know why Jake didn't tell you." Jenn let go of Riley's hand and crossed her arms across her chest. Riley continued, "He didn't want you to know because he was trying to come up with a plan to ask you out. Officially."

Jenn's stomach dropped. She shook her head. "That's probably why he asked me for coffee that day."

Riley shook her head. "He called me after to ask about Mike. He wasn't mad at you, more at himself. Then he didn't want to step in your way either."

Jenn's heart was beating faster. "I don't see what bearing this has right now. Why are we talking about Jake?"

Riley patted Jenn's arm. "The question you asked before. About what's holding you back?" Riley took a deep breath. "Jake." Jenn shot her a look and shook her head.

Standing quickly, Jenn paced in front of Riley. "No, we've each been in a relationship. We've never even talked about that again. We're friends."

She spoke quickly as Riley's eyes followed her. "Jenn, you two were never just friends."

Jenn paused and turned. "What am I supposed to do?" A sense of panic started to fill her chest.

Riley stood and placed a hand on Jenn's shoulder to calm her. "I can't tell you what to do. All I know is that Jake is moving to Boston in a few weeks, and Mike wants to move in with you. Those are two really big things at once. You need to figure out how you feel about both before it's too late." Jenn nodded slowly and pulled Riley into a hug. She felt confused on top of the panic.

Jenn let go of Riley and smiled. "I need to go. I think I need to jog for a bit." Riley nodded and returned to her laundry.

Jenn drove home and changed quickly before heading out on her run. She adjusted her headphones and took off jogging down the sidewalk. There was no direction to her run, she just wanted to clear her head.

The music was loud in her ears as she dodged around pedestrians. Her breaths were even, and her sneakers rhythmically hit the pavement. Thoughts flashed through her head, and she turned a corner and picked up speed. She didn't know the answer. She really cared about both men, but in quite different ways. There was no clear answer and she didn't want to hurt either one.

A car horn honked as she sprinted across a street. She paused by the curb and waved an apology to the driver. Hunched over and breathing heavily, she looked around and realized she was about three miles from her apartment. Stretching her arms over her head and leaning to touch her toes, Jenn was able to catch her breath and continued to jog. She headed back in the direction of home.

The sun was starting to set by the time she got back. She felt emotionally and physically drained as she walked up the stairs. Mike was sitting at the kitchen table when she opened the door. "There you are, I was getting worried." Jenn smiled and grabbed a glass of water.

"Sorry, decided to take a run and lost track of time," she said as she leaned down to kiss his cheek. "How was your day?" Mike began talking about his workday and Jenn nodded along, not really listening. The mixed-up thoughts in her head took over again. She smiled and nodded, pretending to listen to Mike's conversation. Her face went blank as she stared at the wall behind Mike.

"Jenn, are you listening?" he asked, waking her from her daydream.

She nodded. "Just tired. I have a lot on my mind." He leaned back in his chair and crossed his arms.

"Anything I can help with?" he asked. She walked over and sat down next to him.

"No, I'm fine. Really," she said as she took his hand. "I'm going to grab a shower and then I can make us something to eat." She headed into the bathroom and stood in front of the mirror. Her face was red, and her hair was wind-blown. She wished that her head would clear, even for a moment, so she could relax. The warm water of the shower loosened her shoulder and back muscles, but her mind would not relent.

After changing into clean clothes, she came back to the kitchen where Mike had already made dinner. Jenn sighed and sat down at the table. "I could tell you were stressed, so I thought this might help." He placed a plate of food in front of her and leaned down to kiss her forehead.

"Thank you," she said, looking into his eyes.

"Anytime," he replied, kissing her lips. He turned to grab himself a plate and she sat, staring at the food. She had to give Mike a fair chance. He was a good chef, that she knew. And she really cared for him. He was good to her and for her, there were no arguments there. Why then did she feel hesitant? "So, want to let me in on what's going on inside that head of yours?" Mike said, trying to get Jenn's attention.

She pushed the food around her plate before answering. "I've been thinking about what you asked me." She didn't look up but continued to play with the food.

"And?" he asked nervously.

"I am still thinking about it. There's one more thing I need to figure out before I can answer. Is that alright?"

He frowned for a moment and then quickly changed to a smile. "I'll be ready when you are." Jenn finally looked up and smiled. They finished their dinner and then Jenn crashed for the night. Mike rubbed her back as she fell asleep and her thoughts began to wind down. She knew that Jake was leaving for school. She knew Mike was here and they were happy. She drifted off to sleep with her mind going back and forth between those two thoughts.

Chapter 36

Jenn and Riley decided to throw Jake a going away party the weekend before he headed off to Boston. Riley insisted on having it at her house, mostly because it was easier for her and Curt.

The two friends spent the day setting up, and people started coming over around 5. Curt grilled hamburgers and hotdogs as Jenn and Mike set up the fire pit for later. Curt had put a radio in the house window to provide music, and the couple's kids played in a small pool on the side of the house.

Jake and Kelly walked in together with a cooler of beer. Jenn gave Jake a quick hug before grabbing two beers and joining Mike by the fire pit. Jake made his rounds, saying hi to everyone and offering drinks. Jenn watched him intently before Kelly broke her concentration.

"Hi guys," she said as she sat down next to them.

"Hey," Mike said, and Jenn nodded.

"Crazy, huh? Boston," Kelly said before taking a drink of her beer.

"Yeah, he's going to pick up that accent. I'm calling it," Jenn joked, still watching Jake. Mike laughed, and Kelly smiled.

"I hope that it won't get me, then." She turned and looked towards the crowd of people congratulating Jake.

"Excuse me?" Jenn asked, finally bringing her attention back to Kelly.

Kelly turned to face her, "Oh, Jake asked me to come with him. I found a job at a hospital near Harvard. I'm so excited." Jenn fought to control her face, even though she felt her cheeks getting flushed.

"That's great. Awesome," she replied. "Will you excuse me? I need to check on Riley and the kids."

Jenn stood and quickly walked over to the side of the house. "Riley!" Jenn called through gritted teeth. Riley was sitting on a blanket with her little girl wrapped in a towel while her son splashed in the pool nearby.

"You have crazy eyes. What's wrong?" Riley asked, setting the baby down on the blanket.

Jenn took a few deep breaths. "Jake asked Kelly to move to Boston with him."

Riley's jaw dropped. "Why were we not told about this?"

"Kelly just said it in passing, but I think she was trying to get a rise out of me," Jenn said quietly.

"Don't play her game. Anyway, that's your answer,

isn't it?" Riley asked. Jenn looked at her oddly. "Jenn, he's moving away with another girl. Problem solved. Obviously makes your choice easier. It's Mike." Riley picked up her daughter, who was fussing, and rocked her.

"Just like that, huh?" Jenn said, looking back toward the party.

"You can't force things, Jenn. Maybe the timing is just not right for a reason." Riley stood and helped her son out of the pool while Jenn grabbed a towel.

They carried the kids back towards the party. Mike was talking to Curt near the grill and Kelly had joined Jake and his work colleagues. Curt and Mike set out the grilled food and called everyone over to start eating. Jenn and Riley filled the kid's plates before eating themselves.

Mike sat down next to Jenn and rubbed her shoulder. "Are you OK? You took off there for a moment."

Jenn nodded quickly. "Yeah, yeah. I promised Riley I'd come help her with the kids. That's all." Mike nodded and started to eat.

Jake and Kelly came to sit down next to Curt and across from Jenn. Jenn and Jake made brief eye contact before looking away from each other. Mike started polite conversation with Jake about the move and school. Jenn was only paying partial attention to the conversation. She didn't know why Jake didn't tell her about this. Kelly talked excitedly about the move while Jake picked at his food. Jenn was focused on his responses and started to feel nervous for him. He didn't seem nearly as excited as Kelly was.

As dinner wound down, people made their way to the fire pit. Riley and Jenn took the kids inside to put them down for the night. As soon as they closed the door to the house, Riley exhaled. "Oh my god. Jake is so not looking forward to Kelly moving with him."

Jenn stopped and looked at her. "What?" she asked. Riley continued to walk through the house and to the kids' bedroom.

After setting them both in their beds, she slowly closed the door. "Did you not see the expression on his face?"

Jenn shrugged. "Maybe he's just tired from all the packing?"

Riley rolled her eyes. "I bet you she brought it up, and he was too nice to say no." Again, Jenn shrugged.

They walked together back to the yard. Jenn didn't want to make judgements, but this decision didn't seem right to her.

Several people had left, and the rest sat around the fire talking about Boston. "Just don't become a Red Sox fan," Curt joked. Jenn sat next to Mike and sipped on her beer.

The conversation was smooth, and the fire was warm, and an hour passed by quickly. Jenn yawned, and Mike rubbed her shoulder.

"I need a fresh drink. Anyone else need anything?" she asked and stood from the chair.

Jake stood up, too, "Here, let me help you." They walked together in silence to the house. Jenn started pulling out beer cans from the fridge and setting them on the counter.

Jake leaned against the counter and crossed his arms. The silence was deafening. He cleared his throat. "So ..." he finally said.

Jenn turned to face him. "Yeah," was all she could come up with in response. They stared at each other for a moment. "Hey, congrats. Kelly told me the good news," Jenn said, trying to keep her voice even.

Jake shifted uncomfortably. "Yeah, we've been talking about it. I know we haven't been together that long, but I didn't want to stop seeing her. I really like her, and I never have to guess with her." He looked down at his shoes.

Jenn swallowed hard. "Wow, that's great Jake. I'm really happy for you," she replied as he looked back at her. She turned and aimlessly rearranged the beer cans on the counter. "Good for you. You know, Mike's planning on moving into my apartment before school starts again." Jenn paused and inhaled. She didn't know why she blurted that out.

Without turning around, she heard Jake shift and exhale. "Oh, that's great. Yeah." Jenn slowly turned around to face him. He was looking down at his shoes again. "I'm … I'm happy for you," he said quietly.

They stood in silence for a moment. After what seemed like hours, they finally made eye contact. Neither spoke, but Jenn's heart was beating fast. "Well, I guess everyone is moving forward. It's going to be weird not having you around all the time," Jenn said, breaking the awkward silence.

"Yep, moving forward," Jake muttered. Jenn stepped forward toward him, trying to figure out if she should comfort him or not.

He looked into her eyes and smiled. "I'm terrified," he finally said. Jenn paused and reached for his hand. They stood holding hands for a minute or two in silence. Jenn sniffed, not realizing that she had started to tear up.

She let go of his hand and stepped back. "Well, you know I'm only a phone call away. Always."

Jake smiled weakly. "I'm really going to miss you."

She smiled back and stepped forward to hug him. "I'm going to miss you, too. You're going to do great, doc," she whispered in his ear.

He laughed softly and hugged her tightly. "Don't forget about us," she added.

He stepped back and wiped a tear from her face. "How could I?" He paused with his hand on her cheek and she felt her chest tighten. She was overcome with the urge to lean in and kiss him, but she shook her head and stepped back.

"Well, we better get back with these beers," she said with a forced laugh, picking up the cans. Jake nodded, not breaking eye contact. He grabbed a few cans and they walked back outside. Riley gave her a look when she sat back down at the fire pit. Jenn shrugged slightly so only Riley could see, and her friend nodded.

They stayed around the fire talking until Jake decided that he and Kelly should get home.

"Big day tomorrow, need our energy," he said, standing and taking Kelly's hand. Jake made his way around the circle, hugging the girls and shaking the guys' hands. Riley and Jenn walked with him toward his car.

"Well, this is going to suck," Riley said, wiping her nose. "We've never been this far apart."

Jake pulled her into a bear hug and kissed her forehead. "I'll be home for holidays and anytime I need a break. You guys are welcome to visit, too." Riley kissed his cheek before turning back toward the fire. Jake and Jenn stood about a foot apart in silence.

"So …" he said again. She smiled weakly and stepped in to hug him. They stood hugging for several minutes.

"You know I love you, right?" Jenn whispered in his year. "Always have, always will."

Jake inhaled sharply. "I know. I love you too. More than you know," he whispered back. They pulled apart and their faces were inches away from each other. Jenn leaned forward and kissed him gently and quickly. She pulled back and cleared her throat. A jolt of electricity had surged in her stomach. Jake stood very still and looked at her with a blank expression.

Kelly walked up and broke the silence. "Ready to go, babe?" she asked, glancing between Jake and Jenn.

Jake nodded, "Yeah, yeah. Let's go." He gave Jenn one last glance and got into the car. Jenn waved slowly as they pulled away. She took several deep breaths and stood watching the car drive down the road.

Riley came up next to her and looped her arm into Jenn's. "You OK?" she whispered.

"As I can be," Jenn whispered back. They turned and walked back to the fire. The group dispersed and headed home shortly after Jake left.

Mike and Jenn were silent on the drive home, Jenn resting her head on the window and looking up at the night sky.

He didn't say anything until they were in the apartment. "You seem distraught."

Jenn nodded and grabbed a glass of water. "It's a big thing. Riley, Jake and I haven't been apart like this since high school." She sipped the water, and Mike stood with his arms crossed, staring at her.

"Is that all this is?" he asked. Jenn looked at him, trying to figure out his expression.

"What do you mean?"

He shuffled his stance and uncrossed his arms. "You seem *really* upset about this. In fact, you've been a little distant lately in general." Jenn sat down at the kitchen table and tapped her water glass nervously.

"I don't like change. I like comfort and routine. Everything is starting to change." She blurted out. Mike walked over and sat across from her.

"It happens, babe. I'm here to help you through it." He reached out for her hand. She looked up into his eyes and a multitude of emotions flashed through her head. She was so grateful for Mike and she really did care for him. She also was confused by the feeling she just had as Jake left. How can she have one and ignore the other? And which one did she want to ignore?

Jenn smiled weakly and pulled his hand in for a kiss. "Thank you." She stared at him, a little more intensely, willing herself to decide. "Mike?" she said softly.

"Yeah?"

"I think you should give up your lease."

He leaned back and smiled. "Really? Are you sure about that?"

Jenn nodded and smiled widely. "I want you to move in here with me."

Mike stood and walked over for a hug, Jenn standing to meet him. They hugged tightly, and Mike picked her up to spin her around. "I love you," Mike said. She laughed as he set her down, kissing him.

Jenn stepped back, momentarily panicked that she didn't feel that jolt of energy in her stomach. She shook her head and led Mike into the bedroom. She figured, or was hoping, that this was just nerves. A decision was made, and that was that.

Chapter 37

Jake called several days later to say that they were all moved in and gave a tour of his new apartment via video chat. They talked briefly and promised to call often.

Mike started moving things into Jenn's apartment shortly after she made her decision. He was fully moved in before school started.

Everything settled into a nice rhythm, between her work and his work. She started to feel very comfortable with him being there and her nervousness about her choice lessened over time.

She started having her morning coffee dates with Riley now, trying to fill the void that Jake left. They had a little time between their work schedules to meet.

"So, did you talk to Jake yesterday?" Riley asked, sipping her coffee.

"Yeah, he seems good. Really adjusting to school and the new city." Jenn stirred her coffee slowly. She half-hoped that Jake would hate everything about Boston and come home.

"He looked happy when I talked to him," Riley said. "And, how are you doing with everything?" she asked Jenn in a motherly fashion.

Jenn laughed. "Fine, mom. I'm good. Really." She squeezed Riley's hand. They sat in silence and drank their coffee.

"Oh, he's coming back in a few weeks for the holidays. The school gives them two whole weeks, and he and Kelly want to meet up for Christmas dinner," Riley said.

Jenn smiled. It would be nice to be together to celebrate Christmas. "Your house?" she asked. Riley nodded.

They finished their coffee and headed out, Riley to work and Jenn to home. Jenn really enjoyed the holiday season and it would be more complete with Jake being home.

She and Mike were heading to her parents' house the weekend before Christmas and they were having dinner with Mike's parents on Christmas Eve. It was their second Christmas together and they promised to not get each other gifts and focus on friends and family instead. Jake and Kelly got into town the week of Christmas and they all agreed to dinner at Riley and Curt's on Christmas Day.

The trip to Jenn's hometown went well. Her parents liked Mike very much. Jenn also really enjoyed the time with Mike's family.

They came home late on Christmas Eve, stomachs full of a wonderful meal, and carrying a box of presents from Mike's family. They set everything in the living room and settled on the couch.

Jenn stared at the Christmas tree and its twinkling lights. "Good Christmas," she sighed, leaning her head on Mike's shoulder.

"It really has been," he said quietly, kissing the top of her head. "You know, it's been a really good year all around." Jenn nodded and cuddled closer. "Jenn, I'm really glad that I found you."

She sat up to look at him directly. "I feel the same way. You really helped me out of a dark place. Thank you." She leaned in and kissed him.

"You know, I never really knew how great a relationship could be until we happened. This last year has been amazing and I'm so happy." He started to sound like he was rambling, and Jenn thought it was adorable that he was nervous.

"It has been amazing. I never thought I would find a happy place after what happened. You are my happy place." She smiled and Mike looked down at her hands.

"I love you so much. I couldn't ask for a better gift than you," he said. He stood up from the couch and fumbled in his pocket. Jenn took a sharp inhale and held her breath, her heart beating fast.

"Well, I could actually think of one." He slowly got

down on one knee while pulling a small red velvet box from his side pocket. "Jenn, I know I will never find anyone like you ever again. I don't want to find anyone else. I want you, just you. Forever. Jenn, will you marry me?" Jenn had her hands covering her mouth as she started to hyperventilate. Tears filled her eyes as she looked from the ring to Mike.

"I thought we said no presents," she whispered finally.

Mike laughed and took her hand. "I lied." He smiled as Jenn lowered her other hand and held it out to him. He slipped the ring onto her finger and looked up at her. "Is that a yes?" he asked. Jenn was frozen for a moment as she looked at the ring.

Slowly she started to nod her head before managing a weak, "Yes."

He pulled her up into a tight hug and kissed her. She calmed her breathing and stared at the ring. "What just happened?" she asked with a laugh.

"You just got a fiancé for Christmas," Mike joked. She looked back at him and smiled before pulling him into another kiss. She turned him and pushed him onto the couch and climbed on top of him.

"I love you," she whispered as he kissed her neck. At that moment, she had no panic or fear. All she saw was Mike and that made her happier than she had been in a long time.

After Mike fell asleep, Jenn snuck into the bathroom with her phone. She took a picture of her hand and sent it to Riley. It was late, so she didn't expect an answer. Surprisingly, her phone started ringing after a few minutes. She answered it quietly only to be met with a shriek on Riley's end. "Shh, calm down," Jenn laughed.

"Oh my god, oh my god. Did you even expect that?" Riley asked in a rapid voice.

Jenn laughed again. "Not at all. It kind of blindsided me, but in a really good way. It felt right."

Riley squealed again. "I cannot wait to hear the details tomorrow. Happy Christmas!" They said goodbye, and Jenn ended the call. She sat on the bathroom floor for several minutes looking at the ring. She truly had no doubts about saying yes to Mike, but she was nervous to tell Jake for some reason.

She and Mike spent Christmas Day together, making desserts for the dinner that evening. That night, they arrived at Riley's a little early to help set up.

Jenn walked into the kitchen with her desserts, and Riley shrieked and ran over, nearly knocking the pans out of Jenn's hands. "Let me see, let me see!" she squealed. Jenn held out her left hand and Riley sighed. "It's beautiful, Mike. Well done." She pulled Mike into a tight hug and he chuckled. Curt walked over and shook his hand, congratulating him. Jenn and Riley were talking excitedly when Jake and Kelly arrived.

"What's the commotion?" Jake asked. Jenn felt the urge to pull her hand out of view, but Riley grabbed it and held it up for Jake and Kelly to see. Kelly clapped and walked quickly over to see, but Jake stood in place and kept eye contact with Jenn. Jenn tried to read his expression but couldn't. She turned her attention to Kelly instead and started to tell her about the proposal. Jake slowly walked over to Mike and patted his shoulder. "Congrats, man." Jenn watched him closely. Jake had a smile on his face, but it looked strained.

Jenn pulled her hand back after a few minutes and changed the subject. "Riley, the food smells great. What can we help with?" Riley set tasks for Jenn and Kelly while the guys set the table and got drinks ready.

Before long, the sounds of dishes and silverware clinking filled the air. Jake talked about school and Boston while Kelly beamed at him. Jenn listened, but couldn't shake the feeling that he was upset.

After dinner and dessert, they all went into the living room to open presents, with Riley's kids taking center stage. They had all agreed to buy presents only for the kids. Curt put on an old Christmas movie and lit the fireplace while the kids tore open the presents and laughed. Riley sat on the couch behind them taking pictures. Jenn sat on the ground to help the kids with whatever they needed.

After an hour of playing, both kids started to whine, and Riley decided to put them to bed. Curt and Riley carried them upstairs and Jenn settled into a chair with Mike. "So, Boston's working out well?" Jenn asked Jake and Kelly.

Kelly smiled at Jake before answering. "It's been so great. Our apartment is so nice and in a really nice area. My new job is amazing and I'm making some new friends. Jake's doing well in school, of course." Jake smiled and shrugged.

Jenn sipped on her glass of wine. "Of course, smarty pants. I couldn't have gotten into Harvard." Jenn joked. Jake gave a weak smile and sipped his drink.

Kelly didn't notice but continued to talk. "So, Mike. How long have you been planning this proposal?"

Mike put his arm around Jenn. "A while. I mean, I would have proposed right away if I knew she wouldn't have run away. She's something else." He leaned over and kissed her forehead.

Jenn blushed and looked toward Jake. He was staring into his glass. "That she is," he muttered. Kelly shot him a look and he cleared his throat. "Sorry, I'm just so excited for you both," Jake said quickly, trying to cover his tracks. Mike raised his glass and hugged Jenn closer to his side. Jenn blushed and looked away.

Riley and Curt returned and steered the awkward

conversation away from Jenn and Mike. As the fire died down and the wine bottle emptied, everyone decided to head home for the night. Jake and Kelly would be returning to Boston the next day.

Jenn and Jake ended up alone for a moment while collecting coats and purses. "So, getting married?" he asked quietly.

"That's the plan." She was nervous.

"Well, at least this one's not a jerk," Jake replied, smiling.

Jenn smiled back, but she had a knot in her stomach. "Jake, you seem upset." She placed a hand on his arm, and he stopped fussing with the coats. He looked at her and didn't say anything at first.

"You know, I don't know," he finally replied. Jenn was about to ask him to explain what he meant when Kelly walked over.

"Are you ready, babe?" she asked, looking back and forth between Jake and Jenn.

He pulled his coat from the pile and handed Kelly her coat. "Yeah, let's get going." He paused before pulling Jenn into a tight hug. "I really am happy for you." He whispered in her ear. She squeezed him once and then let go.

Jenn turned and gave Kelly a quick hug. "We'll see you guys in a few months," Jenn said as they walked to the door. Jake and Kelly said goodbye to everyone else before walking out to their car. Jenn stood in the doorway and watched as they drove away.

Riley stood next to her and squeezed her arm. "Are you OK?" she whispered.

Jenn nodded, "Yeah, but I don't know what's going on with him," she whispered back. Riley shrugged, and they turned back inside. Riley and Jenn cleared the table while Mike and Curt picked up the living room.

"Thanks for having us," Mike said, shaking Curt's hand and hugging Riley.

"Anytime." Riley replied. Jenn and Mike gathered their things and left for home. It had been a great holiday season and Jenn was happy, but she still worried about Jake. She couldn't put her finger on it, but she knew something was off. She also did not want to discuss it with Mike because she thought it would be awkward. She pushed the thoughts to the back of her mind and assumed that Jake would talk to her if he needed her.

Chapter 38

Jenn entered the new year with a sense of excitement for the future. Jenn had decided to go back to school for her master's degree and would start applying for the fall semester. Her therapist decided that she only needed to come in annually, barring any issues.

She and Mike were doing well but had not started planning for the wedding. Mike understood that Jenn needed time to plan, so he didn't push. They kept in touch with Jake, who was doing well in school and stayed in Boston over the summer to take some extra courses and to do an internship. Jenn missed him, but video chats made the distance a little easier. He promised to be home again over the holidays.

Jenn and Mike decided to move into a bigger apartment over the summer, closer to Mike's new school. His new job was at a high school across town. Jenn was accepted into a master's program and would be able to do most of her work online. She was also given the new job of charge nurse at work. Near the end of summer, Riley found out she was expecting again, and Curt joked that three was enough.

Mike's job transition went smoothly, and Jenn was able to jump into school without issue. Jake entered his second year of med school and continued at the top of his class. Jake said that Kelly had talked about going back to school as well.

The next few months of adjustment went by quickly, and Jenn was glad when the holidays came around. Riley called her one night while she was wrapping presents.

"Hey, Jake's not coming home for the holidays. I just got off the phone with him. He said he was swamped with schoolwork."

Jenn felt her stomach drop. "That awful," she said. Riley promised that they would video chat with him on Christmas day from her house. Jenn hung up with Riley and sent a quick text to Jake.

Sorry you're stuck in Boston for the holidays. We miss you.

She continued wrapping presents and went to bed before she received a reply.

The next day she had planned on last minute shopping with Riley. They were walking around the mall, looking in windows when Jenn stopped suddenly. Riley tried to look and figure out what Jenn was staring at when she saw Kevin and a woman looking at a table of books about 10 feet away from them. Riley tried to pull Jenn's arm to get her to move away, but Kevin looked up and caught both of their eyes. He didn't move at first, but then slowly raised his arm and gave an awkward wave. Jenn stared at him and forced herself to wave back. Kevin whispered something to the woman he was with before walking towards them. Riley inhaled sharply as Jenn squeezed her arm.

"Hi Jenn, Riley," Kevin said as he reached the two of them. Riley looked to Jenn, who hadn't broken her stare, and then back to Kevin.

"Hey Kevin. How are you?" she asked.

Kevin looked at Jenn and then back to Riley. "I'm fine, and you two?"

Jenn finally shook her head and answered. "Great. We're great." She rocked on her heels and looked toward the woman that Kevin was with.

"Man, it's been awhile," Kevin said, snapping Jenn's attention back to him.

"Yeah, almost seven years."

He scratched his head nervously. "I'd love to catch up. Would you want to grab a coffee sometime?"

Jenn looked at Riley and then back at Kevin, pausing briefly before answering. "Sure." Kevin wrote down his number and handed it to Jenn. Jenn stared at it and noticed he had changed it after she blocked him.

The woman walked over from the book table and stood next to Kevin. "Jenn, Riley. This is my wife, Susan."

Jenn and Riley shook her hand. Jenn stared at her and realized she was several months pregnant.

"So nice to meet you, Kevin has told me so much about you both," she said. Jenn and Riley looked at Kevin with confused looks.

"Nice to see you again," Kevin said, taking Susan's hand and turning to walk back to the book table. Jenn waved and then turned slowly to Riley.

"That was awkward," she muttered.

"He seems happy. Maybe he finally grew up," Riley said. Jenn tucked the number into her pocket. She wasn't sure if she would call him or not.

They finished with their shopping and headed home. Jenn was still in a state of shock when she walked into her apartment. Mike must have noticed, because he stopped in his tracks when she walked in the door. "Are you all right?" he asked, walking over to her and placing a hand on her shoulder.

Jenn nodded and set down her bags. "Um, we ran into Kevin," she said, not meeting Mike's eye. "He was with his wife, who is pregnant. He gave me his number and he said he'd love to catch up." She kept looking down, not wanting to see Mike's reaction.

"Well, I think that's great. Isn't it?" he asked after a

moment. Jenn looked up at him and met his gaze. She really took for granted what a genuinely good man Mike was.

"You're, OK with that?" she stumbled over the question.

Mike shrugged. "I think it will help. Maybe, air things out?" Jenn smiled and made a mental note to text Kevin the next day.

Mike and Jenn wrapped presents and watched holiday movies that night. "How is it that you are so OK with me having coffee with my ex-fiancé?" she asked.

Mike paused and thought about it. "I don't know, I just am. I don't see a threat, and everyone has a past."

Jenn smiled and nodded. "You really are a good guy, you know that?" she leaned over and kissed him.

"Yeah, it's a curse and a blessing," he joked. They put the wrapped presents under the Christmas tree and headed to bed.

Jenn was flipping through a bridal magazine while Mike finished up some emails. He looked over at the magazine and smiled. "So, any more idea about our wedding?"

She put the magazine down and looked at him. "Just getting ideas. I still don't think we need to rush anything."

Mike sighed and rolled onto his back, looking up. "I know. I just want to know where we are." He looked offended.

Jenn reached over and took his hand. "We're here. Now. The wedding is just a party, you know? I'm with you and we love each other. That's what's important."

Mike smiled and leaned over to kiss her. "Absolutely." Jenn set the magazine aside and turned off the light. She nestled into Mike's arm and closed her eyes. She always got nervous when he started talking about the wedding because she still had her doubts, though she didn't want him to know that. There was no rhyme or reason to her skittishness, but it was there, and it was nagging. She figured when it was right, she would know.

The next day was Christmas Eve and Jenn and Mike would be having dinner at Mike's parents' house. During the afternoon, Jenn decided to send a quick text to Kevin asking about going for coffee. They agreed on meeting a few days after Christmas. Jenn was nervous, but excited.

The dinner with Mike's mom and dad went well, although his mother asked about wedding plans. Mike steered the conversation and answered well enough to satisfy his parents for the time being.

Christmas day was spent with Riley, Curt, and their kids. After a huge meal and presents, Riley and Jenn decided to video chat with Jake. When he answered, he looked tired and disheveled.

"Hey Jake, how are you?" Riley asked in a worried tone.

He ran his hand through his hair and smiled. "Just busy. Who'd have thought becoming a doctor would be such hard work?"

"We miss you!" Jenn said. "Did Kelly stay with you?"

Jake looked away from the computer for a moment and then replied, "Uh, no. She went home for the holidays. Said she missed her family."

Jenn and Riley exchanged a look. "I'm sorry to hear that. We're sending out your present tomorrow, so keep an eye out for it," Riley said.

Jake smiled. "I'll be back during summer for a week or two. I assume this is only going to get harder, so I better catch a break when I can." They chatted briefly before ending the call.

Jenn stared at the screen after it went blank. "He looks awful. Poor thing." Riley patted her back and they returned to the living room.

After a few more drinks they decided to end the night. Mike and Jenn left with a handful of gifts. Jenn was leaning against the car window when Mike broke the silence.

"How's Jake?" he asked.

Jenn shrugged. "He looks worn out, like he could use a break." She sat up and looked at Mike. "He doesn't talk to us like he used to, and I feel like he hasn't been home in years."

Mike nodded and kept his eyes on the road. "Honey, he goes to Harvard medical school. He's studying to be a doctor. I'm sure no one assumed that would be an easy path." Jenn sighed. She knew Mike was right, but she missed Jake always being there. She wished she could visit him, but school and work did not give her much free time either.

Chapter 39

A few days after Christmas, Jenn found herself sitting in a small coffee shop waiting for Kevin. She was nervous and didn't know what to expect. She had arrived several minutes early and was stirring her coffee absentmindedly, trying to think what she would say to Kevin. He walked into the shop and spotted her sitting by the windows. She waved, and he walked over to the table. Jenn stood and awkwardly hugged him before sitting back down. Kevin went to the counter to order a drink before joining her.

"You look well," he said.

"As do you." There was a pause as she continued to stir her drink.

He chuckled. "Didn't think this would be easy."

She smiled. "I'm sorry, I just don't know what to say."

He nodded and took a sip of his drink. "Can I start?" he asked. Jenn gestured for him to continue and leaned back in her chair. "First, Jenn, I want to say how truly sorry I am." Jenn bit her lip and nodded, crossing her arms. "I was a stupid kid back then and you didn't deserve that." She nodded again, staying silent. "I would say I wish I could take it all back, but not all of it was bad. You know?"

She stared at him. "No, not all of it was bad," she said quietly.

Kevin smiled nervously before continuing. "Second, I hate what you went through afterwards. I feel sick just thinking about it. Curt called me when it happened and yelled at me for hours. I am so, so sorry. I'm glad you are OK now."

Jenn continued to stare at him. She hadn't realized that he had kept up on her after they broke up. "I'm glad I'm OK too."

There was another awkward pause of. "Enough of that. How are you now? Still working at the same place? Or are you running it now?" Kevin leaned forward and folded his hands together, which made Jenn chuckle.

"Same place, but not running it. I'm in school to get my master's degree. I think I might want to teach nursing someday. And this." She said, holding out her left hand to show off her ring.

Kevin reached forward to take her hand and she tensed momentarily. "Wow, congrats. Tell me about him."

Jenn pulled her hand back and smiled, looking at her ring. "His name is Mike, he's a teacher. We've been together two years and engaged one."

Kevin nodded and chuckled. "I'm happy for you.

When's the big day?"

Jenn frowned and fidgeted with the ring. "No date yet. There's no rush. I'm working on school and he just switched from middle school to high school teaching, so things are hectic."

Kevin reached forward and put his hand over hers. She looked up at him. "Jenn, it's fine. I'm not prying, just interested. It's okay to be nervous about this. I was, but my wife wants a big family, so I figured I couldn't wait too long."

Jenn smiled at him. He had grown up. "Well, looks like you're doing fine there."

Kevin beamed. "Yeah, it's a boy. He's due in April."

She nodded and patted his hand. "I'm happy for you." She was overcome with the need to talk about her fears, but she wasn't sure if Kevin was the person she should be talking to. "Kevin, can I ask you something strange?" He leaned back and nodded. She paused for a moment, trying to think of the right thing to say. "Why do you think that I can't plan this wedding?"

Kevin inhaled and leaned forward again. "Don't know if I can answer that." He tapped his fingers on the table, took a sip of his coffee and continued. "Let me ask you this question. Are you one hundred percent sure that you want to marry this man?"

Jenn's eyes widened, and she took a deep breath. "Mike is a great guy and he treats me so well. He loves me, and I love him. We're good together." She rambled and tapped her ring on her cup.

Kevin laughed softly. "You didn't answer the question."

Jenn looked at him and he raised an eyebrow. "Oh god," she whispered.

Kevin moved his chair around the table until he was next to her. "Don't dig too deep into it. I was just trying to clear your mind."

Jenn was breathing quickly, and her chest tightened. "No, you're right. I didn't answer. I don't know the answer." Kevin put his arm around her, and she leaned her head on his shoulder. For a moment she forgot everything that had happened between them. She shook her head when she realized what she was doing. "Well, since you seem to be better at this than I am. What's holding me back?"

Kevin sat back in his chair and whistled. "Well, one, I was a bad example of what can happen in a relationship. Two, maybe there's something or someone holding you back?" He said the last part quickly.

Jenn looked at him, confused. "What do you mean?"

Kevin clicked his tongue before continuing. "Can I

ask something without you getting mad?" Jenn nodded, and Kevin continued. "How's your relationship with Jake been?"

Jenn looked down at her lap and blushed. "He's in Boston for medical school. I haven't seen him in months and he's so busy. Last time we talked he looked so worn out, I'm worried about him."

She looked up at Kevin and he was smiling. "You see, that's your problem."

Jenn raised her eyebrow and shook her head. "He's my best friend, I'm allowed to worry about him."

Kevin laughed and patted her shoulder. "Jenn, he was the only guy I ever worried about during our whole relationship. I don't know how Mike handles it, but I know the truth. He's not just your best friend."

Jenn felt her face flush again. "No, he has a girlfriend and I have a fiancé. He moved to Boston with her. I'm just worried because I am used to having him here."

Kevin nodded. "And now that he's not here, you have more time to think about it? I think when he was here, you two could hide it better. Distance does that, especially when it comes to feelings."

Jenn felt her stomach drop. She couldn't look up at Kevin because she felt embarrassed. "It's OK, Jenn. Relationships and feelings are funny things. But the doubt, that's there because something isn't right. Now, you can either work on your current relationship, or you can try to work out these feelings you are having."

She looked up at him and he was staring at her with a smug look on his face. "You really have changed." Jen smiled weakly.

"Yeah, sometimes it takes a pretty big event to make you realize that you were being a complete ass." Kevin put his arm around Jenn and hugged her. She didn't flinch, and that made her realize that she was finally ready to let go of her past.

"Thank you, Kevin, I didn't know how much I needed this."

He looked at his watch. "I better get home. It was so nice to see you again. Please don't be a stranger." Kevin stood and grabbed his coat.

"I won't. Good luck with the baby and thank Susan for letting me borrow you." She reached up and he took her hand, giving it a squeeze before he walked out of the shop. She watched him walk away, feeling both relieved and confused about what he had said. Was Jake the reason she couldn't set a wedding date? She couldn't bring herself to think that.

Jenn finished her coffee and left the shop, walking through the streets and looking into store windows. She let her mind wander, trying to picture her future with Mike. She didn't have an idea of what she wanted for the wedding or where she saw herself in five years. Nothing had been stable for a long time with her, so she didn't know what to expect.

Her mind wandered to Jake. She couldn't help herself. He knew her better than anyone, and they had been through so much, so of course she would feel a connection to him. After an hour, Jenn realized that her walk was doing nothing to clear her head, so she began to head towards home.

Mike was waiting for her when she got to the apartment. He tried to play cool, but she knew he was nervous about Kevin. "So, how was it?" he asked.

Jenn tossed her purse on the counter and sat down next to him. "Good. Great, actually. He has really grown up, and he apologized for everything that happened. It's like a weight has been lifted."

Mike reached over and squeezed her hand. "Well, then I'm glad that you went." Jenn nodded.

Chapter 40

Jenn had to work that night, so Mike had made dinner. They ate together and talked, but Jenn didn't tell him everything Kevin said. She took a shower and changed into her work clothes.

Mike liked to drive her to work so she didn't have to take the bus. "Have a great night and I'll pick you up in the morning," Mike said as he kissed her goodnight.

"I love you," she said as she got out of the car.

Jenn swiped her badge to get into the building and she made her way to the employee locker room. Nicole was already there, looking through a magazine. "Hey," Jenn said as she punched in for the shift.

She and Nicole headed out to the nurse's station and got the reports from the previous nurses. They started their rounds, and Nicole began chatting about her new boyfriend. Jenn nodded and yawned.

"Am I boring you?" Nicole asked. Jenn shook her head.

"No, I just didn't rest today. Um, I had coffee with Kevin." Jenn kept walking a few steps before she realized Nicole wasn't next to her.

"Excuse me?" she asked. Jenn repeated herself, and Nicole replied "What?" in a scream whisper.

Jenn told Nicole about bumping into Kevin while they were shopping and that she thought that talking with him might give her some closure. Nicole nodded, her mouth hanging open the entire time.

"He also gave me some advice. He's grown up quite a bit," Jenn said.

Nicole shook her head and closed her mouth. "What advice?"

Jenn shrugged. "He just wanted to know why I hadn't set a wedding date yet." They made their way back to the nurse's desk and sat down. Jenn took a drink of coffee and Nicole stared at her.

"And?" she asked.

"Oh, well, he thinks I have doubts," Jenn replied.

Nicole turned to her computer and started typing. "And do you?"

Jenn shrugged again and started typing on her computer. "I don't really know what's bothering me. I mean, my track record stinks. I just have a nagging in the back of my mind that won't let go."

Nicole nodded, still typing. "Well, whatever it is, I

wouldn't commit to a date until you figure it out." Jenn nodded and smiled. Everyone made sense when they told her to wait, but she was afraid of hurting Mike.

Then she frowned. "He's going to want an answer eventually. We can't be engaged forever."

Nicole stopped typing and turned toward Jenn, "True, true. But you can make an excuse right now. You have to focus on school, so you can be done in three years." She turned back to the computer.

"That's a perfect idea. Hopefully, my brain unmixes before then." Jenn laughed. Nicole smiled and winked at her.

By morning, Jenn was exhausted and was happy to see Mike waiting for her. "Good morning, I am so tired," she said, leaning over to kiss him. He brought her a coffee and she drank it quickly, grateful for his thoughtfulness. Once she was home, she collapsed onto the couch and slept for several hours.

Chapter 41

After the holidays, Jenn and Mike went back to their busy schedules and didn't even have time to stop and think about planning a wedding. Jenn was relieved because she hadn't been able to shake her doubt. Occasionally, she thought Mike would bring it up, but he didn't.

Riley had her second son in early April and Kevin's son was born two weeks later. Jenn helped at Curt and Riley's when she got home from the hospital, occasionally taking the other two children out of the house so Riley could have a little time with her newborn. Mike always came along and was great with the kids. Jenn also visited with Kevin and Susan about a month after their son was born. Mike came and met Kevin for the first time, which was surprisingly not awkward.

Between school, work, and helping Riley, Jenn's days and months flew by. She didn't get to chat with Jake as much as before, but his schoolwork had increased as well.

Before she knew it, the school year was over, and she was helping Mike clean out his classroom. The anniversary of her accident came and went without anyone noticing for the first time. Even her therapist, Rebecca, was impressed by her progress. After consulting with Jenn's doctor, they decided to cut her medication in half. But even with all the positives in her life, Jenn still couldn't shake her feeling of doubt.

With school on break for summer, she and Mike were able to spend more time together. Mike even agreed to start jogging with Jenn, and they planned to run a 10K at the end of summer. They spent a lot of time at parks with Riley and her kids.

One Saturday afternoon, she and Riley were sitting on a bench at the park with the baby while Mike chased the toddlers. Jenn was in the middle of a sentence when she stopped. Kelly was walking past with a handful of shopping bags. "Kelly!" Jenn hollered and waved. Kelly looked over and paused, but did not wave. She started to walk away, and Jenn jogged over to where she was. "Hey, Kelly, what are you doing home?" Jenn asked, trying to catch her breath.

Kelly looked toward the park and then back to Jenn. "Um, I've been back for about a month."

Jenn was confused and raised an eyebrow. "A month? What do you mean? Is Jake with you?"

Kelly adjusted the shopping bags on her arm. "No, he's still in Boston."

Jenn stared at her but didn't speak. There was a long pause before Kelly sighed. "Look, we broke up." Jenn's mouth opened and closed slowly, but she couldn't find the words. "I knew he wouldn't tell you," Kelly muttered.

Jenn crossed her arms, feeling offended. "What does that mean?"

Kelly set the bags down. "Oh, come on, Jenn." Jenn looked back to the park where Riley was staring at the two of them. Kelly rolled her eyes. "I was never a match for you. I was sick of trying."

Jenn took a step back. "Me? What do I have to do with anything? I've barely spoken to Jake."

Kelly leaned down to pick up her bags. "Doesn't matter. He's always going to choose you." She turned and walked away, leaving Jenn stunned. Jenn turned slowly and walked back to where Riley was sitting.

She sat down and stared towards the playground while Riley waited in anticipation. "Oh, come on. What was that about?"

Jenn shook her head. "She and Jake broke up and she moved back here a month ago." ·

Jenn heard Riley inhale sharply. "A month ago? He didn't tell me. Did he tell you?" she asked. Jenn shook her head again.

Mike walked over holding Riley's kids by the hands. "Was that Kelly?"

Jenn looked at Riley and then back to Mike. "Yeah, she's home for a visit." Riley gave her a look.

"Oh, that's nice. Is Jake here, too?" Mike asked, setting the kids on the bench and tying the boy's shoe.

"No, no. He had too much going on with school," Riley answered. She lightly elbowed Jenn's side so she would snap out of her trance. Mike didn't notice. "Well, I have to get these guys home for lunch." Riley put the baby in his carrier and gathered up her things.

Mike and Jenn walked to Riley's car with the other two children. Riley buckled everyone in before pausing to make eye contact with Jenn. "Thanks. I will talk to you later," she said emphatically. Jenn nodded and took Mike's hand before backing away from the car.

"Is she all right?" Mike asked with a concerned tone. Jenn nodded and walked over to Mike's car without saying anything. Her head was spinning. What did Kelly mean when she said that Jake chose Jenn? She sat in silence, staring out the window as Mike pulled away.

The silence continued as they walked into the apartment and Jenn sat down at the kitchen table. Mike grabbed a bottle of water and placed it in front of her. "Jenn? What's going on?" he asked. She looked up at him slowly, and he looked worried.

She took a drink of water and halfheartedly shrugged her shoulders. "I don't know."

He sat down across from her and took her hand.

"You need to talk to me. It's not good to keep things in."
Jenn looked up into his eyes. She felt her chest tighten.
Clearing her throat, she told him what Kelly had told her. He
sat silent and nodded, his face not showing any emotion.

"OK? Well, you didn't have anything to do with it,
right? I'm sure he's just stressed with school, and Kelly does
seem to be a little clingy. Don't put this on yourself," he said
as he patted her hand.

She nodded. "Yeah, of course." She forced herself to
smile. The nagging in the back of her head intensified, but
she ignored it.

The truth was that she didn't know what Jake was
thinking. Maybe Kelly was just making excuses for her
failed relationship. Maybe Mike was right. Jenn figured
that Jake would call when he was ready to talk about it.

But weeks went by and she heard nothing from him.
Riley said that he had texted her that he was fine and
working on an internship for the summer. "But he didn't
mention Kelly or anything?" Jenn asked.

"Not at all," Riley replied. Neither of them knew
what was going on, and it was really getting to Jenn. She
was too afraid to broach the topic by calling him, so she just
let it be. Mike tried to support her and encouraged her to
call Jake, but she always said no. Instead, she threw herself
into work and preparing for the next semester of school.
Although he never mentioned it, Mike seemed to be leery of

the whole situation.

Chapter 42

Mike decided to take Jenn out for a nice dinner near the end of July. Jenn was grateful for the night out since she had been working so hard. Mike looked nervous, but Jenn had no idea why. They sat down at the restaurant and ordered their meal. There was little talk between them. He fidgeted with his napkin and Jenn reached across the table for his hand.

Mike looked up and Jenn noticed he looked sad. "Mike? What is it?"

He stopped fidgeting and leaned forward to take both of her hands. "I think it's time we talked about this."

"This what?" she asked, genuinely confused.

Mike smiled weakly. "What's been bothering you this past month." Jenn pulled her hands back and leaned back in her chair. She looked at her hand and fiddled with her ring.

"Nothing has been ..." she started before Mike cut her off.

"Come on, Jenn. I may be a nice guy who won't bring it up, but I'm not blind." She looked at him and noticed his eyes starting to water. She felt her heart beating fast.

"I don't know what you mean." Her cheeks were starting to burn.

He sighed and crossed his arms. "OK. Fine." Then he leaned forward quickly and spoke in a low tone. "No. This needs to be out in the open." Jenn was taken aback. She sat with her mouth slightly open, not saying anything. "Then I guess I'll just say it." Mike inhaled deeply. "You've been distant ever since you talked to Kelly about Jake."

Jenn exhaled. She didn't realize that she had been holding her breath. "I'm … I'm just concerned. He's there, all alone. He hasn't talked to me about it."

Mike laughed. "Of course, he hasn't. He's as stubborn as you are." Jenn looked at him quizzically. "Again, I'm not blind, Jenn. I knew right away that there was something between the two of you."

Jenn sat in silence, her mind racing, trying to find a response to his statement. The waitress interrupted her thoughts by bringing their food. Mike started eating and Jenn sat there, dumbfounded.

She watched Mike carefully as a tear rolled down her cheek. "I don't know how you want me to respond to that," she said after several minutes.

Mike set down his fork and looked at her. "Let's start by speaking honestly for once. I'm a big boy and I can handle it."

Jenn took several deep breaths, trying to stop herself from crying. "Mike, I love you. What is going on?" she said with an air of panic.

He smiled gently and took her hand. "I never said you didn't. I just want to know what's going on in your head." He pulled his hand back and took a few more bites of food. Jenn stared at her plate.

"I don't know what's going on in my mind." She picked up her napkin and dabbed her eyes before looking back at Mike.

"Can I give this a go?" he asked. Jenn's eyes widened, and she slowly nodded. "At least from my perspective." He paused and took a deep breath. "There are some unresolved feelings between you and Jake." Jenn started to say something, but he held up his hand. "I'm not accusing or saying anything bad about it, but it's just a fact." Jenn looked down at her hand again, staring at her ring. "Jenn, I just want it out there. It seems to be looming over you like a dark cloud."

She looked back at him and sniffed. "So, what can I do about it?"

Mike sighed. "Well, I assume that this isn't going to go any further until you figure that out."

Jenn stared at him. "Are you breaking up with me?"

Mike laughed softly. "Not at all. I love you, but I need to know that you are all in this with me."

Jenn took several deep breaths. She looked around her at the people sitting close by, worried that she was causing a scene. No one seemed to notice her.

"So, what are you wanting?" she asked without looking directly at him.

Mike moved his chair closer to her. "I am going to Chicago for a week to meet with an old friend. I want you to talk to Jake, to figure this out."

Jenn looked at him in awe. "How did I end up with such a great man?"

Mike laughed and put his arm over her shoulder. "I know, that darn curse again."

Jenn managed a weak smile. "After you get back, we can start planning then. OK?" Jenn leaned into his side. Mike nodded and kissed her forehead.

They left the restaurant and headed home. Jenn held on tight to Mike's hand the entire drive, feeling a sense of panic. She wasn't sure if it was the panic of Mike leaving for Chicago or the fact that she had to confront Jake.

Mike left early the next day and Jenn spent the morning trying to come up with a plan. She was nervous to call Jake, let alone air out all their dirty laundry.

She talked to Riley briefly, and Riley was on Mike's side. Jenn half-hoped that Riley would tell her it was a horrible idea, but she encouraged her to call Jake.

Jenn paced through her apartment, formulating a plan. Each time she sat in front of her laptop to call Jake, she panicked and began pacing again.

She was pouring herself a cup of coffee when her computer chimed. She turned it towards her to check the notification and nearly choked on her coffee.

Jake had sent a message saying, *Hey, I need to talk to you. When can we chat?*

Jenn's heart was beating rapidly, and she felt flushed. She took a large drink of coffee and tapped her fingers on the kitchen counter.

After a few minutes she pulled the computer toward her and replied, *I'm off today, so anytime.*

She hit send and a moment later a notification came across for a video chat. Jenn inhaled and pushed the accept button. Jake popped up on the screen. He looked tired and hadn't shaved in a few days.

"Hey Jenn," he said awkwardly.

Jenn gave a wave and sat down with her computer at the kitchen table. "How are you?" she asked.

Jake smiled and shrugged. "Been having a bit of a rough patch, but I'm working through it." He ran his hand through his hair, which was also longer than usual. They sat in silence for a minute.

"So?" Jenn asked with anticipation.

Jake cleared his throat and fidgeted in his seat. "So, I got an email and a text saying that I needed to talk to you." Jenn opened and closed her mouth, unable to answer. "Yeah, your best friend and fiancé are quite persistent."

Jenn blushed. "Oh god, what did they say?"

Jake laughed. "Well, Riley is Riley and was pretty direct. She said that you two knew what had been going on and I need to talk to you about it." He took a deep breath. "Mike said that you had been upset and needed to talk to me about some things." Jenn nodded but couldn't find the words. Jake smiled. "It's unfair that he's such a nice guy, you know." Jenn nodded again.

She thought about it carefully before answering. "Yeah, I guess there are a few things I need to talk to you about." Jake nodded and leaned back in his chair.

Jenn paused before continuing. "Why didn't you tell me that you and Kelly broke up and she moved back?" Jake opened his mouth but was cut off. "And why have you been avoiding us? We haven't seen you in a year and you hardly talk to us."

Jake adjusted his seat awkwardly. "I've been talking to Riley and Curt a lot."

Jenn's jaw dropped. "What? So, you've just been avoiding me?" Jake nodded slowly, and Jenn crossed her arms in front of her. "What the hell?" She was angry.

Jake leaned forward toward his computer. "What good would it have done to tell you any of this, Jenn?"

"Um, it would have stopped me from worrying and imagining the worst."

Jake sighed. "Worse than the truth?"

Jenn looked at him, confused. He looked at her intently. "Can you honestly say that you wanted to know about my break-up or the mess that is in my mind?" Jenn bit her lip and nodded. He raised an eyebrow. "What will that accomplish?"

Jenn shrugged. "I don't know, but I want to know what's going on. I've been so confused, and I miss you so much. I'm worried about you." Jake chuckled to himself.

He took a drink from a water bottle next to him and returned his full attention to Jenn. "Fine. But I need to ask something of you first."

Jenn nodded, "Anything."

"Jenn, I need this to be a completely honest

conversation. Even if you're afraid to hurt my feelings."
Jenn felt her chest tighten and she nodded slowly. Jake
adjusted himself in the chair again and leaned forward.
"OK, full disclosure," he muttered. "Kelly broke up with me.
We hadn't been good for a long time. I think it started after
Mike proposed to you. I couldn't shake the feeling that it
wasn't right with her. It wasn't a pretty breakup." He sighed.
"She accused me of not committing to her because I was still
in love with someone else." He looked away for a moment.
"I didn't see it then. But the more I thought about it, the
more I feared that she was right." He looked back to Jenn. "I
distanced myself in hope that those feelings would go away.
I begged and prayed that they would because they are killing
me."

Jenn felt a tear fall down her cheek before she knew
she was crying. "I can't, I can't shake them. No matter how
I try." He paused and stared at her. Her hands were
trembling. "I know there's nothing I can do about them
either. I waited too long. It's just hard." He sniffed and
looked down at his hands.

Jenn sat in shock. She couldn't speak, and her heart
was pounding in her ears. "I know I also can't ask anything
of the other person because she is happy now, happier than
I've seen her in years. I can't be a part of destroying that."
Jake met her gaze again and stopped talking.

Jenn inhaled and exhaled deeply. "I don't know
what to say, Jake."

He nodded. "I just want honesty here."

Jenn inhaled deeply. "Mike is right, I've been confused for a while. I accepted his proposal, but I've had a nagging feeling in the back of my mind ever since. I thought that it was just because of my past, but I don't know if that's true." She fidgeted with her ring. "I met with Kevin over the holidays and we aired out everything. It felt really good, but he told me the same thing that everyone always does."

"And that is?" Jake asked.

Jenn looked at him. "That I'm always confused because I won't admit how I really feel."

He nodded and pushed on. "And how *do* you feel?" She glanced away from the computer and paused.

She looked around her kitchen and her eyes came to rest on her fridge. The front was covered with photos of friends and family. She found a picture of her and Jake, smiling and laughing about something.

She smiled. "That I've always known how I felt about you, but I would never admit it."

She heard him sigh. There was silence between them. "Thank you for being honest." She looked back at him and his eyes were watering.

"That doesn't help anything, does it?" she asked.

Jake picked up a tissue and wiped his eyes. "I fear that it doesn't, but I needed to know." He forced a smile.

Jenn felt more tears on her cheeks. "So, what am I supposed to do?"

Jake shook his head. "I can't answer that for you." They stared at each other. "I think we should use this time apart to think it over. I can't ask anything from you, regardless of what I want. I just wanted you to know the truth." He took a deep breath. "You've always been it for me, Jenn, since I was fifteen. I knew it then and I know it now. We just can't seem to get the timing right."

Jenn let a sob out before controlling herself. "Damn it, Jake."

"I said honesty, sorry. All I ask is that you keep it in mind and be honest about it. I won't tell you to leave Mike, he's a great guy. I won't beg you to choose me, it's not my style. I'll be all right, one way or another. I'm going to be a doctor and do great things. I just wish that you'd do them with me." Jake finished and smiled at Jenn, who was openly sobbing now. She took several breaths to control herself. She didn't know how to respond.

Jake cut her off before she could say anything. "I'm sorry to cut you off, but I have to get back to studying. I promise I will call you more. Please, take care of yourself. Remember what I said. You know it's the truth." He smiled and pressed the end call button.

Jenn sat with tears in her eyes, staring at the blank computer screen. His words echoed in her ears as she sat alone in silence. She slowly closed her laptop and laid her head on the kitchen table. She couldn't stop crying. She was glad to know the truth, but she didn't know what to do with it. Mike would be back in a week. What would she tell him?

She sat up quickly and called Riley. Riley listened quietly as Jenn described the conversation with Jake. After Jenn finished talking, Riley remained silent. "Riley? Please. What do I do?" Jenn asked between sobs.

She could hear Riley sigh deeply. "Jenn, you know I can't answer that for you."

Jenn nodded and wiped her nose with a tissue. "I can't answer it either."

"Fine, my advice to you. This is all I'm going to say. You need to take this time alone and really think about this. I mean, REALLY think about it." Riley replied.

Jenn looked down at her ring. "I'm scared."

Riley frowned. "I know, sweetie. The truth is in there somewhere, you just need to find it. I won't give my opinion because whatever you choose is for you, not anyone else."

Jenn forced a small smile and nodded. "I know, I know. Ugh, this is not going to be fun."

Riley shrugged. "But think of the reward."

Jenn looked back to the pictures on the fridge. "Thank you for talking to me, Ri. I need to get some schoolwork done."

"You're OK, right?" Riley asked. Jenn looked back to her and nodded. They exchanged goodbyes and ended the call.

Jenn stood and walked over to stand in front of her photos. There were photos of her family and Mike's family, photos of friends and photos of her and Mike together. She looked from one to another, studying her face in them. There wasn't one where she looked happier or sadder than the next.

She pulled down a photo of her and Jake and a photo of her and Mike. She sat down at the table and placed both in front of her. She stared at both, willing herself to imagine each scenario. Her life with Mike was great. He was a good man, and he took care of her. He made her feel safe. Her friendship with Jake had several ups and down, but there was a passion with it. She cared deeply for him, and she was always happy when he was around. It was an impossible choice. Jenn picked up the photos and put them back on the fridge, away from one another. She obviously would not be able to sort out this dilemma in one night, so she took to her homework to keep her mind occupied.

The next few days brought no further clarity, so Jenn picked up extra shifts at work to keep busy. Nicole had the same thoughts as Riley did about the entire situation. She did, however, suggest a possible third solution.

"Well, if you can't decide right now, don't," Nicole suggested as they were cleaning out the stock room.

Jenn paused and looked at her. "What do you mean?"

Nicole shrugged and pulled a box off the shelf. "I mean, if you can't choose between them right now, take your time. This is a big decision, you know that. It wouldn't be fair for either of them if you hurried to decide and ended up making the wrong one. I say, lay it all out on the table, be honest with them both. Then, take your time, take care of you. When you're ready to make the decision, it will be easy."

Jenn thought about it. "That was the best advice I've gotten in a long time, and I see a shrink." She laughed.

Nicole smiled. "Why, thank you." They finished their rounds for the night. After gathering their things, Nicole hugged Jenn tightly. "We're still young, you know. Everyone is always in a rush nowadays. You can't rush this."

Jenn squeezed her once. "I know." They said their goodbyes and Jenn walked towards her apartment instead of taking the bus.

After grabbing a coffee, she walked slowly and enjoyed the morning sun. Her thoughts were becoming clearer on the situation, and she knew that she couldn't decide right now. There were so many pieces to this puzzle.

By the time she reached her apartment she had decided that she was not going to decide. Not right now. Nicole was right, she had time. She had to finish school and take care of herself and pray that the answer came to her when the time was right.

Chapter 43

Mike came home from Chicago after a week and he seemed happy. They spent the first night back together talking about the city and the friends he reconnected with. She decided not to bring up anything and just enjoy the time together. Mike didn't push either.

It wasn't until Jenn talked about getting ready for the school year that Mike's expression changed. "I, um, have some big news," he said nervously. Jenn kept a straight face, but a lump had formed in her throat.

"Oh yeah? What is it?" she asked.

Mike took her hands and squeezed, giving Jenn a sense of dread for some reason. "The reason I went to Chicago was to interview for a job." Jenn stared at him silently. He finally met her gaze. "Yeah, I, um … the friend in Chicago is a teacher and he told me about a job opening at a private school up there. I put in a resume and they wanted to meet with me." Jenn nodded slowly. Mike cleared his throat. "They want me there as soon as possible."

Jenn slowly pulled her hands back into her lap. "So, you're moving to Chicago?"

He put his hand on her knee. "I am." Jenn turned away from him for a moment, collecting her thoughts.

"Had you already made up your mind before you visited?" she asked in almost a whisper.

He didn't answer at first. "I think I had, subconsciously."

Jenn turned back to him, tears in her eyes. "And what am I supposed to do? I can't go to Chicago."

Mike reached out and pulled her towards him. "I know you can't. I also know that you need time to figure out all the things going on. I thought, maybe, it would be easier if I wasn't here." She opened her mouth slowly, but she couldn't answer. Her heart was beating fast.

"So, that's it?" she asked.

He smiled his crooked smile and shook his head. "Not at all. I just think we have hit an impasse." He sighed and took her hand. "Jenn, I know what I want. I love you. I know you love me too, but I also know that you are unsure of what you want." Jenn started to interrupt but he stopped her. "No, it's fine. I promise. I'm not upset about it. If we choose to spend our lives together, it needs to be an honest and complete decision. You're not there yet." Mike put his hand on her cheek.

Jenn looked down at her ring and felt a tear fall. She didn't know how to respond. "When will you leave?" she asked in a small voice.

"School starts in two weeks, so sometime next week."

She looked up at him. "So, what does that mean for us?"

Mike leaned back and crossed his arms. "I'm not really sure. This has never happened to me before."

Jenn laughed softly. "Yeah, me neither. Why are you such a great guy? You could be a complete asshole and make this a lot easier." She knew it was a weak joke.

He chuckled. "Sorry, you're not getting off that easily."

She leaned forward and kissed him softly. "I do love you, you know."

Mike smiled. "I know, I love you, too."

They spent the next week together as if nothing had changed. The day of his move, Jenn felt a panic starting in her chest. She wasn't good with change, even if the change was good. Mike hugged her tightly as they stood together next to his car. "I will be back to visit for the holidays, and I will call as much as I can."

Jenn laid her head against his chest. "I'm going to miss you. Be safe." When they pulled apart, they stood face to face in silence. Jenn reached up and kissed him. The kiss was soft but had a feeling of finality to Jenn. Mike put his hand on her face and smiled before turning and getting into his car. Jenn watched him pull away and stood there for several minutes once he was gone. She held up her hand and looked at her ring again, but it suddenly felt heavy.

She knew that Mike had told her that nothing would change, but the feeling hit her in that moment that everything had changed. She walked slowly back into her apartment, which felt empty. Standing in the center of the kitchen, she began to cry again. The laptop was on her kitchen table and she felt the urge to call Jake, but she was afraid it would make this situation more confusing.

She called Riley instead. "Oh Jenn, I'm sorry. Why didn't you call me sooner?"

Jenn shrugged. "I don't know, it didn't feel real until right now."

Riley nodded. "Hey, come down to the school and help me set up my classroom. The kids are here with me." Jenn nodded and hung up the call. She sat at the table, staring at the wall. Pulling out the phone, she sent a quick text to Jake.

I miss you, hope you are well.

Her mind was a mess, but she smiled as he texted back.

Same.

Chapter 44

Jenn threw herself back into work, school and spending time with Riley and her family. She spoke frequently with both Jake and Mike, but her feelings still weren't clear.

When the holidays approached, Jenn made one big decision. She and Mike met shortly before Christmas for dinner. She was nervous, but Mike seemed calm and collected.

"You don't need to be nervous. I know what's coming," he said with a smile.

She bit her lip and pulled her engagement ring from her finger. He sighed and took it from her. "I am so sorry."

He reached out and took her hand. "You have nothing to be sorry about. I asked for honesty. Is it hard? It is, but I know you can't force anything either."

Jenn smiled weakly. "You are such a decent person. I can't even explain it."

He laughed. "I'm not going to look at this like a tragic event. It's not the end of something. You are a good person, Jenn, and I don't want you to be out of my life." He reached for her hand. They sat in silence, holding hands across the table.

"You won't lose me. I'm here. I just don't want to hold you back. You have so much to offer. I want you to be happy." She smiled at him.

"I'm going to be sad for just a moment, but I promise I am OK. I love my new job and Chicago is great. I can finally be a true Cubs fan without ridicule." He laughed, and Jenn joined him.

After dinner, Mike walked Jenn to her car. "Until next time." He held out his hand. She laughed and pushed his hand away, pulling him into a hug. He squeezed her tightly before stepping back. They looked at each other for a moment before leaning in for a final kiss. He turned slowly and walked away. She leaned against her car and watched him. Jenn wasn't sure how she felt at that moment, but she knew she had made the right decision.

The rest of the holidays were tough since she had to explain to everyone about her engagement coming to an end. Everyone was supportive and worried at the same time. Jenn had to promise everyone that it was a mutual decision and that she was fine.

The only person she hadn't talked to about it was Jake. She didn't know what she would say, because the end of her engagement was not her choosing him. She was truly choosing herself for now. She was a year away from finishing her master's degree and that's what she wanted to focus on.

Sitting at her kitchen table on New Year's Eve, she poured herself a glass of wine and opened her laptop. She didn't know if Jake would be out celebrating or not. She tapped her fingers on the table and thought about what to say. Holding her breath, she pushed the video chat button. Jake answered after several rings. He looked better, clean shaven with a fresh haircut. He was buttoning the top button of a dress shirt. "Hey," he said.

"Wow, you look nice. Going out?" Jenn asked.

He nodded. "Yeah, some med students are going to this big New Year's party at the school."

"That's great. I won't keep you."

"No problem, did you want to talk about something?" Jake asked.

Jenn looked down at her hand, now missing the ring. "Yeah ... I wanted to tell you ..." she started to say but was cut off a female voice coming from off screen at Jake's apartment.

"Hey, babe, are you almost ready?" the woman called. Jenn's stomach dropped.

Jake looked embarrassed. "Uh, yeah. Give me a minute." He looked back at Jenn with apologetic eyes. "Jenn, can I call you tomorrow?" he asked. Jenn nodded, biting her lips to stop herself from crying.

"Sure, sure. Happy New Year's, Jake," she said before hitting end. She closed her laptop a little harder than she wanted to. She decided not to tell Jake about her breakup. The timing was, again, not right.

******

The start of the new year brought with it the promise of new beginnings. Jenn decided that she would focus on her wants and needs and not worry about relationships. She missed the physical contact, but she also realized that she didn't need it. She was satisfied with her work and she was doing well with school. She was also closer to Riley than ever before.

Riley asked her a few times about Mike and Jake, but Jenn just brushed the questions aside. She kept in contact with both, but they were also swept up in their own lives. Riley told Jenn that Jake was only casually dating the girl from New Year's, but Jenn said it wasn't her business. Mike told Jenn he had also started dating an old friend from school, but Jenn said it wasn't a problem. Everyone was moving forward in their lives and Jenn was happy to be taking care of herself for once.

1 year later

Chapter 45

Jenn entered the last semester of her master's program. She spent most of her time at work or working on her thesis.

She had kept her promise to herself and hadn't been out on a date since her last meal with Mike. The last time she spoke to him, he was doing well and was moving in with his new girlfriend. Jenn was relieved to not feel jealous over this, but happy.

Jake was in his last semester of medical school and had started looking for residencies. He was in the top 5 percent of his class. They never talked about relationships when they video chatted, but Jake was aware that she was no longer with Mike. Jenn never wanted to ask him about his love life because she didn't want to know if he had moved past her. And she felt guilty about not wanting him to move on. Her feelings for him were still uncertain, but she did know that it hurt to think he would be with anyone else. Luckily, school kept her so busy that she didn't have a lot of time to dwell on it.

As the end of school loomed, the workload increased. Between work and school, she didn't have a moment to herself.

Riley took her out for a drink a few weeks before

graduation to give her a break. "Thank you, I needed to relax," Jenn said, sipping on her cocktail.

Riley nodded. "Me too. I feel like I'm with kids all day and then kids all night. I needed an adult, other than my husband, to talk to."

Jenn looked out across the bar. "Man, I feel old. Old spinster Jenn."

Riley rolled her eyes. "I don't know if you can qualify as a spinster if it's your choice."

Jenn gave her a playful shove. "Eh, no one wants this mess."

Riley shook her head. "Yeah, right."

Jenn glared at her. "Why, you have a hot guy waiting for me?" she asked. Her face flushed a little and she took a quick sip of her drink.

Riley laughed. "Even you can't say that without getting nervous. You are so funny, Jenn."

Jenn laughed awkwardly. "I don't know what you mean."

Riley stopped stirring her drink and looked at her. "Really?" Jenn looked down at her drink, feeling embarrassed. "Jenn, I'm just teasing you. Come on." Riley reached out and put her hand on Jenn's arm.

Jenn looked back at her, feeling sad suddenly. "It doesn't matter," she whispered.

"What doesn't?"

Jenn picked up her drink and downed it quickly. "The timing never works. I don't think it ever will."

Riley rolled her eyes again. "If we're talking about the same thing, then you are always wrong." Riley took a quick drink. "Jenn, you know all you have to do is tell him you're ready."

Jenn looked away and stared out across the bar. "But am I?"

"Are you?" Riley came back at her.

"That's the thing Riley, I still don't know. How do I know?"

Riley took another drink and looked intently at Jenn. "All right. Tipsy Riley is going to lay down some truths for you." Jenn smiled and nodded. "Miss Jenn, you are in love with Jake and it's been driving me nuts watching you fight it." Riley took a deep breath. "Stop being such a chicken shit and do something about it." She emptied her glass. Jenn stared at her with her mouth agape.

"Well, thanks tipsy Riley, for that." Jenn laughed. "It's just that easy?" Riley nodded without saying anything.

Riley ordered two more drinks and reached for Jenn's hand. "It *is* that easy if you allow it to be."

Jenn looked at her and smiled. "So, what's our plan?"

Riley shrugged. "You're the one that's kept him waiting this long. Better be something big." Riley took a large drink and hiccupped.

Jenn chuckled softly to herself. She knew Riley was right. Riley giggled and pointed towards the bar. "There's a guy over there that has been staring at you for at least twenty minutes." Jenn smacked Riley's hand down before turning around to look. The man quickly looked down at his drink, embarrassed that he was caught staring.

Jenn turned back to Riley and shrugged. "Don't think I need to pick up a guy in a bar. I'm getting too old for that." She stirred her drink, watching the ice float in a circle.

Riley giggled again. "Told you so."

"You are such a know-it-all when tipsy Riley comes out."

Riley pulled the straw out of her glass and chewed on the end. "It is what I do, I drink and I know stuff, or something like that. Just like the guy from that book you love." She pushed the straw back to the bottom of her glass and attempted to slurp the last drops.

Jenn laughed and pulled out her phone. "If you're starting to compare yourself to fictional characters, I think it's time to call Curt." Curt answered after a few rings and said he'd be there to pick them up shortly.

Riley attempted to order one last drink before Jenn cut her off. "Ri, time to go. No more drinks for you." Jenn pulled her coat from behind her and put it on before helping Riley put on hers.

The man from the bar approached Jenn as she was gathering her purse. "Leaving already? I was hoping to get you a drink."

Riley burst into giggles and Jenn shushed her. "Sorry, I have to get my friend home. She doesn't handle her alcohol well."

The man didn't move at first. "Can I at least get your number?"

Riley continued to laugh, and Jenn smiled carefully. "Sorry, I don't want to be rude, but I'm really not interested right now." The man looked offended.

"Yeah, she's going to go after the man of her dreams and they're going to get married," Riley slurred.

"Oh my god. You, go." Jenn pushed Riley toward the door. She mouthed "Sorry" to the man and followed Riley. "You are out of control," Jenn muttered.

They stepped out of the door and saw Curt's SUV parked a little down the road. Jenn herded Riley toward the car and opened the passenger side. "She's in rare form, you're welcome," Jenn joked. Riley giggled.

"Do you need a ride?" Curt asked.

Jenn looked in the back and the three car seats with sleeping kids. "No, thank you though. I'll make my way."

Riley grabbed for Jenn's hand. "Now, promise me Jenn. You go and sweep him off his feet." Jenn smiled and patted her hand. Curt stared at Jenn with a quizzical look. Riley turned to face him. "She's going to Boston."

Curt inhaled and nodded. "I see. Well, it's about time."

Jenn rolled her eyes. "You too? Is everyone so sure of Jake and me? You know, besides me."

Curt laughed. "He's a great guy, Jenn. I know I haven't known him as long as you have, but I have talked to him a lot over the last couple years. He's been waiting for this, believe me." He smiled and patted Riley's head.

Riley turned back to Jenn. "Let me know when the wedding is."

Curt and Jenn both laughed. "You'll be the first to know, Riley." Jenn leaned over and kissed her forehead before closing the car door and giving a small wave. She stood on the sidewalk and watched the car drive away.

Jenn figured she needed a walk to process and decide what to do in the situation. She turned around and nearly ran into the man from inside the bar.

He smiled at her, "So, now that she's gone, can I get you that drink?"

Jenn looked toward the bar and then back at him. "I'm sorry, I meant what I said." He pouted, trying to get some sympathy from Jenn. "Really, I am headed home. Thank you anyway." She walked around him and headed up the block toward her apartment.

The cool night air felt refreshing as she walked. She took several deep breaths, trying to wrap her mind around everything that Riley and Curt had said.

Jake was graduating in a week and he would be a doctor. He hadn't made up his mind about where his residency would be. Jenn didn't know what she would say to him or how she would make it work if he stayed on the East Coast.

She felt anxiety starting to rise in her chest. Shaking her head, she tried to think of the positives. Jake was her best friend and she knew there was an undeniable connection between them. He knew her better than anyone, besides maybe Riley. The physical attraction between them was electric when they were together. It was never a question of whether they would be together, but more of a question when. She always knew they would be together in the end.

Jenn stopped walking suddenly and looked forward without really focusing. "Oh my god."

It was as if she had run into a brick wall. Everything in her mind was beginning to clear. She wasn't afraid to be with him. She wanted to be with him. She could see it in front of her, her whole future with him. The anxiety in her chest disappeared. She giggled and nodded to herself. "Well, what do you know?" she whispered. Her pace quickened as she walked toward her apartment.

Once she made it home, she pulled out her laptop and started looking for plane tickets to Boston for the next weekend. There was no nagging voice in the back of her mind; she was very calm as she bought the ticket. She also fought the urge to call Jake to let him know that she would be at his graduation, but she figured that it would be better as a surprise.

Chapter 46

Jenn spent the next week finishing up her thesis since she would be graduating the week after Jake. She worked the Friday night before she left for Boston, and she couldn't wait to tell Nicole about her plans. As soon as they finished report, Jenn began to ramble on about her decision and her trip.

Nicole could hardly hold in her excitement. "That is so romantic and exciting! I'm so happy for you."

She hugged Jenn tightly. "Thank you for not saying that it was about time or something like that. That's usually the response I get," Jenn said as she stepped back from the hug.

Nicole nodded and smiled. "I'm saying it internally, don't worry."

The night flew by, and by morning Jenn's excitement level was high. She stood in the locker room and waited for Nicole to get her things, so they could walk out together. "So, when is your flight?" Nicole asked as they walked out of the building.

Jenn glanced down at her watch. "Flight is at noon. I have a hotel room booked for tonight and the graduation ceremony is tomorrow."

Nicole giggled and hugged Jenn again. "I'm so happy and proud of you. I'm glad you took the time to make the right decision." Jenn nodded. She didn't feel nervous or worried about her choice. For the first time in a long time, she was confident and ready for the next step.

"I'm ready. I can't wait to see him." Jenn stepped back and adjusted her bag on her shoulder. Nicole waved as Jenn turned to walk toward the bus stop.

"Good luck!" Nicole yelled after her. Jenn gave a thumbs up and hurried toward the bus that was pulling up. She was surprisingly wide awake when she got home. She started packing a few things into a carry-on and double-checked her ticket information.

After eating a quick breakfast and drinking two cups of coffee, she decided to call Riley. "How excited are you right now?" Riley asked.

Jenn paced in the living room while she talked. "I just want to go already. I'm ready." Instead of her normal anxiety, Jenn experienced the unfamiliar feeling of butterflies in her stomach.

"Well, Curt talked to him last night, and he was really bummed that we couldn't make it this weekend. He asked about you, but Curt said you were stuck working." Riley had been instructed not to ruin the surprise.

"I hope he doesn't suspect anything." Jenn continued

pacing. Curt had been her ears while she planned out her trip. He talked to Jake and asked questions about the graduation ceremony. Curt also let it slip that Jake was currently single and free for Jenn to swoop in.

"So, what's the plan?" Riley asked.

Jenn stopped pacing and thought about it. "I don't really have one. I'm going to find him after the ceremony and tell him. I'm going to tell him that I'm ready."

Riley let out a high-pitched noise of excitement. "I can't believe this is finally going to happen!"

Jenn looked at her watch. "I have to get going, I want to get to the airport a little early." She and Riley said their goodbyes and Jenn gathered her bags.

Her nerves started acting up a little on the drive to the airport and as she checked in. After making it through the check point, she decided to grab a drink to calm herself. It was barely 11 a.m. so she felt a little guilty having a drink, but there were several other people at the bar with her, so the guilt was short-lived. As she drank, she texted Jake to congratulate him and to apologize for not being able to make it to his graduation. He replied that he was sorry she had to work and that he would be home soon to visit. She smiled to herself.

The announcement came that Jenn's flight was boarding, so she took a final drink from her glass and thanked the bartender before heading to the gate. After a quick bathroom break, she took her place in line at the gate and waited. She thanked the woman scanning the tickets before heading onto the plane and finding her seat.

After stowing her carry-on above her, she settled into the seat and looked out the window. She watched the workers loading luggage onto the plane and she jumped slightly when someone sat down next to her. "I'm sorry, dear. I didn't mean to startle you," said an older woman with grey hair. She smiled.

"No problem, I was just daydreaming." Jenn smiled back. The woman dug into her purse, pulled out her phone and shut it off. Jenn followed suit and then stowed her purse under her chair. She looked back out of the window and noticed the workers starting to back away from the plane. Jenn didn't realize it, but she started to fidget in her seat.

The older woman smiled at her. "Nervous about the flight?"

Jenn forced herself to stop moving. "No, I'm excited."

The captain came over the loudspeaker to announce that the plane would be taking off shortly. The usual pre-flight duties began, and Jenn listened to the announcements and instructions without really hearing them. All she could think about was Jake.

The plane started moving as the flight attendants made their way to their seats. Jenn adjusted her seat belt and leaned her head back. "I'm not a fan of the takeoff." Jenn whispered to her seatmate.

She smiled at Jenn and patted her on the hand. "I usually just say a good solid prayer and close my eyes." Jenn nodded and closed her eyes.

The plane reached the runway and started to pick up speed. Jenn squeezed her eyes tight and felt her stomach flip as the plane lifted off. Once it leveled out, she opened her eyes to find the older woman smiling at her. "Told you it works."

Jenn laughed. "I'm Jenn," she said, holding out her hand.

"Cindy," the woman replied, taking Jenn's hand and shaking it. Jenn turned and looked out the window as the plane climbed through the clouds. "So, what takes you to Boston?" Cindy asked.

Jenn turned and looked at her. She didn't know why, but she felt like she wanted to tell Cindy her whole story. Maybe it was because she was older and motherly, or maybe it was because Jenn wanted to get it off her chest. "Well, it's a long story," Jenn started. "Would you like to hear it?" Cindy smiled and nodded cheerfully.

Jenn started from the beginning. She told Cindy

about her two best friends. She told her about Kevin and their failed relationship. She even told her about her hospitalization and recovery. After telling her about Mike and that failed relationship, she stopped and took a deep breath. "So, now I'm here. Going to see Jake to surprise him because it took my dumb self this long to realize something that I should have figured out years ago." Cindy had listened and nodded along without interrupting as Jenn rambled. "I guess better late than never, right?" Jenn asked.

Cindy chuckled. "That, my dear, is quite the love story." She reached out and patted Jenn's hand. "From what little I know, I can't tell you what the right answer is. I will say that when you talk about this Jake, you have a different tone in your voice."

Jenn bit her lip and thought about it. "I just hope he hasn't given up on me after all this time."

Cindy shook her head. "If he lasted through all of that other stuff, he's still there waiting." She smiled again.

Jenn couldn't help but smiling back. "Thanks for listening to my rambles. I'm so nervous for tomorrow."

Cindy took a drink of water and looked back at Jenn. "I think what you're doing is romantic, and I think he will be pleased to see you there." Jenn felt like she wanted to hug Cindy, but she held back.

Jenn steered the conversation to lighter topics, asking

about Cindy and her life. It turned out that Cindy was a retired nurse and was recently widowed. By the time they were descending into Boston, Jenn felt oddly connected to Cindy.

Once they landed and gathered their belongings, they walked together to the gate. "Well, Jenn, I wish you the best of luck. Tell Jake he's a very lucky young man." Cindy turned and held out her arms for a hug.

Jenn stepped forward and hugged her without hesitation. "Thank you again for the conversation. Have a great visit with your family." Cindy waved and walked towards the luggage claim.

Jenn looked around and found the way to the rental cars. She picked up a set of keys and headed to the parking ramp. After looking up the directions to the hotel in her phone's GPS, she drove out of the airport. The hotel wasn't that far away, so she stopped to pick up some food before checking in.

She settled into the hotel room and pulled out her phone. She texted Riley to let her know that she had made it safely. Then she texted Jake to wish him luck tomorrow.

She pulled out a notepad from the bedside table and started to scribble down her thoughts about what to say to Jake tomorrow. She was having a hard time putting down all the emotions that had built up over the many years. She crumpled several pieces of paper before she wrote down what she thought was the best idea. She set the pen down and smiled at what she had written. After carefully tearing the paper off the notepad, she slipped it into her purse.

It was not very late, but Jenn hadn't slept on the plane like she had originally planned. She changed into her pajamas and climbed under the covers, turning on the TV for some background noise. She fell asleep quickly, images and thoughts running through her head about the next day.

Chapter 47

Her phone buzzed early the next morning, waking her. It was a text from Nicole, jokingly telling her to "Go get yourself a doctor." Jenn smiled and rubbed her eyes. It was only 7 a.m. She rolled onto her back and stretched.

She was hungry. Throwing on a sweatshirt, she headed downstairs to the continental breakfast area. As she turned the corner, she stopped quickly and pushed herself against the wall.

A blonde woman stood next to the breakfast buffet, filling a travel mug with coffee. Jenn stared and prayed that the woman would not turn around, but she looked straight in Jenn's direction. Pausing, she stared toward Jenn before breaking into a smile.

It was Jake's sister Jessica. "Jenn? What the hell are you doing in Boston? Does Jake know you're here?" She walked over and gave Jenn a hug.

"Um, no. It's supposed to be a surprise," Jenn said shyly. Jessica smiled and stepped back.

"Well, he's going to be so excited to see you!" she said. Jenn blushed and looked down at her feet. "Are you alone?" Jessica asked, looking past Jenn to see if anyone was joining her.

Jenn nodded. "Yes, I am. I was just coming in to see Jake." She looked up at Jessica.

"Come on, I'll have a coffee with you." Jessica led Jenn back to the breakfast area and sat down at a table while Jenn grabbed a coffee. "I haven't seen you in years."

Jenn nodded and took a sip of coffee. "After you left for college, I think." Jessica leaned back in her chair.

"So, how are things?" she asked. Jenn shrugged. She was unsure of what to tell Jessica. She didn't know what Jake had told her.

"Um, good, I guess. Just working and finishing up my master's degree."

Jessica smiled, "You two smarty pants. No wonder you guys are best friends."

Jenn sipped her coffee and looked around the room. "Are your parents here?"

"No, they stayed at Jake's apartment. I needed a night to myself." She was a journalist who traveled a lot and never settled down. Jenn was envious of her freedom in a way but thought that it would get lonely. "Jake tells me that you were getting married, but you called it off. How are you doing with that?"

Jenn choked on her coffee a little and set down the cup. "You guys talk about me?"

Jessica laughed out loud. "Oh, honey, he's talked to me about you since he was fifteen." Jenn felt her cheeks start to burn. "Relax, Jenn. I'm not here to judge. I'm just curious." She paused. "Why *are* you here?"

Jenn felt her heart start to beat quickly. "Um, well. I needed to see Jake."

Jessica set her cup down and crossed her arms. "You know, when he told me about you for the first time I thought, oh no. He's in love." She chuckled. "Then he told me that you two were just friends. But whenever I watched you, there was always a feeling that it was more than that."

Jenn fidgeted in her chair, feeling nervous. "Yeah. That's funny," she said quietly.

Jessica stared at her with a smirk on her face. "Then he told me about your college boyfriend and you getting engaged. Then about your breakup and what happened after. I thought that the cycle would never end."

Jenn looked at her, confused. "Cycle?"

Jessica leaned forward. "You see, he would get his hopes up every time something would go wrong in your relationships. Like, each time it might be THE time for him." She looked intently at Jenn. "He never gave up hope." Jenn stared at Jessica and was lost for words. Jessica continued, "I hoped that one of the girls here would break the cycle, but they just couldn't. You have this hold over him, Jenn."

Jenn looked down at her coffee, a strong feeling of guilt rushing over her. "I know, but you don't understand…" she started to say, then paused.

Jessica sat without breaking eye contact, urging Jenn to continue. "You see, you two *are* idiots." Jenn laughed loudly without meaning to, then clasped her hand over her mouth. Jessica laughed as well.

"That's the understatement of the century," Jenn finally replied after she caught her breath. They sat in silence, staring at each other. "Are you going to give me the big sister threat or speech?" Jenn asked.

Jessica shook her head. "Does that mean that you're finally going to do something about it?"

Jenn smiled shyly and nodded. "I'd say it's been long enough."

Jessica clapped and made Jenn jump. "The only big sister thing I will say is that you better take damn good care of my little brother." She stood up, walked around the table to Jenn and placed her hand on Jenn's shoulder. "And that it's about damn time."

Jenn reached up and patted Jessica's hand. "I guess I'll see you after the ceremony. Oh, and please keep this between us." Jessica made the motion of locking her lips and throwing away the key before waving and walking away. Jenn sat for a moment and smiled. She finished her cup of coffee and headed back to her room to get ready.

She redid her hair several times and stood in front of the mirror feeling nervous about her clothing choice. After psyching herself up, she sat on the bed and looked over her notes about what she wanted to say to Jake.

Her conversation with Jessica made this moment feel so much bigger than it was. He had been waiting for her to come to her senses for a long time, so she had to make this worthy of his wait. Her stomach was a knot. After another cup of coffee, Jenn mustered up the courage to head over to the ceremony.

The traffic was heavy, and the parking lot was overflowing when she pulled in. After finding a parking spot, she sat in her car and scanned the crowd. She did not want to run into Jake's family, so she stayed in her car until the crowd thinned out.

When she couldn't wait any longer, Jenn made her way to the ceremony area and found a seat in the back. From where she sat, she could see Jake's family near the front. Her heart was beating fast and she took several deep breaths to calm down. Someone walked by her and handed her a program for the ceremony. Jenn thumbed through the pages and found Jake's picture. She touched it gently with her fingertips and her stomach did a flip.

Someone walked on the stage and asked everyone to turn off their cellphones and to not use flash photography. Jenn reached in her purse and pressed the volume button of her phone. She adjusted herself in her chair, the excitement growing.

Music started to play as the crowd settled into their seats. The graduates filed in. Jenn found Jake near the middle of the group and she leaned down slightly so he wouldn't notice her. She smiled. He looked very handsome in his graduation gown.

A man stepped onto the stage to give the opening remarks. Jenn was moved to tears. Several other people spoke before they announced the distribution of the diplomas. The graduates stood. Jenn had to control herself when Jake's name was announced because she wanted to cheer loudly.

After everyone had their diplomas, the director of the medical school made one last speech and congratulated everyone. A loud cheer came over the crowd and graduation caps flew into the air. Jenn stood and clapped loudly, tears in her eyes.

After the ceremony had ended, the graduates were joined by their friends and families, taking pictures and receiving flowers or gifts.

In the chaos of the moment, Jenn slipped out towards the parking lot. It took her a few minutes to find Jake's car and stand beside it. She pulled a card out of her purse that she had purchased. It was a generic "Congrats Grad" card, but she didn't know what to get Jake in the situation. He deserved something phenomenal, but she couldn't think of anything tangible.

Jenn smiled and thought, *I guess I'll just have to do.*

After about 30 minutes, people started to come out to the parking lot and cars started dispersing. Jenn waited until she saw Jake's parents walking with Jessica to the far side of the parking lot where their car was. Jake was with them, and they paused briefly to hug him before they walked away. Jessica caught Jenn's eye and smiled, winking at her.

Jake looked at his sister and then turned around to see what she was looking at. His expression was of utter surprise, and it made Jenn's heart beat even quicker. Jessica squeezed his hand before he turned and walked toward Jenn without breaking eye contact, his smile growing the closer he got. "What the hell are you doing here? I thought you were working."

"Yeah, I lied about that. I couldn't figure out what kind of graduation present to get you, so I thought maybe I would do." She tucked the card back in her purse. Jake stopped about a foot in front of her and they stood, staring at each other without talking.

Jake laughed and pulled her into a tight hug. "Damn good present, though," he whispered in her ear. She started laughing as he picked her up and spun her around. They held each other tightly until he finally set her down and let go. "I can't believe you flew all the way here for this. Thank you, that's amazing."

She shrugged and smiled. "How else am I supposed to celebrate such a momentous occasion with my best friend?"

Jake smiled. "My god, I've missed you," he said, reaching up to brush a stray hair behind her ear.

"Yeah, I know what you mean. It seems like forever since I last saw you."

There was a moment of awkward silence before Jake cleared his throat. "So, how long are you in Boston for?"

Jenn looked up at him. "I have to head back to St Louis tomorrow. My finals are next week, and I graduate next weekend."

Jake nodded and reached for her hand. "That means we have two things to celebrate." Jenn took his hand and looked at it. She bit her lip and looked up at him. He smiled at her and her heart fluttered.

She stepped in front of him, so they were face to face, and she cleared her throat. "I'm so proud of you, Jake. I always knew you would do great things in your life. Now you're a doctor. I'm in awe of you every day."

Jake squeezed her hands. "Thank you." His voice took on a worried tone. "Are you OK? You look nervous."

Jenn met his gaze and nodded. "I am *very* nervous."

Jake squeezed her hands again. "Do you want to sit down somewhere and talk for a minute?" Jenn shook her head. She kicked a rock on the ground and felt her chest tighten.

"No, I need to do this now before I chicken out."

Jake put his hand under her chin and made her look into his eyes. "So, say it then." Jenn met his gaze and forced herself not to look away.

"Here goes nothing," she started and cleared her throat. "Jake, you and I have been doing this back-and-forth, will-they-or-won't-they dance since we were fifteen years old. That's a long time." Jake laughed and nodded. "I am forever grateful that you stuck by my side through the best and worst of it. You are my best friend and quite literally my hero." Jenn took a deep breath and stepped closer to Jake. "I'm sorry that it took me so long to figure it out. But I just wanted to tell you in person that … it is figured out." She felt her cheeks burning as she looked into Jake's eyes.

He smiled. "What exactly is figured out?"

She took another deep breath and paused. There was no backing down. "Jake, I love you. I've loved you since I was fifteen years old. I've just been too much of an idiot to admit it. But it's always been there." She looked down again, feeling embarrassed. "I don't expect anything from you, but I needed you to know that. I'm so sorry that it took me this long." She exhaled sharply, and it felt as though she had been holding her breath for hours. She was afraid to look up at him.

There was a moment of silence before Jake pulled her closer. She looked up at him and he had tears in his eyes. Jenn was suddenly nervous until he smiled.

"I can't tell you how long I've been waiting for you to say that."

Jenn laughed and pulled her hands away from his before wrapping them around the back of his neck. "Well, I'm not a doctor, so we *all* can't be brilliant." Jake laughed and put his arms around her waist. "So, where do we go from here?" Jenn asked.

Jake laughed. "Well, I think we should go celebrate with my family."

Jenn nodded. "OK, then what?"

Jake thought about it. "Well, I have to complete my residency. I've applied to several hospitals."

Jenn bit her lip. "Did you apply to any St. Louis area hospitals?"

Jake laughed. "Some of the first I looked into, why? Is there something special about St. Louis?" he asked, his eyes gleaming.

She chuckled softly. "I hear that there is a girl in St. Louis who is dying to finally take you out on a date."

Jake leaned his face closer to hers. "I see. Is that your way of asking me out, Jenn?"

She smiled. "Most definitely." She pulled his face towards hers and kissed him softly. His arms tightened around her waist as he pulled her body into his. Jenn felt fireworks in her stomach as the heat raced to her cheeks. She closed her eyes and felt like there was no one else in the entire world.

She didn't know how long they stood there before Jake finally loosened his grip on her. He pulled away and stared into her eyes, stroking her cheek. Jenn was overwhelmed with happiness in that moment.

Jake kissed her once more and took her hand. "I love you Jenn, more than you know."

"I love you, too."

Jake opened his car door and she got into the passenger seat.

She didn't know what to expect in the future, but she knew that they would be all right. Jake pulled out of the parking lot and drove off towards downtown. Jenn took his hand and squeezed. Jake glanced at her briefly with a smile and then returned his gaze to the road. Jenn leaned her head against the cool window and watched the buildings pass by. For the first time in a long time, she felt no anxiety and no doubt. This is where she was meant to be.

5 Years Later

Chapter 48

Jenn turned a page in the book she was reading as the morning light shone through the dusty windows of her sun porch. She adjusted the blanket on her lap, blocking out the cool morning air. A smile formed on her face as she read. After finishing a chapter, she took a sip of warm coffee. The sun was coming up over the houses in her neighborhood, reflecting off the morning dew on the grass.

This was Jenn's favorite time of day, and she took a deep breath, closing her eyes. The silence was interrupted by a shuffling sound coming over the monitor that sat on the table next to her. It was followed by a small whimper. Jenn sighed, placed a bookmark in her book and set it down on the table.

Before she was able to stand up, Jenn heard a man's voice come over the monitor. "Oh, sweetheart. Daddy's here." Jenn's heart skipped a beat as she smiled at the monitor. "Come here, come here. Let's not cry. Mommy's taking a little break, but Daddy has you." Jenn leaned back in her chair and listened. "Mommy was up all night with you, so Daddy could rest before work. Let's give her a minute or two of peace. She's such a good mommy," he continued in a gentle voice.

Jenn felt tears form in her eyes and wiped her nose.

The baby continued to whimper, and Jenn could hear the man shushing gently.

After several minutes the whimper turned into a soft cry. "Well, looks like I'm not going to win this battle. Let's change that diaper and go find Mommy." Jenn adjusted herself in the chair and took another drink from her coffee cup. She smiled and pulled the blanket around her shoulder.

Jake appeared at the sliding door with a small bundle wrapped in blankets. He smiled at Jenn, slid the door open and stepped out onto the porch. "I think someone is hungry," he whispered as the baby fussed in his arms.

Jenn put out her arms and he gently handed the baby to her. She looked down at her daughter and smiled. She stroked the baby's cheek, and all was calm.

"I wish it was that easy for me," Jake whispered as he pulled a chair next to Jenn.

She looked at him and smiled, "Well, you aren't the food source, so I win in that department." Jake grinned and leaned back in his chair. Jenn adjusted the baby and began to feed her. She watched the baby nurse, a warm sensation forming in her chest. "I'm so happy," Jenn whispered, a small tear rolling down her cheek.

Jake reached over and took her hand, squeezing gently. "Me too." Jenn looked up at him and smiled. "I'm going to grab a cup of coffee before my shift starts." He headed inside.

Jenn watched him, then returned her attention to the baby. The silence was broken only by soft sounds coming from the baby as she nursed.

Jake returned after a few moments and sat down again. He was wearing his blue scrubs and his hair was messy. "You should probably brush your hair, so you don't scare off your patients," Jenn teased.

Jake laughed and ran his hand through his hair. "As long as I do my job, I don't think they would care about my hair sticking up." Jenn adjusted the baby and picked up her coffee. She looked out the window again. The sun shone brightly now, warming the porch.

"Sorry I have to work this weekend. I'd rather be here to celebrate our anniversary," Jake said.

Jenn looked back at him and shrugged. "It's fine. We'll celebrate another night."

It was their third wedding anniversary. Jake had been accepted into a residency in St. Louis shortly after graduation and he and Jenn were married in a small ceremony after dating for two years.

Shortly after their second anniversary, Jenn found out she was expecting their first child, a daughter they named Reagan. Jenn was on maternity leave from her teaching job at a local community college.

They had moved to a neighborhood close to Riley and Curt after they found out Jenn was pregnant. Jake was working in the ICU of the hospital where he did his residency.

They finished their coffees in silence as the baby fell asleep while still nursing. Jenn rocked her gently and smiled at Jake.

"I've got to get going." He stood up, walked over to Jenn and kissed her, then leaned over and kissed Reagan on the top of her head. "I love you girls."

"We love you, too." Jenn watched him walk back into the house and listened as the car started and the garage door closed. Jenn looked back down at her sleeping baby and smiled.

Everything had fallen into place for her. It had been a long and sometimes painful road, but she would not have changed any of it. Every heartbreak, every trial had brought her to where she was today. She still bore the scars, but they faded more with each passing day. She knew she was right where she belonged. The future didn't scare her anymore, because with Jake by her side she knew that everything would be all right.

Jenn smiled at her baby and stroked her hair. "And she lived happily ever after…" she whispered.

About the Author

Elizabeth is a wife, mother of three and a Registered Nurse. Writing is her form of therapy and she loves including parts of her life in her books. She has enjoyed writing and reading stories her entire life. When she's not working or chasing after her kids, she loves to play soccer and hike. She resides in Moline, IL with her husband, Derek, and their three children.

I want to thank my husband, Derek, for always believing in my writing and pushing me to do more than let my stories sit on the computer. Thank you to my sister, Susan, who has always loved books and who I look up to every day. She is always there to offer up wonderful books and I have learned to always listen to her suggestions. My parents, who always showed us the wonder that a book has to offer. And to my co-workers, those who read my books first and encouraged me to pursue this adventure. Thank you for your kind words and belief. And to many of my patients that have listen to me babble on about wanting to be an author, thank you for listening and believing in me. Thank you all for your help, whatever form it came in. I would not have had the strength without all of you as my support. From the bottom of my heart, thank you.

CPSIA information can be obtained
at www.ICGtesting.com
Printed in the USA
BVHW040156200620
581815BV00011B/48